CRISPR

Horizon's Wake, Book I

A Novel By
Lincoln Cole

Published by Lincoln Cole, Columbus, 2018
lincoln@lincolncole.net
www.LincolnCole.net

Cover Design by M.N. Arzu
www.mnarzuauthor.com

"It has become appallingly obvious that our technology has exceeded our humanity."

Albert Einstein

This book is dedicated to the following people who helped make it a reality: Alan Schmidt, Amanda Vey, Lori Jordan, Katelyn Charles, Dark Trope Films, and Chantalia Jordan. Thank you all so very much for your support!

Prologue

"Do you think Andrew knows?"

"It's possible. Not likely, but possible. It doesn't matter if he knows, though."

"Why not?"

"It's too late for him to stop us now. We've come too far. The transport is scheduled to leave in two days. He's too busy with his agenda to worry about what I'm doing."

"You're sure?"

"I'm sure. Besides, the boat will keep him too concerned for him to worry about anything else."

"He took the bait?"

"Hook, line, and sinker. He spent a fortune hiring a team to destroy the cargo. He has no clue it's just a distraction."

"Perfect. He won't even know what happened until it's too late. You said he—"

"Careful. Just say the package."

"Sorry. You said the package would be in a transport truck?"

"Yeah. A single guard and unarmed driver. That was the minimum I could send without raising any red flags."

"That shouldn't pose a problem. I'll use the same team protecting the boat to pick up the package."

"Good. So, you're ready for the pickup, then?"

"Beyond ready. I can't believe it's happening finally. I contacted my friend this morning. He assured me that everything would go smoothly."

"Excellent."

"Thank you, Madison. For everything. I need you to know how much I appreciate—"

"Don't thank me. Not yet, at least. Once we do this, they won't stop hunting you. Ever."

"I understand—"

"No, you don't. You think you understand, but you don't

know Andrew like I do."

"I've got a place outside their reach. In a week's time, this will all be over."

"Nothing is outside his reach."

"I promise you; this place is. Everything is in order, and in two days' time, I'll be out of the country."

"I hope to God you're right."

"I am. I'll send you a postcard when we get there."

The silence from the end of the line spoke volumes.

Wallace said, "What? What is it?"

"Let me ask you something, and be honest. Do you think I'll still be alive to get it?"

"You better be. You should run."

"I will. As soon as the transport leaves, I'll get out of here."

"I can send you the location—"

"Don't."

"You sure?"

"It's better this way. Then, if they catch me, I won't have to lie."

"All right. But as soon as things calm down, I'll find you."

"You better."

"I will. You said you're sending some files?"

"Notes and details. A USB drive will hold the information. The package won't have any tracking chips, so you will have a small head-start, but they will have satellites and surveillance programs to track you. I copied everything I had access to and included all my notes. It isn't proof, but it should give you enough to start an investigation."

"I don't care about that."

"You should. With what Andrew has planned, we should all feel afraid. Promise you'll get the word out no matter what happens to me."

"I promise. I've got friends. Once I show this to the right people, they will bring him down."

"Just ... don't squander this chance, Wallace. It's the only one we'll get."

"I won't. Relax; everything will be perfect. In two weeks, we'll sit sipping Martini's on the beach."

"I told you; the odds of this going in our favor—"

"It'll work. I made a mistake, Madison, and right now, I'm correcting it. They won't know what hit them."

8

"I hope you're right."

"I am. And I promise that I'll find you when this is all over with, and we'll make a new life together."

"Okay. Look, I need to go. They'll wonder where I am if I don't check in. Just make sure you're there to pick up the package. Two days. Don't forget."

"I won't. Stay strong."

"You too, Wallace. Stay safe."

Chapter 1
Ocean City, Delaware

1

The rippling ocean waves crashed against the hull of the cargo-shipping vessel, The Lonely Spirit. The ship lay a few hours outside of a port in Delaware, scheduled to dock in the wee hours of the morning. Apart from the occasional gust of wind tearing across the deck, the waves were the only thing diminishing the profound silence of the night.

Quinn Walden enjoyed the night. He relished the isolation of the empty deck while the rest of the crew stayed down below. For this reason, he didn't mind spending the night as The Lonely Spirit's lone topside guard. Everyone else huddled below deck, out of the cold.

A few would seek sleep, but most would stay busy losing the wages they hadn't yet earned for this job. Immature kids with more ambition than intelligence. Quinn envied them, remembering the days when he could afford such frivolity with his earnings.

The lights of Delaware's port shone in the distance. They didn't seem as if they grew any nearer, but regardless, the vessel made good time on its way to the docks. It would please Quinn when they landed because it would mean they had reached safe harbor.

Until then, the threat remained.

If a threat existed at all. He now thought it had all been a false alarm. Quinn slipped his radio free and clicked on the mic, lifting it up to his mouth.

"Everything good on your end?"

"Nothing to report," a woman's voice replied, followed by static.

"I haven't seen anything either."

"You probably won't. Keep your eyes peeled anyway. If they plan on trying something, they're running out of time."

"All right. Keep me updated."

This time, no response came, as expected. Since they'd first begun this trip back in South America, the woman on the other end of the line had remained tight-lipped. Quinn had never met her; although, he'd met some of the crew with whom she worked.

The woman oversaw the ship's security, though Quinn hadn't met her or even learned her name. Some outside company hired to keep the cargo safe, and not a part of the original crew. She was somewhere on board, but it was a big ship, and she kept to herself.

He'd met some of her team, however. Two burly and ugly men who usually lost money right along with his crew. Ex-military, both seemed better at following orders than giving them.

For the first few days of the trip, the security chief had insisted that they didn't need a night watchman. She had told Quinn he could relax because he wasn't doing any good anyway. Now, though, she didn't even bother. They both knew that Quinn enjoyed the night air. Not even armed, if a threat did occur on the cargo vessel, he wouldn't prove any help in stopping it.

He slipped the radio back into his pocket, watching the waves crash against the hull. Quinn liked the flicker of the ship's floodlights casting shadows upon the water, which bounced in chaotic and beautiful patterns that captivated him.

The effect got lost in the daylight. The way the waves flowed struck him as rhythmic and poetic—a dance separate from human understanding. It would have been perfect if it wasn't so damn cold.

Quinn drew his coat tighter around his shoulders and blew warm air into his hands. Before too long, he would need to refill his thermos with ̇coffee. And his bladder felt full from the first round, so he would need to hit the head, too. Maybe a smoke, even, if he could bum one off the guys below deck.

He'd run out of cigarettes a couple of days ago but refused to buy them when the ship left Brazil.

It didn't just come down to him being too cheap to buy them: the corner shop he'd stopped in only carried packs with the impotence-warning label. He didn't mind the labels with deformed babies or cancerous lungs, but no way would he pay for a pack with a warning label that he might never have kids.

12

Well, more kids.

The heavy metal door that led below deck flew open. Music poured out, ripping Quinn out of his reverie with a jolt. He glanced over in annoyance to see who had just come above deck, but the doorway stood out of his sightline.

"Cut out that racket!" he shouted. "I can't hear myself think."

The heavy door closed again, drowning out the cacophony. Heavy boot steps came his way, and then someone walked around the corner.

It took a minute to recognize the bundled-up man, but Quinn felt relieved to see Jimmy Pitts trudging toward him. His younger friend rubbed his hands together and scowled at the wind.

"I don't see how you can stand this frigidness," Jimmy said with a groan, leaning against the railing beside Quinn and staring out at the sea.

"Not much choice is there? No one else wanted this shift."

"No one *needed* this shift. The owner hired security, remember?"

"Which doesn't automatically let us off the hook. *We* are supposed to keep the cargo safe. Not some crew of jackass outsiders."

"*We* are supposed to make sure the ship keeps running. The port is *right there*. We're safe."

"You think they figured it out?"

Jimmy shrugged. "Whoever planned to hit us must have figured things out."

"Maybe. Either way, we won't be safe until we dock and get paid."

Jimmy scoffed, "You can be such a worry-wart, you know?"

"Who says worry-wart? You sound like an old woman."

"It's something my grandma used to say, I think."

"Ah, makes sense. Is it the wind messing with your brain? The only person I've ever heard use that phrase was my mother."

"Hmm. Maybe that was where I heard it?" Jimmy said, grinning.

Quinn flashed him a look. "Oh, you got jokes tonight?"

"Jokes for days."

"That right?"

"Well, maybe minutes with this cold."

"Nah, man. It ain't so bad."

13

"I would have asked for more money if I were you since you're taking all the night shifts out here in the cold. A larger cut, I mean."

Quinn shrugged. It didn't sound like a bad idea, and maybe he could raise the issue on their next run. For certain, he wouldn't object to more money, and Jimmy did have a point. He agreed, "Maybe."

"Plus, since you're up here at night, you get the hotty all to yourself."

"The hotty?"

Jimmy pointed at the radio in Quinn's pocket. "The woman on the other end of that line."

"Oh. You've seen her?"

"Nope. But she sounds hot."

"Just because she sounds hot doesn't mean she *is* hot," Quinn said. "Haven't you heard of phone sex lines?"

Jimmy shrugged. "Sounds hot is good enough for me right now. Maybe once we're back on dry land that will change."

"What if it's a man with a high-pitched voice?"

"Then *he* sounds hot." Jimmy shrugged. "I don't even know why they bothered hiring the security team. They're getting paid a fortune to do nothing."

"How do you know what they're earning?"

Jimmy waved a hand in annoyance. "You know what I mean. Mercenaries and private security teams make bank."

"Do they? Where's your proof?"

"Shut up. All I'm trying to say is we haven't seen another ship for three days, and even if one *did* come into range, we would pick it up on our radar scans long before our security team could see anything. We're paying them to do nothing."

"*We're* not paying them anything."

"The owners, I mean. Stop being contrary. Whoever's cargo we're hauling is the person I'm talking about."

"You don't think the threat is legit?"

"No. I think someone got their panties in a bunch. They should have just paid us more."

"I can't say no to that. We don't even know what our cargo is. Not that I give a toss one way or another. All I'm saying is *someone* must care, or they wouldn't have hired a private security team to get it to Delaware safely."

Jimmy shrugged. "Sure. Either way, you might as well just

14

come inside and let them earn their dough. No sense in doing their job for them if you don't get paid."

"Nah, I'm good."

"You sure? The guys would agree to let you in on the game—"

"You're out of money, aren't you?"

Hesitation. "What?"

"You ran out of money, didn't you?"

Jimmy laughed mirthlessly. "Yeah. I hoped you could front me some change."

"Like the last time? Or the time before that? Should have known this wasn't a social visit. I'm still waiting to get paid back, you know. Have you been to the bank recently?"

"As soon as we hit shore."

"That's what you said last time."

"It's coming. With interest."

Quinn smirked and shook his head. "Sure it is."

"So, you'll front me?"

"Hell no."

Jimmy sighed. He reached into a hidden pocket and drew out a flask. "Suit yourself. A few hours and we'll dock and have done with this run anyway. You know when the next run happens?"

"Our next trip isn't for a couple of weeks, and the weather is supposed to get a lot warmer."

"Cool. A few weeks, huh? Might be I'll hit up Atlantic City when we get there."

"You'll end up broke in a week."

"Or rich enough to quit this shit."

"Nah, broke."

Jimmy shrugged. "Most likely. What about you? What will you do with your weeks off?"

"Head back to Detroit for the downtime. Haven't seen Sally or the new baby in months."

"Third, right?"

"Fourth," Quinn said. "She's my third girl."

Jimmy whistled, handing the flask over to Quinn. "You need this more than I do, brother. You Catholics sure do pop 'em out. I can barely keep up with the names—couldn't imagine how Sally feels."

"More mouths to feed." Quinn took a long drag before passing back the flask. The liquid burned all the way down his

15

throat. Cheap stuff. He wiped his mouth with the back of his glove.

"I hear that."

A long while passed in silence, with the two of them staring out at the ocean and enjoying each other's company. Quinn realized that his friend didn't want to leave him up here alone, but Jimmy shook and shivered from the deep chill.

"Don't worry about me," Quinn said. "I'll stay up here and finish my shift, and you can head on back inside. The cold doesn't bother me."

"You sure?"

"I'm sure," Quinn said, reaching over and patting Jimmy on the back. "Thanks for coming out to check on me, though. I appreciate it."

"Appreciate it enough to cover me?"

"Not tonight. I might head to Atlantic City with you, though, when we hit the shore. Maybe I'll play some slots."

"Slots? Women play slots. You should get out on the tables."

"I prefer the games that come with a lot of bells and whistles. The flashier and louder the better."

"To each his own, I guess. Need a nightcap?" Jimmy asked, offering up the flask again.

"Sure."

"Just hang onto it. Only a bit left anyway."

"Nah. Let me just finish it off and—"

Quinn attempted to unscrew the lid while wearing his gloves, but it proved slippery on the fabric. In the process, he lost control of the metallic canister, and it dropped out of his hand.

The flask hit the deck with its first bounce.

It went over the edge of the cargo ship with the second.

Both men stared after it in awe, unable to speak.

Finally, Quinn gulped and pushed himself away from the railing. He cleared his throat. "I know what you're thinking, but I'm *not* going in after it."

"For God's sake, Quinn. That was a gift from my brother. You're buying me a new one."

"Yeah, okay."

"And a bottle of whiskey for my troubles. It had better be expensive and—"

"Let's not go crazy here," Quinn said, laughing. "New flask: no problem. More cheap swill, done. Top shelf? Hell no."

16

"It was from my *favorite* brother."

"You only have the one."

"Good point. I accept your offer. I'm heading inside," Jimmy said, rubbing his hands again and blowing on them. "If you want to stick around out here and freeze your nuts off, that's your problem."

Quinn nodded after Jimmy as the younger man walked away. Then he leaned his back against the railing to look up at the night sky. After a moment, the heavy door opened and closed again, leaving him alone on the deck once more.

The whiskey settled on his stomach, and it felt good. It had turned out to be a good night

Chapter 2
Ocean City, Delaware

1

"Just one guy on deck again," Jensen said into the headset microphone, typing a command into his computer and shifting between camera images rapidly. "The same guy as before."

"The other guy left?"

"Back below deck. You're clear. If you're going to jump, then do it now."

Jensen paused on the final camera, which focused on Malcolm, who stood near the loading ramp of the plane, decked out in a black amphibious HALO suit and parachute.

"Did I mention that you look like a badass?" Jensen said. "Be honest—you only took this job to do a nighttime HALO jump."

"I took the job because they were desperate and willing to pay a fortune."

"Uh huh."

"Besides, we're too low for an actual HALO jump."

"Couldn't talk him into flying higher?"

Malcolm ignored Jensen, put on his altitude mask, and walked toward the end of the ramp.

"Makes sense," Jensen said, playfully. "Since you're so cheap anyway. You never want to pay top dollar for anything."

"I don't like this," Malcolm said, his voice tinny in the speakers of Jensen's computer.

"Too close to shore? You wanted to hit them at the end of the trip when their guard came down."

On the tiny computer screen, Malcolm shook his head. "No. My gut. Something about this job feels off."

"It seems legit."

"Too legit," Malcolm said.

19

"Too legit to quit?"

Malcolm ignored him. Instead, he asked, "You didn't find anything odd?"

Jensen said, "Not in the time I had. I would have run a more thorough sweep, but you only gave me a day. What are you thinking? The security is too lax?"

"I don't know."

"I did think the same thing."

Malcolm didn't reply immediately. Jensen tapped his fingers against the door of the car, wondering what was going through his boss's mind. He didn't like to rush him, but they were running out of time.

"Should we call it?" Jensen asked, glancing at the back seat behind him. Amy sat bundled up in her coat, staring out the window, and barely paying attention to him at all.

She provided backup in case the boat made it to shore, setting up distractions for their getaway after they destroyed the cargo.

Amy wanted to be up there with Malcolm, Jensen knew, but Malcolm had insisted on boarding The Lonely Spirit alone.

"We'll miss our window," Jensen said. "Your jump is in thirty seconds, so I need to know if we're calling it."

A few seconds passed.

"No," Malcolm said, finally. "It's just paranoia. We'll move forward with the plan. You're right. It's legit."

"I'm right?" Jensen said, sounding incredulous. "Hang on— let me start recording, and you can repeat that."

"Shut up. Focus."

"All right then," Jensen said, tapping on the keyboard. "Twenty seconds, boss. Hope you're ready to get wet."

Malcolm didn't reply. Jensen couldn't imagine doing what Malcolm was about to do. His boss wouldn't be able to see the water below him until it was too late, which meant putting his life in the hands of sensitive and expensive equipment.

While Jensen trusted his computers, electronics could fail. Even if it didn't, he wouldn't be willing to risk his life so readily. One minor malfunction and ...

Jensen blinked and forced away the thoughts. That was why he wasn't up there in the plane getting ready to swan-dive a few thousand feet to the water below. And why he never did those kinds of things. He wasn't dumb enough to risk his life, not when there were alternatives.

"Are you ready? Fifteen seconds."

"Count it down," Malcolm called over the headset.

"I did say this was a bad plan, right?" Jensen said. "Borderline suicidal, putting so much trust in altitude meters—"

"Just count it down," Malcolm said, clicking the button to lower the ramp on the Cessna. The pilot would close the ramp once Malcolm had gone and never mention to anyone that he'd had a guest on his plane for the last few hours. Jensen didn't know where Malcolm had found the guy, but it made their job of getting close to the smuggling vessel quite a bit easier.

"Okay," Jensen said, watching the monitor. "Here it goes: five ... four ..."

"Three ..."

"Two ..."

"One ..."

"Jump."

Jensen sucked in a shuddering breath. Even down here on the docks, he felt trepidation in the pit of his stomach just imagining what was about to happen. On the screen in the cargo bay of the plane, he watched as Malcolm disappeared into the darkness below the aircraft.

"Game on."

2

Wind whipped past Malcolm's clothing, and the drop of his stomach registered the sensation of falling, but he couldn't see anything. The drone of the plane's engines had gone in an instant, replaced by the violent rush of air pummeling his body.

This made for his fifteenth jump from this height, but only the third ever at night. The other two similar jumps hadn't happened in this kind of dark, though, with the clouds above blocking all moonlight. It felt like a vacuum—suspended in air and utterly weightless—and as if he could fall forever.

The drop had a bottom, however, and if he weren't careful, he would hit the water with a sickening thud that would tear him asunder. Then the only luck he could count on was if he died from impact instead of drowning.

How long had he been in the air? Two seconds? Twenty? A

minute?

Without the perspective of the environment around him, he lost all awareness of time and height. He glanced at the dial on his wrist. Six thousand meters. He couldn't have jumped that long ago.

Or the dial read incorrectly.

Not a pleasant thought.

"Fifty-eight hundred meters," Jensen called out over the headset.

Just hearing Jensen's voice filled Malcolm with relief. It brought enough to know he wasn't alone. A few seconds passed, and then Jensen said, "Five thousand meters."

Jensen continued to count down the altitude as the seconds ticked by. Malcolm passed through the clouds, and tiny dots of light grew in the distance—from the city outside the port, but it didn't give enough to get his bearings. He had to trust Jensen and the equipment for his survival.

After what felt like forever—though less than five minutes— Malcolm had reached a safe altitude at which he could pull the chute.

"You're clear, boss."

Malcolm pulled the strap to release the parachute. His body jerked upward into the air. Then a gust of wind caught hold of him and ripped his body to the side, which felt both exhilarating and terrifying.

He lived for this. And though he couldn't see the billowing cloth material above his head, he could feel the change in his rapid descent as the chute caught the air and he guided it down.

Directly below him, a speck of light glistened. From this height, it looked like the flame of a candle. That light was his target. The Lonely Spirit. A shipping vessel carrying the cargo he was tasked to destroy.

Malcolm kept an eye on his altitude gauge as he descended, still unable to make out any actual water below. Two more minutes passed with minimal change, and he realized he must be getting close to the water level now.

Here came the most dangerous part of the entire jump: he would have only a few seconds to react from the moment of impact until he became fully submerged, and in that time, he would have to free himself from the parachute before it dragged him under.

On top of that, he would also need to obtain an idea of where he'd landed in comparison to his target. If the current picked him up and carried him too far away from the cargo vessel, then it would prove impossible for his team to find and rescue him before he went adrift completely.

To steady his nerves, Malcolm took a few deep breaths and waited.

Jensen's voice came over the headset, "Any second now—"

Malcolm received only a split-second view of the night-black sea before he crashed into it. He landed harder than anticipated, and the frigidity of the water overwhelmed him instantly. His suit was designed to protect him from that cold, but it still shocked his system.

The suit kept him dry and insulated, and so, once he made it out of the water, he would warm up in a hurry. Malcolm released the latch on the parachute, slipping it free and letting it go. It washed away at speed, dragged in the undertow.

Then he turned his attention to spotting his target. Light glimmered in the distance to his east, about eighty meters away. It came straight toward him.

"Perfect trajectory, Jensen."

"Of course. Perfect timing too," Jensen said. "I have the ship's GPS and, contrary to popular belief, I *can* do basic mathematics to line up things like this."

"Basic?"

"Calculating the jump point based on multiple factors like wind, vessel, and aircraft speed and directionality to put you two hundred meters ahead of the ship in its exact path *is* basic mathematics, right?"

"It is actually about eighty meters."

Jensen fell silent on the other end of the line for a moment. Then he said, "You didn't let me finish. Two hundred meters, give or take."

"That's a lot of take."

"Everyone's a critic."

"Still, good job."

"Does that mean I get a raise?"

"Don't push it."

Malcolm took a moment to do a gear check while the ship approached: his pistols nestled in their holsters at his sides—a pair of Smith and Wesson M&P9Ls, and his night-vision goggles and Jensen's little drone hung pinned to his vest in plastic sealed wrapping. Not waterproof, he would have to manage without them until he climbed onboard the ship and out of the frigid water.

In addition, he had several pounds of explosive foam in spray canisters to eliminate the cargo. Though not as stable or destructive as he would have liked, they didn't require a detonation cap to ignite.

A few high-priority crates were all he needed to go after, and with luck, he would get in and out with no one onboard the ship any the wiser.

Malcolm yanked off the altitude mask and took a breath of the chilly night air. "I thought you said it would be a warm night."

"It is," Jensen said. "We're nice and toasty on the docks. Right, Ames?"

Malcolm didn't hear anything from Amy. She remained upset that he'd left her behind on this run. He'd considered sending her on the jump instead of himself but had changed his mind at the last minute. No sense in risking her unnecessarily. And he didn't believe her ready for something like this.

"What Amy said, I dare not repeat over the line," Jensen said. "But, yes, she is downright fiery out here."

"At least we have cloud cover."

Malcolm didn't worry about getting spotted. When he looked up at the sky above him, he realized that, if anything, the night would only get darker. It was supposed to rain, but he hoped that the inclement weather would hold off until this job was over with.

Malcolm bobbed in the water and waited while the spotlight grew gradually, adjusting his position occasionally to make sure he lay in its path.

The cargo ship towered above him, and he aligned himself with the current to get as close as possible to the side of The Lonely Spirit. He held a hook in his left hand and waited patiently for the moment to strike.

The current threatened to drag him away, but he managed to get his right hand on one of the hull's ridges and punch the grappling hook through the fiberglass siding of the vessel. The boat moved slowly, but even then, the rushing water made it difficult to maintain his grip. It dragged him along as he started to pull himself up.

His hand slipped from the ridge, and suddenly, he hung loose, dragged down under the waterline behind his hook.

He managed to catch a breath of air before his head got sucked under, and he twisted around and lost all perspective. Without any light, it became impossible to tell which direction was up.

Lungs burning, Malcolm struggled against the current to reach the surface and realized he wasn't making any progress. He forced himself to relax and grabbed hold of the wire, using it to pull himself alongside the hull of the ship, praying the hook would have a secure enough grip in the side of the vessel to support his head.

Finally, he managed to get his head above water, and this time, he locked both hands on the ridges and pulled the upper half of his body out of the sea. His muscles throbbed, and his vision had tunneled from lack of oxygen, but otherwise, he remained unscathed.

"Malcolm, you there?" Jensen's voice sounded in his ear. It amazed Malcolm that the earbud hadn't jarred loose when he got pulled under.

"I'm here."

"What happened?"

"Undertow," he said. "Switching to the headset."

He took a moment to catch his breath. Though still panting lightly, he now gained better control of the situation.

He climbed higher so that his legs hung above the sea. Now it was all or nothing: he released the hook and let it fall. It splashed into the water and disappeared. He wouldn't get a third chance.

Resolute, Malcolm climbed higher up the side of the hull, opening the plastic bag on his chest. Then he donned the night-vision goggles and activated them. The ship wasn't well lit, which would give him a significant advantage over the crew.

Next, he put on a slender headset as well, which would give him better connectivity to his team. Though not waterproof like the bud, it had better sound quality.

"You still there?" he said.

"What?"

"Can you hear me?"

"Hang on. Let me turn you up," Jensen said. "Say something."

25

"Better?" Malcolm whispered.

"Whoa. That's loud," Jensen said. "Lots of feedback. I told you we should have sprung for a throat mic."

Malcolm cupped his hand around his mouth and the microphone. "How's this?" he said as loudly as he dared. A string of cursing came from the other end, along with a loud thud. Malcolm smiled.

"Not cool," Jensen said. "Not cool at all. I almost fell out of the car."

"Is anyone in the control room of the ship?"

"No, just that lone guy on the deck. They don't seem too worried about security. I hacked their controls already and piggybacked into the system. On your signal, I'll stop the boat and kill the lights."

"How long will that last?"

"They can turn them back on pretty easily with manual controls, so make sure you're quick."

Malcolm hesitated. "Limited security," he said. "Only one guard. Why wouldn't they have more?"

"This isn't a smuggling ship," Jensen said. "The cargo is mostly legit."

"We're only after three cases, right?"

"That's all," Jensen said. "You sure you want to blow up whatever it is? Could be worth a fortune."

"They paid us to blow it up."

"What the client doesn't know won't hurt him."

"But it might hurt us. They're giving us plenty to do this job. We'll not take any extra risk or betray the person who hired us."

"Fine. I just wanted to register my reluctance to blow up something before checking its price tag."

"No security," Malcolm said. "Must not be worth that much."

"Maybe that's what they want you to think."

"Maybe," Malcolm said.

He couldn't shake the feeling that something was wrong with this situation. If the crates weren't worth a lot, then why had they paid so much to destroy them?

They had done a full recon of the ship and found nothing amiss. The crates weren't registered, and most likely, the crew didn't know they were aboard. The crew ran its own security, but no one had military training.

Malcolm would have preferred having a few more guards

patrolling the ship. At least then he would have known the threat. Then he could plan for it.

What he didn't know could undoubtedly hurt him.

A second longer he hesitated and then dragged himself over the edge of the deck; the single guard—a man named Quinn, from Jensen's recon—stood at the opposite end of the ship, leaning against the railing and not paying attention to anything at all right then.

There seemed no chance he would see an attack coming. Malcolm slid himself under the ship's railing and to his feet. Then he quick-stepped the thirty feet across the deck to the lone guard, while at the same time, he drew a seven-inch blade from a hilt on his shoulder.

Quinn didn't react until Malcolm reached only a few steps away, and when he began to turn and open his mouth to shout, it was too late.

Malcolm put his hand over Quinn's mouth and held the blade to his throat. "Not a peep," he muttered into the man's ear. "Got it?"

Quinn nodded.

Carefully, he dragged the man away from the railing and out of sight. Quinn didn't react at all except to allow himself to be dragged. His body shook with fear.

"You'll wake up with a headache in about twenty minutes, and when you do, it'll be fine for you to head into the control room and call the coastguard. Let them know what happened, but if you even so much as try to give them a description of me, know that I'll come looking for you. Got it?"

Again, Quinn nodded.

"Good."

Malcolm pulled his hand back and punched Quinn in the back of the head with the butt-end of his knife. Quinn collapsed to the deck like a sack of potatoes. Malcolm checked his pulse to make sure hadn't died, and then he stood up.

"Deck is secure."

"Tell me when to cut the power," Jensen said. Malcolm moved over to the metal door that led below deck. He tested it to make sure it stood unlocked. It did.

Earlier, he had memorized the layout of the ship and knew his route perfectly; through the dining area, down the stairs, and all the way across the hall to the cargo hold. If he encountered any resistance, then so be it.

In the region of four or six men stood between here and there, but once he had control of the engine room, he had control of the ship.

"Hang on. Someone's coming. Guess we couldn't plan for things to go this easily, huh?"

Malcolm flipped on his night-vision goggles and made the sign of the cross. "Here goes nothing."

Chapter 3
Ocean City, Delaware

1

"Three Aces. Read 'em an' weep."

"Three aces? Wow, that's tough to beat ..."

"I don't like taking your money, but I'll still take it—"

"But, you know what's even tougher ... a whole *mess* of clubs."

Henry's face paled when Jimmy laid his cards down on the table; Henry had already engaged in the process of leaning forward to scoop up his winnings, and now, he leaned back into his seat slowly with a groan.

"Are you kidding me?" he asked.

"Afraid not." Jimmy wrapped his arm around the pile and dragged it in front of him. "My children thank you."

"You don't have any children," Henry said, bleakly. "Can I at least have my watch back?"

"Oh, you mean this watch?" Jimmy slid the metal band over his wrist.

"That cost me three hundred bucks, man."

"You shouldn't have bet it."

"You shouldn't have won."

"What can I say? It's my lucky night. I'll tell you what. Give me three hundred bucks, and we'll call it even," Jimmy said.

Henry blew out air. "I don't have three hundred bucks."

"You will when we hit port and get paid in oh, say, two hours. I'll just hang onto this until then."

Henry stood up from behind the table and grabbed his coat. "Weren't you out of money?"

"Was. Not now."

Henry grumbled and headed for the stairs. He threw his coat on and grabbed a box of Marlboro cigarettes. "I need some fresh air," he said, "and I'm out of money."

"We can keep playing on credit."

"Screw you." Henry pushed open the door and disappeared out into the night.

Jimmy watched him go and turned back to the other players. His friend Kenny burst out laughing. "I don't know who will be more pissed. Henry when he realizes you played on stolen money or Quinn when he figures out you pinched his wallet."

"I'll pay Quinn back with interest," Jimmy said. "Henry? Who cares?"

2

Outside, on the deck, Henry lit his cigarette and took a long drag into his lungs. He held it for a long minute before blowing it out through his nostrils. Then he walked over to the railing, using his thumb to scratch his nose and letting out a deep sigh.

"God damn it," he mumbled. "God damn clubs."

He stared out at the water, puffing on the filter. A gust of wind whipped past him, and he pulled his hood over his ears.

"Why would anyone stay out here willingly in this shit?" he called out, turning to face the front of the boat. He couldn't see Quinn in his field of vision, so he assumed the guy must have fled into the control room to escape the cold.

Quinn was a loner, anti-social as hell. It bugged Henry, but not enough for him to mistreat the guy. It wasn't as though Quinn was intentionally a loser. The poor guy just couldn't help himself.

And now, Henry had to admit that he didn't want to be around the other crew members either. His stomach twisted, and he didn't know what he would tell his girlfriend about the money he'd just lost. His wallet had grown a lot lighter.

It hadn't turned out to be a good night. But he couldn't afford to lose that watch either. Maybe if he told Quinn that Jimmy stole his wallet, they could team up on the little bastard, and he could get it back.

"Quinn, you out here?" he asked. "Yo, Quinn."

He stopped, noticing something odd out of the corner of his

30

eye. When he turned, he saw a wrapped-up body tucked behind boxes. Quinn. Henry rushed over, eyes wide, and knelt. "Quinn? You okay?"

He shook the form, and Quinn let out a groan and swatted at him.

"What the hell happened?" Quinn mumbled, rubbing his head. "What's going on?"

Then, without warning, everything stopped. The spotlights blinked and went out, the rumbling of the engine disappeared, and the boat ceased its forward trajectory. They sat dead in the water, entirely at the mercy of a calm sea.

The cigarette fell from Henry's lips. "What the hell?"

Then came gunshots.

3

When the man walked out onto the deck to smoke, Malcolm had hidden out of the way. That meant one less enemy he would need to worry about when things got messy, and it made his entrance easier: now, he wouldn't have to open the door and make noise to get inside.

Satisfied, he gave Jensen the command to cut the power. A few seconds passed, and then the engine went out, and as soon as Malcolm felt the ship buckle under his feet, he stepped below deck into The Lonely Spirit's mess hall.

Sounds of shouting and confusion reached him. With his goggles, the area lit up clearly. Beforehand, he had loaded rubber bullets into his pistols. He had come here to knock them out, not kill them. Without hesitation, he aimed and fired off a series of three shots—two into the first guard's chest, and one into the leg of the second.

The men barely reacted to the intrusion, and Malcolm went through that room and into the stairwell in only seconds. A door opened on his right, and a night-blind guard stumbled into the hallway, carrying a shotgun. Malcolm didn't bother shooting, but instead, launched a series of kicks into the bloke's knee, groin, and head. The guy dropped the gun and collapsed to the ground in the fetal position, showing no desire to resist further.

The door at the end of the hall swung closed in front of him, and a lock clicked on the other side. That entrance led to the cargo room, precisely where he needed to go to finish the job.

Malcolm reached down to his waist and yanked one of the canisters of foam explosive out of his hip bandolier. He stepped up to the door and knelt, spraying the foam over where the lock would sit on the other side. Then he ignited it.

A sharp and localized explosion struck against the lock, and he followed that up with a kick just under the bolt to knock the door loose. The practiced maneuver took less than twelve seconds, and then he dashed inside the lower decks.

The ship remained powered off, and hissing came from the engines down below as they cooled off. In front of him lay the cargo section he wanted. It held the containers he needed to destroy, but he found this door locked as well. For a second, he paused to listen. Movement sounded on the other side of the door in the hold.

"There's a guy on the top deck running to the control room," Jensen said over the headset. "He can switch off my remote control of the ship. When he gets there, the lights and engine turn back on, and I'm out of the game. You have about twenty seconds left."

"Plenty of time."

This door was flimsy wood. He kicked it open and stepped inside, raising his pistols.

A shot came from the right corner of the cargo room, and then another from only a few feet to his left. Two enemies, both of which seemed without night vision. Blindly, they fired at him in the darkness, but he could see them perfectly.

He raised his pistol and fired off four rounds, two at each man. A moment of awkward hesitation followed, and then two thumps sounded when their bodies hit the floor.

Everything went quiet. Malcolm stayed close to the left wall and moved deeper into the room, making sure no one hid behind any of the crates in the storage. The critical containers lay up ahead. The rest, no more than a bunch of boxes he didn't need to worry about.

Except ...

They sat empty, he realized.

Malcolm's heart leapt into his chest. This was wrong. This was very, very wrong. The cargo hold should have been loaded to the brim with goods for a trip like this. Instead, the entire cargo room held nothing but empty crates.

32

"It's empty."

"What is?" Jensen asked.

"The hold. Everything. Everything is empty."

"What do you mean? I know for a fact that when they left South America two days ago this—"

The sound of gunshots coming through the headset interrupted Jensen.

"Jensen? What the hell is happening?"

More gunshots and shouting from Amy and Jensen's end. Then, everything on the other end of the line went silent.

"What's going on?" he shouted.

He didn't get a reply.

A trap—he'd walked into a trap. The boxes weren't here, which meant someone knew he was coming.

However, just realizing it was a trap didn't do him a lot of good in his current situation. His contact had hired him to destroy specific cargo, and now—it seemed—someone else had been hired to prevent that. The unknown person, or persons, had managed to stay one step ahead of his crew, which meant they knew his exact plans and location.

The empty crates didn't form part of the plan. They acted as collateral.

Suddenly, the lights came on, and his goggles went dark, the light filters cutting off the night vision before it blinded him. Malcolm stumbled to the side from the sudden disorientation and bounced off the wall. He cursed and ripped the goggles off, dropping them to the ground, and then he blinked rapidly to clear his vision.

A few seconds passed, and then he froze. Against the wall, only inches in front of his face, sat a clock detonator, counting down. On the floor, next to it, lay a crate, only this one wasn't empty.

Several pounds of plastic explosive filled this one.

The counter reached ten seconds.

"Good to see you, Malcolm," a voice called out behind him. "I've waited for this day for a long time."

He turned. Jeff Tripp stood in the doorway, an assault rifle leveled at Malcolm. The ugly, balding man grinned from ear to vile ear.

"I'll enjoy killing you."

Malcolm didn't hesitate or think.

33

Instead, reacting on instinct, he turned and sprinted toward the opposite wall of the ship.

Jeff opened fire.

Malcolm ducked low behind the empty crates as he ran. His body jolted from the impact of bullets thudding into his bullet-proof vest. A few missed the protective plating and tore into him, but he forced himself to keep moving.

Halfway across the cargo hold, he ripped the bandolier of foam explosive from his hip and threw it at the wall as hard as he could. The metal wall had no reinforcement, and hopefully, it wouldn't hinder him much.

The shooting stopped, and the door slammed shut behind him, but he ignored it. He focused and kept running, raising his other pistol. This one, he had loaded with real bullets.

Malcolm waited until the bandolier hit the wall and then fired at it.

His first shot missed and thudded into the wall next to the bandolier, but the second hit the flying package.

It exploded, spreading flames back into the room but also doing significant damage to the thin metal wall. Malcolm held his arm up to protect his face and kept running. He didn't have time to stop and check if his plan had worked.

At speed, he stumbled into the wall, crashing through the softened material and out into the open air beyond just as the C-4 erupted behind him. This explosion felt much worse: it sounded loud, a lot more so than Malcolm would have expected, and then something hit him from behind. Or several something's; he couldn't be sure.

The air wrapped around him when he fell. Malcolm closed his eyes.

He hit the water face-first and at an awkward angle. Pain rushed up his spine, but whether from the explosion or the landing he couldn't tell for sure. For a second, he blacked out from the pain, and when he came to, he swam frantically for the surface. When he broke through, at last, he sucked in a breath of much-needed air.

Violently, he flailed about. His body didn't work as well as it should. In a panic, his mind screamed at him, yelling for Malcolm to swim harder. However, he pushed the idea down. He needed to relax and tread water, not give in to the panic.

Malcolm struggled to gather his bearings. To his left, flames

34

blazed throughout The Lonely Spirit. In front of him lay the port, only a few hundred meters away.

One of his legs throbbed, as well as his lower back, and he grew weaker by the second. Most likely, shrapnel from the explosion had punctured him. He suspected blood loss but couldn't address that right now.

"Jensen," he mumbled, grabbing for the microphone and speaker attached to his ear. The dunking under water might well have destroyed it, but he had to try. He clicked the power button. "Jensen, can you hear me?"

No response came. Was the mic working or not? "Get out of there. Jensen? Can you hear me? It was a trap. Get Amy and get out of there."

Still no response. Only static on the other end. Malcolm prayed that they hadn't died.

Somehow, he doubted his prayers would get answered.

His arms gave out as he slipped toward unconsciousness. It would only take minutes before he found a watery grave. His injuries put his body into shock. He tried to fight it, but it proved futile. He had died already—it would just take his body a while to catch up.

More time passed, probably minutes, but it felt like hours. Exhaustion crept in, and Malcolm became delirious.

"I told you no one was supposed to get hurt!" someone called from behind him. A female voice, though she sounded far away.

"I will not pass up a chance to kill Malcolm. No matter what you say."

Something grabbed his arm, steadying him. He tried to look up but felt too tired. Slowly, he sank further into the abyss. "Help me."

"Just let him die," the man said again. "It's over for him."

The hand on his arm disappeared. Then came a sound, like a gunshot, but muffled. Malcolm continued to slip, and his head went under water, but then something caught him.

"Don't worry; I've got you," the woman's voice said. Malcolm didn't feel worried. The water soothed. It didn't even feel cold anymore. He wanted to drift away into its embrace.

"This is a disaster," the woman mumbled. "No one was supposed to get hurt. Damn it, Malcolm, stay with me. Don't you dare die on me."

35

The last thing Malcolm heard was the sound of a helicopter approaching, and then he knew no more.

Chapter 4
Concord, New Hampshire

1

The front lock of his hotel room buzzed a second before the door opened. "Finally, you're back," Lyle said, tapping a few keys on his laptop to lock the screen and spinning in his chair. "How did your trip go?"

In the doorway, Kate Allison hesitated for a second, staring at Lyle curiously. Finally, she strode into the room and set her bags on the table, giving him a funny look.

"How did you know it was me?"

"Who else would it be?"

"I could have been someone trying to kill you."

"Who would want to kill me?" he asked, all innocence.

"You *are* a wanted fugitive."

Lyle shrugged. "Fugitive, maybe. Wanted? Probably not. Besides, asking how I knew it was you is a silly question. I'm hooked into live feeds from all of the hotel's cameras."

"I came up a rear access stairwell. No cameras."

"No *hotel* cameras," Lyle said. "I put a couple of my own in there, just in case."

"Ah. I didn't notice them. You're getting better at this."

"Being a criminal?" he asked. "I've always been good with electronics. It's the 'wanted by the FBI' part that still feels new to me."

"Only for questioning."

"Oh, is that all they want to do? Ask me a couple of questions and then lock me in a box for the rest of my life?"

"You should stay more careful."

"Maybe. At least I made the most-wanted list."

"Barely."

"Forty-seven isn't barely, if you ask me."

"They only track fifty."

"And I'm among those fifty. Are *you* on the list? ... I didn't think so."

She shrugged. "In a month or two, you won't make the cut at all."

"That's assuming I don't get in trouble again," Lyle said. "Speaking of which, do we have a new job? I'm itching to get in trouble again."

"Ah, well, getting into trouble depends on whether or not we get caught. And, yeah, we do have a new job. Why, you anxious or something?"

"Bored would better describe me. I've stayed cooped up in here for two weeks. It would pass the time more easily if my partner was here with me and not out of the country working side jobs she won't tell me about."

She narrowed her eyes. "How did you know I left the country?"

"Tracking chip," he said, waving his hand in dismissal. "In your coat. The inseam."

"I lost that coat."

"I know. Made it *way* harder for me to keep tabs on you. I lost you once you popped over into Brazil."

Kate stared at him for a long minute, standing in the doorway. "Is that how it's going to be, with you spying on me every time I'm gone for a couple of days?"

"You left without saying anything. If you told me where you planned to go and treated this like a partnership, I wouldn't *need* to spy on you."

"Partners trust each other."

"Exactly!"

"I told you I had a job."

"And *nothing* else. I wanted to make sure you were safe. I could have helped."

"Not with this one."

"Why not? I thought we were a team?"

Kate sighed and rubbed her forehead. "You've given me a headache. I don't have to tell you *every* single time I step out for a couple of days."

"No," he said. "You don't. And it isn't that I don't trust you or anything. It would be nice if you let me know, though."

"Point taken. I didn't mean to bail like that. I just had some business to take care of and didn't want you involved."

"Apology accepted."

"I wasn't apologizing—"

"So, what's the new job?"

Kate didn't respond immediately. Instead, she walked over to the window and drew aside the heavy hotel curtain. Sunlight poured into the room, and Lyle hissed in mock pain. He covered his eyes with his arm.

"Ah, it burns!"

"So dramatic. Sometimes, I just don't know what to do with you. How did you manage during my absence?"

"Manage? Are you kidding?"

"What?"

"Two weeks," he said. "You went for two weeks. I ran out of food and had to go to the supermarket. Twice."

Her lip curled up. "Did you wear your disguise?"

Lyle stood and grabbed a frilly red dress from the floor. With a frown, he shook it in her face. "Did you find this funny? No way in hell will I wear a dress."

"I left a makeup kit, too. I even found your base-color rouge."

"Ha. Funny."

"No one would recognize you in drag."

"I found a place that doesn't have cameras. I don't stand out exactly."

"Nope, you don't," she said. "Twenty-something white guy with average features and brown hair. Hard to believe they didn't recognize you."

"Ouch. When you put it like that—"

"And no muscle mass," she added, grinning. "Plain face. Kind of frumpy looking."

"Too far. Now you've gone too far. Frumpy? What does that even mean?"

She walked across the room to where Lyle stood and wrapped her arms around his neck before leaning in and kissing him softly on the lips. "All right. Too far."

"I've been doing pushups."

"Have you?" she asked. "Lots of pushups but no showers, huh?"

He shrugged. "I think I showered a couple of days ago. Maybe."

39

"I can tell. Shower, shave, and I'll come back in an hour or so with food."

"What? You're leaving again?"

"Only for a while," she said.

"I have food here." He pointed at the table. Old wrappers and candy bars covered it, as well as half-empty bags of chips and soda.

She frowned at it and then laughed. "You picked up Heath bars?"

He shrugged. "You said they were your favorite. I got a six-pack."

"Then why's there only one left?"

"I bought them five days ago. At least there's still one."

She picked it up from the table. "I can see that. You got my favorite candy bar and then ate all of them except one?"

"You disappeared for two weeks."

She slid it into her pocket. "I guess I should feel glad you actually saved me the one. It'll make a good dessert after we get some real food in our stomachs. Then we can go meet our newest client."

Lyle perked up. "We meet him today?"

"No. Tomorrow. Today, we drive."

"Where?"

"Texas."

"You're kidding? That's, like, twenty hours."

"More like twenty-eight."

"Who's the client?"

"I don't know. Peter just gave me an address and a time to meet him. Easy job, he said. Just pick up a package and drop it off."

"That's it?"

"That's it. Except ..."

"What?"

"We have to drive straight through, so I hope you're ready for a lot of traveling."

He groaned. "Can't we fly?"

"What part of 'FBI's most wanted list' don't you understand?"

"Fine, lots of driving."

"And an easy job."

"Sounds too good to be true," he said. "And when it feels

40

that way, it usually is."

"Oh, I forgot to mention that the men who have the package right now also carry guns."

"Ah, there it is," he said. "Why doesn't anyone simply leave the packages unattended? Like, maybe for our next job, we can steal Amazon packages from someone's porch."

"We don't need any toothbrushes or electric razors."

"Is that all you think they sell? Ye of little imagination."

She shrugged. "In any case, the job is still a cake walk. As long as my partner in crime gets himself clean-shaven and doesn't smell like a hermit when I come back. If you don't take a shower, then the hardest part about this job will be getting the client to agree to overlook your stink."

Lyle laughed. "Fine."

"I'll be back."

"All right. See you soon."

Kate nodded and headed out of the room. She closed the door behind her, and Lyle let out a sigh.

"Food, huh?" he asked, taking out his cellphone and punching in his unlock code. It popped to life with a map of the surrounding area, along with a little dot moving away from his position toward the parking lot.

This tracking chip, he'd put in the Heath candy bar Kate had in her pocket. When all else failed, he could trust her stomach to get the job done.

Luckily, she hadn't felt hungry when she arrived.

"Let's see where you're *really* going."

2

When the little blinking dot stopped moving, Lyle wished he'd brought along a disguise. Not the dress, of course, but something to make him a little less conspicuous walking into a hospital full of cameras.

In most situations, he would have felt willing to take his chances and hope that he wouldn't get spotted. However, entering a hospital didn't seem like the greatest plan in the world for a wanted fugitive.

Why on earth had Kate come here?

Naturally, he reminded himself, getting inside didn't

necessarily require that he leave his car. He found a parking spot near the back of the lot and grabbed his laptop from the rear seat. The hospital had multiple Wi-Fi networks, and after a little searching, he found the hidden security network with the cameras.

It took no time at all to gain control and get full access to the system. Most of the hallways, and even a good deal of the rooms, had cameras in them for monitoring patients and visitors. He scanned back through the timestamps to when Kate arrived, found her, and tracked her through the hospital up to one of the rooms on the third floor.

That room lived in the ICU recovery ward—lucky because it had a ceiling-mounted camera for patient care at a nearby nursing station. Most suites had a modicum of privacy, but that didn't seem to apply for intensive-care patients.

Lyle pulled up the image and jumped back through timestamps to the live feed. Kate sat in a chair beside a bed. On that bed lay what looked like a sleeping man with rugged features and curly black hair. Maybe in his early forties, muscular, and well toned.

"Who the hell are you?" Lyle muttered to himself.

Perturbed, he pulled up the hospital records for the patient and combed through the information. The room was registered to a man named Jason Coleman, though a quick check showed a bogus social security number. The admission came as the result of multiple gunshot wounds sometime in the last couple of days, and he discovered transfer paperwork from another hospital.

Lyle backtracked the transfer and found that it, too, was fake. Not even a good forgery, but enough to convince the hospital, it seemed. That pretend transfer form tracked back to another one in Delaware, and there the trail ended. Lyle tried to run facial recognition on the guy through a government database but got no hits.

A glance at the camera showed the guy waking. Kate reached over and, tenderly, grabbed his arm, steadying him. They spoke, but the camera feed had no audio. Apparently, the hospital's invasion of privacy stopped short of eavesdropping.

Lyle had no clue what the two said. He leaned in close to the monitor, trying to read their lips. No good, though, as he had no clue or training in lip reading.

Stumped for the moment, he mused over other options to

overhear their conversation—maybe hack Kate's phone and turn on the microphone, or see if he could access the nurses' call system and use it to listen in—then, all of a sudden, Kate reached into her pocket.

She pulled out the Heath bar.

Lyle froze, fingers hovering over the keyboard.

"Uh-oh."

She unwrapped the plastic and broke off a chunk of the chocolate, handing it to the injured man on the bed. Then she did a double take, spotting the tiny strip of metal attached to the bottom of the candy bar.

Lyle had done a great job resealing the package (it had only taken him six tries), but the jig was up.

Kate glanced around the room, spotting and staring directly at the camera.

"Oops."

Slowly, she drew her phone from her pocket, pressed a button, and held it up to her ear. Throughout the entire motion, she kept staring at the camera.

His phone rang. Lyle gulped and rubbed his hands against his pants.

"Okay, Lyle, just relax. You can do this. She doesn't know anything, so just play it cool."

He answered, "Hey, just finishing my shower and—"

"You're outside, aren't you?"

"What do you mean? I'm still back at the—"

"You speak too fast, and your pitch goes, like, two octaves higher when you lie," she said. "We need to work on that."

He took a deep breath. "Fine. I'm outside in the parking lot. I felt curious about where you were going since you just got back into the country."

"You could have asked."

"Would you have told me?"

She hesitated. "Probably not."

"Exactly."

"Fair enough."

"Who's your friend?"

Her expression soured. The guy lay staring up at the camera now too, a bemused expression on his face.

"Jealous?"

"Of his muscular arms and chiseled jaw? Not even a tiny bit."

43

"He has perfect abs, too."

"Pfft. I've got a great ab as well. ... Just the one. ... Seriously, though, who is he? That the client?"

"Bring your car around to the loading bay."

"What? Why?"

"I need to get him out of here. Since you're outside anyway, you might as well make yourself useful. Do me a favor and cut all the camera feeds for a couple of minutes. We don't need anyone asking silly questions about where he went."

"What are you talking about?"

Kate flipped the phone closed and put it in her pocket without answering. Then she stood and walked over to a nearby wheelchair. After unfolding it, she wheeled it over to the bed. Sorted, Kate put the phone back to her ear. Again, his phone buzzed.

Lyle answered.

Kate said, "Cameras off?"

"You know this guy got shot a couple of days ago. Twice. He got shot twice."

"He's stable now."

"He got shot two times. That's two separate bullets."

"I can count, Lyle. Are the cameras off?"

He sighed, typing out a series of reboot commands into the network. "Off."

"Good. Meet me at the door in two minutes."

"I don't think—"

The line went dead once more. Lyle growled in frustration, dropping the phone onto the seat next to him, and started the car. He drove around the side of the hospital to the equipment loading and unloading dock and parked.

"She thinks I'll just do *anything* she asks any time she needs it," he muttered. "One of these days ..."

A minute later, the door opened. Kate wheeled the man outside. His expression seemed one of pain, but he didn't look like the type of person to complain. Lyle rolled down his window. He accused, "You knew I would follow you. You *knew* I would track you here."

Kate shrugged. "I checked all my pockets and clothes for a tracker after I left. I had started to believe you wouldn't show up, and that I would have to call you to come meet me here. The candy bar was a neat trick, though. Didn't see it coming."

44

"Thanks."

"How long did it take to reseal the package?"

"Forever. The plastic kept melting."

She laughed. Lyle climbed out and opened the rear car door, and together, they helped the injured man inside. Lyle had a million more questions for Kate about who this guy was, but he knew better than to ask her anything at a moment like this.

The guy appeared a lot more intimidating in person than on the screen, Lyle noted. Even injured, Lyle felt certain the guy could take him in a fight.

"Who is he?" Lyle asked.

"I can hear you," the man said. He had his eyes closed, and he winced in pain when they moved him.

"Fine, who are you?"

"None of your business."

"That so? I don't think you're in much of a position to object to my questions right about now."

"Then go ahead and try to make me talk."

"Tempting," Lyle said. "But I'll let it slide this time. Usually, I like to know who I'm working for when we take on a new client."

"He isn't the job," Kate said, closing the vehicle door.

"He isn't?" Lyle stared at her.

"Just a friend who got himself into a rough situation. We're doing him a favor."

Lyle scratched his chin. "We do favors now?"

She scowled at him. "Get in the car."

"All right," he said.

Kate went around to the passenger side, shoved his laptop and equipment onto the floor and then climbed in. A second later, they got back on the road and headed toward their hotel.

The guy in the back was drugged, Lyle realized, and after a few minutes of traveling, the guy fell fast asleep.

"Like a baby," Lyle said. "Who is he?"

Kate blinked at him, drawn out of her thoughts—distracted. Something he wasn't used to from her.

"I told you, just an old friend."

"How did he get shot?"

"He had a job in Delaware. Barely made it out alive."

"Delaware? The state?"

"No, the chestnuts. Of course, the state."

"What was the job?"

"Off-the-books cargo shipment. Someone hired them to destroy the goods."

"Them?"

"His team."

"Where are they?"

"Dead," the man said from the back seat. Lyle glanced in the mirror. The guy had woken. "All of them died."

His voice quivered ever so slightly when he said it. Then he clutched at his bandaged side and grimaced in pain.

"Died? How?"

"Mercenaries hit us. Blindsided the whole team. I should have died, too, like the rest of my squad."

"Everyone except Kate, you mean?"

"No," Kate said. "I was in Brazil on a job when I heard. Rushed back straight away and got him moved before they could finish the job."

"Thanks for that," the guy said. "I don't remember much from the last two days, but I'm sure I wouldn't be here without you."

"Who did the hit?"

Their muscled companion shook his head. "No clue who paid for the job, but I recognized a couple of the bastards who pulled it off. I plan to start digging, and once I find—"

"You can't," Kate said.

"What do you mean?"

She let out a sigh, shifting in her seat. "Because you've been blacklisted."

3

"What are you talking about? Blacklisted? The job went sideways, but that's not enough to put me on burn notice."

"The report is that you went rogue and murdered your team. It's being floated, and six international agencies have cut ties already."

"What?" he asked, shocked. "You've got to be kidding me. Who put out the notice?"

"It doesn't say. Probably the same people who hit you when they found out you'd survived. They didn't want you asking the wrong questions."

"God damn it."

"I knew the reports were crap as soon as they came in. That's how I found out you'd landed in trouble. You could never turn on your team or—"

"Wait, wait, wait," Lyle said. He slammed on the brakes and swerved the car off the road. "You're telling me that we have a *burned* asset in our car? I thought we were supposed to stay clear of burned assets?"

"Look, it doesn't matter. The report went international as of this morning."

"So, he has a target on his back?"

"Basically. That's why we couldn't leave him in the hospital. Too many people will come searching—"

"For us," Lyle said. "Since we're harboring him, they will come looking for *us*. *You* were the one that told me never to mess with anyone burned and to always play by the street rules. This doesn't sound like playing by the rules to me."

"This is different."

"How is this different?"

"Malcolm is an old friend."

"Oh, so he has a name now?" Lyle shifted in his seat to glance back at the man. "Malcolm, is it? What is your opinion on the matter? Should we harbor a burned asset?"

Malcolm glanced between the two of them. He appeared, vaguely, like a small kid who didn't enjoy seeing his parents argue. "He's right. I appreciate you saving my life, Kate, but if someone burned me, then this isn't your problem. I can get out and—"

"No." Kate turned in her seat to face Lyle. "Look, I should have told you about all of this—"

"Damn right you should have."

"But I didn't have time to get your approval. Malcolm is an old friend, and I'll *not* leave him alone after he got burned for something he didn't do. So, your choices are to put the car into gear and take us back to the hotel or get out."

Lyle stared at her for a second, huffed, and then turned to face forward.

"Fine, but I want to make sure my disapproval is noted."

"Then consider it on record. It'll only take a couple of days to get Malcolm back on his feet and sort out this mess, and then he'll be on his way. I promise."

Lyle felt unconvinced. He'd spent the last two years working with Kate, and she'd never once mentioned partners that she used to work with, much less muscular men with whom she, clearly, had history.

No, something else hid there. Maybe an old flame, a fling, or something more. Lyle bit back his jealousy, put the car into gear, and drove them back to the hotel. The rest of the trip passed in silence. Kate wouldn't even look at him.

Never a good sign.

Chapter 5
Houston, Texas

1

Andrew Carmichael stared out through the boardroom window at the sprawling city below. He had rented a conference room on the seventy-third floor of this tower for just that reason. Everything seemed so small down below, like an ant farm scurrying about.

It had cost a fortune to hold his meeting here instead of his own offices, and it proved highly impractical for a business expense, but that didn't matter. It seemed a small price to pay for the ability to convey his influence and wealth over the other people in the boardroom with him.

"Um ... sir?"

The interruption came from behind and to his left, out of the mouth of his newest secretary in a series of unfortunate hires. He grimaced in annoyance but didn't answer her: he reckoned she wouldn't break the streak.

The eyes of all his investors bored into his back, as well as the occasional whisper as they attempted to judge his intentions. He imagined that he must cut a regal figure standing here, tall and handsome in his tailored navy suit, and hair perfectly coifed as he posed by the window.

Thus far, he'd kept them waiting in their well-cushioned chairs for a full thirty seconds. He could practically taste their anxiety. They reeked of nervousness and weakness underneath their expensive attire and affectations. His inattention produced the desired impact.

Keep them guessing. Carmichael used silence as a tool to establish control over the conversation. He *needed* to oversee this conversation: his project had reached a critical junction. A misspoken word or second-guessed intention could bring his entire house of cards crumbling down around him.

He checked his watch: another twenty seconds and he would begin.

The trick of using a pause before speaking he had learned from watching videos of the charismatic leaders in the world, including–no, Andrew admitted, *especially*–Adolf Hitler. A deplorable man and fascist leader, to be sure, yet Hitler had been a genius public speaker. *He* knew how to control a crowd and keep entire nations on their toes wanting more.

Andrew felt the pressure to speak from just the ten people at the table behind him: he couldn't imagine standing in front of hundreds of thousands at a podium and counting off a full minute before speaking.

"Sir? We are ready for you."

Andrew's jaw clenched at the repeated interruption. This secretary had turned out much like her predecessors, and Carmichael chided himself for selecting yet another timid little girl.

She appeared a docile creature who refused to look him in the eyes when he spoke, so he'd thought she would make for the perfect help. He liked that about her because she understood that their relationship was not one of equality. He was the boss, she the help.

She was new, though, and he hadn't yet had "the talk" with her about how he did business. In meetings, her duty was to take notes and document transactions, but it was never, ever, to speak without his consent. Moreover, he would not allow her to question his decisions.

Once this meeting ended, he would have to reconsider keeping her around.

He glanced at his watch again: a minute and five seconds of silence would have to do. Andrew drew a steadying breath, plastered on his business smile, and turned to face the board of investors.

Nine in total, plus his secretary, sitting spaced around an oval table. Six men and four women, all dressed to the nines. Fen Wu, his secretary, sat in the rear corner of the room, an iPad in hand. She shook in her seat when he surveyed her, and shrank under his gaze.

"Thank you, Fen."

50

Andrew smiled at the investors. He reminded himself that when he spoke, he must address the women as often as the men. The last thing he needed was for anyone else to lie to a reporter that he was a misogynist.

CDM Pharmaceuticals didn't need any further negative publicity just now.

"I called this meeting," he said, clearing his throat, "because I plan on taking CDM public in two months and—"

"It's a mistake," George Trinple said. A fat and balding man, he had loose jowls and saggy skin. "We know why you asked us here, boy, and this visit is just a courtesy."

"I agree," Emily Perkins said.

Hers was the opinion Andrew most worried about swaying in this meeting. Shapely and attractive for a woman in her mid-fifties, she had a reputation in the industry for going toe-to-toe with anyone. Full of strong opinions, she held a no-nonsense attitude.

Andrew hated her.

"If we go public right now, then after only a few weeks of being live, our stock prices will plummet," she said. "CDM only has two drugs on the market, and Camlodien is only six months old—still in its infancy. No one in the market will bet on us. We'll crash, and then we'll get absorbed into one of the big three pharmaceutical companies and lose everything for which we've fought."

"On the contrary, I intend to do the absorbing," Andrew said. "By the end of the fiscal year, we will—"

"In what reality? In the one we live in, CDM remains too weak to stand on its own."

"I don't appreciate the interruption, Emily. You've missed the point entirely. This isn't about Camlodien but our other offerings. We will become the first company to bring a successful gene therapy to commerce. A thing both practical and affordable in an entirely unclaimed market."

Emily shook her head. "Your therapy isn't market ready. You admitted so yourself. And, at best, the initial offering will solve a problem that affects one in five thousand people. Most won't even seek treatment, let alone something untested and unproven."

"Correct, in that the trials for this particular gene therapy remain ongoing, but you have it wrong about the viability of *my*

51

company. We received this year's contract to create and distribute the latest flu vaccine, which is due to begin shipment in a few weeks."

Emily remained argumentative, "The flu has proven tame this season. It is likely we won't even recuperate our initial investment."

"I invested in the vaccine for public relations and relationship building more than profit or revenue."

"Oh, so you're in the charity business now? How will that line our pocketbooks?"

"It isn't about the bottom line—"

"It is clear that the pieces of this puzzle are not aligned right now to take the company public."

Andrew grew annoyed to see that she held some sway with the other members of the board, who sat nodding in agreement.

"I've heard many reports that this year's flu will be significantly worse than most," he said, deviating back to the vaccine. "We will stay poised to turn a profit from it as well as build goodwill."

"It hasn't happened yet, and the season is halfway over. Unless something changes fast, we're looking at one of the tamest flu seasons in the last thirty years. Vaccinations are down almost forty percent year over year."

"Florida got hit the hardest, and it is mostly finished with the flue," George said, grinning smugly. "This morning, on the news, I heard that the number of reported cases has dropped, and the cases reported are mild. Emily has it right: this has turned into a terrible vaccination season, and there's no way we'll turn a profit."

"People just aren't scared," Andrew said, nodding. "And I agree that without people getting sick it could be an abysmal season—"

"I don't think that people *not* getting sick counts as an abysmal season," Emily said with a small laugh. "But the point still stands. If anything, *that* contract was bad for the company."

Andrew shook his head, "It remains revenue and profit just for manufacturing the vaccine, and that has resulted in company growth even if no payouts."

"It didn't bring enough to translate into profit, and certainly not enough to equal market share. We know the numbers, Andy, and they don't look good. If anything, this setback should delay our public offerings, not speed it up."

"You forget that we also have an exclusive patent for Camlodien for the next seven years."

"What about it? It provides a useful anticoagulant," Emily said, frowning, "but just having one solid pharmaceutical on the market won't earn enough to carry an entire company. Our competitors have portfolios of twenty to thirty drugs. We don't even have another medicine on a market path yet."

"What if Camlodien proves enough to carry us, though? What if it *is* enough to solidify our entire future?"

Andrew's question hung in the air as everyone around the table exchanged confused glances.

"Camlodien doesn't require patients to go in for regular blood tests like Warfarin or Heparin. In many trials, it has shown itself up to four times as effective as its competitors with fewer negative side effects."

His words surprised them, and they exchanged more looks. Even Emily appeared caught off-guard by the possibilities, and it took her a moment to recover. "What trials are those?"

"Internal studies for patients with Factor V Leiden thrombophilia."

"You haven't told us about those."

"Nothing to tell before now."

Emily wore a chagrined expression, "What are our patient numbers? How much usage could we expect out of it?"

"Five percent Caucasians and around two percent international."

"How many seek treatment?"

"Lower, but by all indications, the number is growing—"

"So, it isn't a condition that many people bother to treat outside of necessity, and there are direct market competitors with more brand recognition?"

Annoyed, Andrew said, "Inferior competitors."

"Yet, more established. Why haven't we trialed *new* drugs that treat conditions like heart disease or diabetes? We could hit considerably higher acquisition numbers even in the over-saturated market than something with a five percent population coverage rate."

"Our price point and cost of acquisition would be lower on a drug like that."

"Yes, but we would make up for it in volume. Why not print

53

a few generics?"

"And soil the brand? CDM isn't—"

"It could become an excellent source of revenue prospects and solidify our portfolio while—"

"I'm not here to argue strategy," Andrew said. "That is *not* why I held this meeting." The words came out harsher than intended, and the expressions of many in the room soured. They had taken Emily's side. The woman had won the hearts and minds of the board.

Piss ants,, all of them.

"I agree that the drug has value," Emily said, savoring her victory, "but it comes nowhere near a game changer. We need to expand, make a few targeted acquisitions, and *then* consider taking the company wide. We need to learn to walk before we can run."

"Walk? You would have us crawling on our knees if you could, wouldn't you?" Andrew spat out the words.

A few audible gasps sounded, but Andrew didn't care. He pressed on, "You bought out your uncle's share of CDM Pharmaceuticals not because you wanted to help grow *my* business, but because you wanted to stifle it. You wanted to stifle *me*."

Rattled, Emily shot to her feet. "I didn't want to stifle anything. I am offended by the accusation."

"The truth is never offensive. All you've done is question my decisions and leadership at *every* turn."

"Then maybe if you started making better decisions ..."

With fingers splayed on the table, she didn't finish the statement; just let the implication hang in the air. Andrew understood that she wanted to replace him as CEO of his company and worked actively to build an alliance with the other board members against him. She wanted his job, which meant she sought to take his company out from under him.

His company.

This meeting should have solidified his position of overseeing CDM, and in a matter of minutes, she had managed to weaken and jeopardize his company's future. If they didn't take the company wide during the required window, then all his hard work would come to naught.

Never would he have sold her an investment share of CDM, but her uncle hadn't told Andrew that he'd fallen on hard times.

That had happened four months ago. Andrew would have helped bail him out, or at least bought up the shares. Instead, Andrew had ended up stuck with this predatory woman who wanted everything he had.

"In any case," Emily said, retaking her seat, "supplies of Camlodien have remained limited, haven't they?"

"Artificially." Andrew waved a dismissive hand in the air. "We have a surplus in reserves, but keeping our public supply low helps to inflate the cost and perceived value."

"If we have the drug, we should sell it. Or, at least, we should give it away overseas in a philanthropic gesture. You said you had an interest in charity, and that would make an excellent source of positive public relations."

"We will, once demand for the product increases."

"When will that happen?" The woman just wouldn't let up.

Andrew couldn't say much without tipping his hand. "It is unclear, but all signs point to new tailwinds soon. We have prepared for any eventuality."

"As have we," Emily said, standing once more. "*Any* eventuality. I appreciate you taking the time to speak with us today, but I must say that your arguments have not convinced me, and I feel surprised by your shortsightedness. I side with George and many others on this issue: CDM Pharmaceuticals cannot and must not go public right now. We have much to consider from this conference. We need a few shake-ups and changes before we can reconvene to consider a public trade offer."

Shake-ups that included a change of leadership. Andrew could hardly believe that she would behave so brazenly in front of the board—even going so far as to call an end to *his* meeting. She must have more control over them than he'd imagined.

"We know how hard you've worked for this," George said, standing as well, "but right now, the company just doesn't have the maturity for such a venture."

Andrew's hands shook, so he stuck them into his pockets, forcing the fake smile to stay planted on his face. He needed the unanimous approval of the investors to move forward with his plan. Six of them, maybe eight, would fall into line with little effort, but convincing Emily had turned out to be a lost cause. He had hoped to charm her, but clearly, that wouldn't work.

This meeting should have shown them positive figures and statistics, using the company's upward trajectory to win the argument. That, though, hadn't worked. If anything, Emily had gained traction in her war against him. Carmichael had lost this battle.

He wouldn't lose the next.

"I'm aware I won't convince you this afternoon that this is the proper course for our company, so let's table the discussion for now. Thank you all for coming."

He walked over and opened the door, making it clear that the meeting had officially finished. Some members left, while others milled around and held private conversations. Andrew made his way around the table, shaking hands and offering empty platitudes as he ushered them out of the room.

Finally, he made it to where Emily and George stood. A few months ago, he would have considered George his closest ally. Amazing how things changed when a skirt entered the picture. The two had become thick as thieves already, locked in a private conversation, which they halted as soon as he strode up.

"I apologize for the interruption," he said, turning to Emily, "but if you wouldn't mind, I would love for the opportunity to meet with you this afternoon and walk you through our facility. If I recall correctly, you haven't received a personal tour yet."

She eyed him suspiciously. "No, I haven't."

"If you allow me to show you some of our upcoming projects, I feel confident I can sway your opinions."

"I don't think so." Emily shook her head. "I have made up my mind on this. And other things."

"Humor me," Andrew said. "Wouldn't you find some value in visiting CDM Pharmaceuticals' home-base and laboratories?"

"I suppose it would be worth understanding how the day-to-day workings of the company fit together," she said after a moment. "Who knows what the future holds?"

"Of course," he said affably, though through gritted teeth. "You never know."

"Fine. I need to stop in at my office, and then I will be ready."

"Great. I'll have a car pick you up in about an hour."

2

To prepare for his meeting with Emily, Andrew returned home. He had spoken with Monroe Fink about his next steps, but already, he had doubts. Maybe he had taken her insults too personally and had let her get under his skin.

It was too late to go back now. Instead, he changed clothes and set off to meet the caterer for his upcoming gala. He had scheduled the charity dinner party over the weekend as a celebratory gesture for taking the company wide.

Probably, he should cancel the gala, but right now he felt too livid to even think about it. At this point in time, he considered the event still on, and he also intended to have his congratulatory dinner.

"Where is the caterer?" he asked his butler, once he had finished changing.

"The basement," the man said.

"What? Why would she go down there?" Andrew rushed below stairs.

The butler hurried to catch up. "You said to give her full access."

Andrew cursed in frustration. Why, oh why, did everyone surrounding him prove incompetent?

He headed along the underground hall. The lights shone, and a woman stood a short way further on.

"You shouldn't have come down here," Andrew said. "The gala takes place upstairs in the ballroom and *maybe* the dining room and—"

"Do you put all of your computers in prison?" The woman turned to face him.

"Excuse me?" Annoyance flared.

A smirk twisted her face, but upon seeing his furious expression, it turned into a frown. "I'm sorry, I didn't realize ... I just wanted to see the property."

"This doesn't form any part of what you *need* to see."

"Again, I'm terribly sorry."

"What did you mean about prisons?"

She turned and pointed at his server, surrounded by a cage that looked somewhat like a prison.

"I meant it as a joke," she muttered.

Andrew blew out a breath and forced himself to relax. "Apologies, I just ... I've had a rough day."

"I understand."

"It's called a Faraday cage. It blocks electronic signals."

Interest lit her features. "Why?"

57

He forced his business smile on. "I like having my secrets," he said, as playfully as he could muster. "And I don't enjoy when people snoop around."

She returned the smile. "Of course. I'm terribly sorry. It won't happen again."

"Think nothing of it."

"Well, everything seems in order. I'll set up tomorrow for the party and get everything in line. What time would you like to serve dinner?"

"Seven," he said. "No, wait, seven-thirty. I want to make sure everyone has a chance to show up."

"Of course," she said. "You have a lovely home, Mr. Carmichael. Thank you so much for the opportunity to help you with this event." Then she turned and headed for the exit.

Andrew watched her leave. Then he glared at his butler. "No one is permitted down here, understood?"

The butler nodded.

"Next time, I won't be as forgiving."

He checked his server to make sure nothing had been tampered with and then headed back out of the basement. He had a most important meeting to get to.

Chapter 6
Beaumont, Texas

1

"You're looking me up, aren't you?"

Lyle froze, fingers hovering over the keyboard.

"Uh, what? Why would you say that?"

"It's what I would do with someone I don't know. A full background check if possible."

Lyle sat in the front seat of the little Chevrolet Cruze they had rented for their cross-country excursion. It turned into an exhausting and hot drive with Kate determined to make the trip in one straight shot with no breaks. Which meant a whole lot of driving and not a lot of sleeping. Twenty-five hours straight, so far, in separate shifts, and for some reason, it felt like Lyle had taken the brunt of night driving.

Finally, they had crossed into Texas about an hour ago and now closed in on their destination. Kate drove this shift, Lyle rode in the passenger seat, and Malcolm lay in the back. He barely seemed to notice the gunshot wounds anymore, and Lyle wondered just how many times this man had gotten shot in his life.

"Actually, I've finished the background check on three international servers and am waiting for a full facial scan on two more. I don't trust readily-available information, so I'm looking deeper."

"Honest, huh? That's refreshing."

Lyle shrugged. "What can I say? I'm an honest guy."

"Find anything interesting?"

"Six aliases and a sordid history, but all of the identities I found are fakes."

"My real name *is* Malcolm."

"Malcolm Caldwell," Lyle said, nodding. "Six years in the military before going private, but even that identity is forged. At least partially."

"How can you tell?"

"I did a circumspect search of top-level events and known contacts. About half of them are mocked-up. The fakes, though not easy to spot, don't hold up under intense scrutiny."

"Ah. So, you figured out the family is false?"

"Yeah," Lyle said. "But I haven't managed to find your real one yet."

"Would it be impolite of me to ask you to stop searching?"

Lyle gave another shrug. "No, but I can't promise I won't. Nothing nefarious, just curiosity, like a puzzle. I'd like to figure out which pieces of this puzzle are real and which ones are just clever fakes."

"You could ask me instead."

"I didn't say I wanted the answer. I enjoy the challenge, but I don't care as much about the result. How much did it cost to create these forgeries?"

"Enough," Malcolm said, sitting up in the seat. "Too much, maybe." He groaned, clutching his side, and then leaned forward.

"You all right?" Lyle asked.

"Fine. To answer your question: I don't have much family. Just my parents, and I had them cut out of my life to keep them safe. The military deployments and contract work both exist, as do certain criminal actions you'll find in a deeper search. The social life is bogus, but the person is real."

"Why would you create a fake identity using your actual name and real details from your life?"

"A good lie feels more real when the truth gets sprinkled throughout. How deep did you have to dig before you realized the identity was a fake?"

"Point taken."

"Plus, I *like* my name. Easier to remember, and most people don't even care."

"Sure. The one thing I haven't found is any reference to your current or past crews. How do you know Kate?"

"We're old friends."

"Friends?"

"I'm sitting right here," Kate told them.

Lyle kept his focus on Malcolm. "Friends?"

"Just friends," Malcolm said. "If that's what you mean."

"I'm trying to figure out why I've never heard of you before."

"It wasn't relevant," Kate said. "I haven't spoken with Malcolm in years."

"But you were willing to risk everything to come rescue him when he got in trouble?"

"He's saved my life many times before," Kate said. "Just returning the favor."

"Seems like a pretty big favor to—"

"What did you find out about our *actual* job?" Kate glared at him. "You know, what I *actually* asked you to look into."

Lyle shrugged. "Oh. That? I did that yesterday."

"Did you, now? And, what, you forgot to tell me?"

"You were sleeping. I guess I did forget."

"You could have woken me."

"Wake you up? Not a chance—I don't want to die."

She groaned. "Fine. What did you find?"

"Not a lot. Stephen Blake, oil mogul worth about fifty-million dollars in off-shore accounts and investments. Keeps to himself, donates a lot to charity, and likes to go to ritzy parties."

"Any enemies?"

"None that I can find."

"Family?"

"One kid, seven-years-old. At boarding school. And has minimal contact with his father. Wife passed away during childbirth. Both of Blake's parents died of natural causes before he reached twenty-five, and no brothers or sisters. A couple of cousins but with almost no ties. In general, he seems to keep to himself."

"There has to be something. Dig deeper. Why would he want to hire us?"

"I dug," Lyle said. "Nothing to find. The guy looks squeaky clean. Not even a sealed juvenile record. I guess we'll have to talk to him to find out what he needs."

"We'll get that chance any minute. We're about ten minutes out."

"You said he wanted us to steal something for him?"

"More or less. Slight risk."

"And he'll pay us two-hundred-thousand dollars for a one-day job? Seems a bit ridiculous if you ask me."

61

"Would you like to help him negotiate the price downward?" Kate asked. "Maybe we can get him to agree to twenty thousand?"

"Funny," Lyle said. "Something just seems off about this."

"It's an easy win," Kate said. "Don't look a gift horse in the mouth."

"That saying refers *specifically* to the fact that you *should* look a gift horse in the mouth. It comes from the idea that you should look at a horse's teeth to determine its age because a gifted horse *might* be a much older horse than you think."

"You can tell a horse's age from its teeth?" Malcolm asked.

"I can't," Lyle said, "but that isn't the point. The point is that if something seems too good to be true, it usually is. The saying contradicts the point you're attempting to make."

"So, what you're saying is we should only take jobs that seem impossible?"

"At least then we would understand what we were in for. This just bugs me. I don't even know what the job *is.*"

"What if it is as simple as Peter said? We pick up a package, drop it off to the guy, and then collect our money."

"Can't be that easy."

"Do you mean to be so negative?"

"I want to be realistic. *No one* is this clean, and it's the squeaky-clean people who usually have the darkest secrets."

"I can attest to that as true," Malcolm said. "It's never the ones you expect."

"See? Even the bullet sponge agrees with me."

"Look, we've almost reached his place. Let's meet the guy, talk to him, and if you still think he's hiding something, we can take a pass on the job."

"Really?"

"Hell no," Kate said, laughing. "Of course we're taking it. I just want you to shut up."

2

"Wow, I guess that's what fifteen million gets you," Lyle said, whistling as they pulled up at the Blake family estate. It looked enormous, comprised of the main house, two guest houses, and an employee cottage in the back. Four fountains decorated the front lawn, a twelve-foot-tall gate fronted it, and countless security cameras surrounded it all.

As they drove up to the main entrance, they passed by dozens of workers tending the grass. Mowing, trimming, and mulching: it looked like a never-ending job. Lyle absorbed it all with a bit of envy. One day, this might have become his life before everything went to hell. He'd been on course to make a fortune and retire at thirty-five.

That was before he made it on the FBI's most wanted list.

"I bet he has a huge pool," Kate said.

"Three of them, actually." Lyle glanced at the satellite image of the property again. "One of them is indoors."

She muttered something he couldn't make out, pulling the car to a stop in front of the large double-door entrance of the manor. A valet hurried over and opened the driver's door for her. Another man, this one dressed like a butler, who had a bald head and trimmed goatee, opened Lyle's door, and he climbed out.

"Welcome," the man said. "Mr. Blake awaits you inside."

"He's expecting us?" Lyle asked.

"Of course."

"Then I guess we shouldn't keep him waiting."

The butler moved to the backseat and opened the door, but Malcolm didn't climb out right away. Instead, he glanced at Kate. "I'll stay in the car," he said.

The valet frowned at him. "Mr. Blake would prefer to have you come inside—"

"I'll stay in the car," Malcolm said. "And the car will stay right here.

The man gulped and nodded. "Of course. I'll be right over there if you need me."

Lyle and Kate followed the butler up the steps toward the front door. By the time they reached the top, Lyle stood panting.

"That out of shape?"

"Screw you."

"Are you about done giving me crap about Malcolm?" Kate asked.

"Almost," Lyle said. "I just wish you had told me something about all of this beforehand."

"If I'd had time, I would have," she said. "I hadn't planned to keep him a secret."

"But, you did."

"Boy, it would be nice if you trusted me occasionally."

"I trust you," Lyle said. "I just don't trust *him* yet. When did you become so sentimental, anyway? I thought you didn't like people?"

"I like you, don't I?"

"That's different."

"Is it?"

"Yep," he said. "Totally different."

The butler opened the door and held it. They walked past into the manor. Enormous, the foyer sprawled around—three stories high with a balcony and split staircase climbing to the second floor. Everything seemed muted in color—brown—and uninviting.

Lyle hated it. His version of this mansion would have much more vibrancy. "Nice place," Lyle said, regardless. "Spacious. The gas bill must be astronomical."

The butler ignored him, turning and gesturing down the hallway to the right. Lyle and Kate moved deeper into the building and found themselves in a living room with multiple couches and chairs. It also sported the biggest fireplace Lyle had ever seen; a tall man could stand up straight inside it, and his head still wouldn't reach the top.

It held no fire just now, and the room itself felt quite drafty. A lone man sat in one of the chairs, holding a notepad and jotting notes into it and not seeming to realize they had arrived. He wore a bathrobe and had a gray beard.

This version of Stephen Blake did not look like the pictures Lyle had seen. The beard was new, as were many gray hairs. It appeared as though he had become a recluse sometime in the last couple of years.

What, Lyle wondered, had triggered that?

Finally, Stephen saw them enter and stood quickly, setting his notepad down and striding across the room eagerly to greet them.

"Ah," he said. "Thank you so much for coming. It's good to see you again."

"Again?" Lyle asked.

"Of course," Kate said, ignoring Lyle and shaking the man's hand.

"How was your flight?"

"We drove," she said. "It was scenic."

"Excellent. Please, have a seat."

64

Lyle picked the comfiest-looking chair in the room, which still ended up too hard and cold for his butt. He'd never understood why people insisted on filling their residences with aesthetically pleasing and entirely uncomfortable furniture.

He hadn't sat down for more than a second before a servant appeared at his arm with a tray. It held biscuits, cookies, tea, and coffee.

"Oh, thank you. I'm starving."

Lyle took a handful of cookies and a cup of tea. Without a table nearby, he laid them out on his lap with a napkin.

Kate and Wallace each waved away the offered tray.

"I asked you here today so that—"

Lyle took a bite of his cookie, and the crunching sound echoed throughout the spacious room. He stopped, mouth filled with crumbs and stickiness, and the other two turned to face him. Kate looked extremely annoyed.

"Sorry," he said with his mouth full, chewing slowly. Even then, each time he bit down, the sound carried. Kate narrowed her eyes, watching him chew. Finally, he swallowed the mushed food and took a sip of his tea.

"Are you quite finished?"

"One more bite?"

"No more bites."

He sighed, wrapping the cookies in the napkin and sliding them into his pocket for later. Sarcastically, he muttered under his breath, "No more bites."

"I heard that," Kate said, turning back to face Wallace. "Please, continue."

Wallace glanced between the two of them, frowning. "Yes ... um ... where was I? Ah, yes, the reason I asked for your help today was that I have a job for you. There is a package I would like you to ... err ... steal for me."

"What does it contain? Are we talking something like an Amazon box?" Lyle asked. "I told Kate already that I would love to steal one of those."

Wallace didn't crack a smile. "It isn't any of your concern. It is a strictly need-to-know item. I have the route through which it will be transported in five hours' time. All I need for you to do is pick it up and bring it to me."

"But you won't tell us what it is?" Lyle asked

"You will find out as soon as you collect it."

65

"Then tell us now," Kate said. "I don't much enjoy surprises."

"No one must know until the item is secured. Even my servants and employees do not know. I'm sorry, but I will not budge on this issue. Hence why I've offered so much money."

"Is it drugs? It's drugs, isn't it?" Lyle asked.

Kate flashed Lyle a quick look, and he fell silent, holding up his hands in submission.

"Let's talk payment," Kate said.

"Two hundred thousand, all on delivery."

"Half up front."

Wallace shook his head. "I negotiated the terms with Peter, just like the last job. Upon successful and *safe* delivery of the package to me, I will pay the full amount. He assured me that my asking price included this term."

"Fine," Kate said. "We just bring it here?"

"Yes. Bring the package to me *immediately* after acquiring it, and I will have the money ready. All cash, non-sequential. You can get paid and go on your way by tonight."

Kate hesitated for only a second before nodding. "Very well. Give us any pertinent information, and we'll be on our way."

"Wait a second," Lyle said. "You need to tell us what this package *is*."

"Lyle." Kate scowled.

"No, I'm serious. I need to know. The fact that he doesn't want to tell us means he thinks we might turn the job down if we found out. Or that he doesn't trust us, and I'm not sure which is worse. So, what is this mysterious package? Is it a biological weapon? Are we stealing something from the military to help you become a domestic terrorist?"

Wallace studied Lyle. "I assure you, it is nothing of the sort."

"Is it something I can carry, or do we need a truck to get it? Here, I'll guess: does the name of this item start with a 'D'?"

"I apologize for my associate here," Kate said, staring pointedly at Lyle. "He's never been good at keeping his mouth shut."

"I don't think we should take the job."

"It is nothing dangerous," Wallace said. "You have my word."

"Then why won't you tell us?"

"Lyle," Kate said, softly. "I think you should wait outside."

He began to open his mouth to speak up again, but the withering look she shot him shut him right up. He threw his

66

hands in the air. "Fine."

He stood and headed for the exit. Along the way, he spotted the tray of leftover cookies. He shoved all the remaining biscuits into his pocket in protest, making sure to do it loudly, and then headed back out the main entrance of the manor.

The car still sat out front, and Malcolm had laid out in the backseat, fast asleep. Pointedly, the valet ignored Lyle, facing away and reading a magazine off to the side of the steps.

Lyle climbed into the passenger seat, shutting the door quietly so that he wouldn't wake the other man. Then he sat in the car, fuming and annoyed.

He didn't have as much experience in this life as Kate, sure, but that didn't make him any less of a partner in this venture. Lyle had lost practically every aspect of his old life when Kate had first shown up, and even though it wasn't her fault, and she had saved him, he still felt a little twinge of anger whenever he thought about everything that had been taken from him.

He could have started over, changing his identity and moving out of the country, but he hadn't. Instead, he had stayed with Kate, becoming her partner in crime and putting his computer skills to use. How much of that was because of her?

How much of it was *for* her?

The truth of the matter, if he were honest with himself, was that he had fallen in love with her. Lyle had loved her since the day she'd exploded into his life, and he'd given up everything to pursue that love. Unrequited puppy love, he knew, mixed with a close friendship and camaraderie.

He had never said as much aloud to her, and he didn't know if he ever would. Instead, he had accepted the fact that they would probably never become anything more than friends and compatriots, but he had, at least, felt that he had made headway and that she trusted him.

Boy, had he got it wrong.

"I can hear your brain gears grinding up there," Malcolm said.

Lyle jerked in his seat, letting out a shocked gasp.

Malcolm chuckled then said, "Sorry, didn't mean to scare you."

"Yeah, you did."

"Maybe a little. What's on your mind?"

"Nothing."

"Sure there is."

"Nothing that concerns you, then."

"Want to talk about it?"

"What part of 'nothing that concerns you' did you not understand?"

"You're pissed about something, and clearly, you want to talk about it."

"No, I'm not, and I don't. And, again, it is none of your business."

"No, it isn't." Malcolm nodded. "But if you want something to distract you, how about you help me out with something."

"Like what?"

"Figure out who did this to me. Who burned me and killed my team. The job was solid, but someone knew we would be on that ship."

"What were you stealing, anyway?"

"Destroying not stealing. Some cargo, pharmaceuticals, but that's as far as I knew. I didn't think it was a big deal, and I definitely didn't expect anyone else to come after us."

"You lost your team?"

Malcolm didn't respond for a while. Then he said, "Yes. Both died. I wasn't sure at first, but I sent out a couple of messages last night that only they would recognize. Nothing came back."

"Maybe they haven't seen it yet."

"No, if they were alive they would have responded."

"Sorry to hear it."

"Me too. That just means I need to figure out who did this so I can get justice for my team."

"You mean vengeance?"

"One and the same right now."

Lyle sighed. "Fine. I did some digging while searching into your past, but I haven't had any hits yet. There's only so much I can do, though, without more information."

"What do you need to know?"

"Who hired you? What was the job? Who might have it in for you? We don't know that the hit was even related to the job you were on, or if it was because of something else."

"You mean like an enemy from my past?"

"It's possible, isn't it?"

"Yeah."

68

"Did you get a good look at the people who shot you?"

"One of them I know for sure, but I don't remember much of what happened. It's all a blur."

"Retrograde amnesia. It'll come back to you slowly. Who is the one person you know for definite was involved?"

"Jeff Tripp," Malcolm said. "But I'm pretty sure he's dead."

"What? You killed him?"

"No. I'm also not sure who did. I just get this ... feeling. I'm sure he's dead, I'm just not sure how I know."

Lyle tapped on his laptop, drawing up reports around the incident and parsing through information. After a minute, he turned back to face Malcolm.

"Nothing useful in police reports. I checked all incident and hospital records for gunshot wounds within a hundred miles of the shooting, and nothing stuck out. A couple of bodies, but no way to verify them right now."

"So, we have no leads?"

"Nothing so far," Lyle said. "But having a name to look for helps. I'll track down known associates and scan anything about Tripp. I've got a few-dozen feelers out there right now, so hopefully, something will turn up."

"Thanks."

Lyle shrugged. "Don't mention it."

They sat in silence for a couple of minutes. Lyle tapped on the computer and searched for further information about Wallace Blake and his business interests. He wanted to know what the man was doing and figure out what he was after. What might someone as rich as him want to steal?

Lyle must have missed something because the job didn't feel right. It sounded too easy, which meant there was an important detail they didn't have.

Something else bugged Lyle, though; why had he said it was nice to see them again? Had Kate worked for him in the past? While driving down here, she'd acted as if she didn't know Wallace, but clearly, they had some history there.

Recent or distant, though? How many more secrets had Kate kept from him? What could this package hold that had such value?

"Why would you help me?" Malcolm asked.

"What?" Distracted, Lyle jerked.

"You said you've searched things about the hit already. Even before I asked, you'd looked into it. You don't know me, so why help?"

"Your team got murdered, and you were burned, so I figured—"

"You don't even know me," Malcolm said. "I get why Kate's helping me. We're old friends. But not you. You don't even seem to like me that much."

"Kate and I are a team," Lyle said. "She might not trust me, but I trust her, and if she says you're worth helping, then I'll help."

"Last I checked, Kate wasn't big on teams. That's why we stopped working together. She couldn't trust anyone, and I got tired of the lies."

Lyle's teeth ground together. What Malcolm had said struck a little too close to home.

"Either way, I trust her," Lyle said. "She isn't one to take in strays, either, so you must be important to her."

"Maybe once," Malcolm said.

The front door of the mansion opened, and Kate walked down the steps. She climbed into the driver's seat and handed Lyle a USB drive.

"That has the location and timing," she said.

Lyle plugged it into his computer and synced up the map. It looked about an hour's drive from their current location, somewhere in the middle of back country roads. He skimmed through the rest of the information.

"A moving truck," he said. "Are we sure this object isn't huge? Are we stealing the truck?"

"No. They will track it if we take something that big. The item isn't large, and Wallace assured me that we will find it easy to transport."

"We trust his assurances?"

"We trust his money."

"Do we?"

"Yes," Kate said. "We haven't had a high-paying job in six months, and something this easy only comes around occasionally. Peter vouched for Wallace, and even if I don't trust the client, I trust Peter."

"It still doesn't feel right," Lyle said.

"If you want to sit this one out, that's fine," Kate said. "I can handle it alone."

"No. I'll help. I won't leave you out there on your own."

Kate turned to Malcolm, "What about you? Do you want in?"

"No." Malcolm shook his head. "The last thing you need is to get seen working with me. Plus, my side is killing me, and I could use a nap."

"All right. Let's find a hotel for you to hang out in and then get this job done. Once we drop off the package, I promise we'll turn all of our attention to helping you."

"Thank you."

"Don't mention it."

Chapter 7
Houston, Texas

1

In a rush, Andrew headed back across the sprawling city of Houston. His run-in with the caterer had made him late for his meeting with Emily Perkins, and he wanted to get there before she showed up to speak with Doctor Monroe Fink. Unlike everything else that had happened, the good doctor wouldn't let him down.

After everything else had gone wrong today, he needed something to go right. He had spoken with Monroe on the phone to ensure he had everything ready for when Emily arrived. The doctor had assured Andrew that things were in hand, and all of Andrew's doubts and misgivings had washed away.

The moment had come to set things in motion.

By the time Andrew reached the offices of his company, he felt in a huff and out of sorts. He chided himself for allowing Emily to bait him as she had in the board meeting. She had manipulated him, and his emotions got the better of him. The meeting had done irreparable damage to his reputation.

No doubt it also helped her in her campaign to become the new face and CEO of CDM Pharmaceuticals, and if he guessed correctly, she'd come only a few weeks away from officially presenting the idea to the other board members.

He wasn't about to let her steal his company.

Luckily, he had something else in mind for her. Andrew would kill two birds with one stone, so to speak. He smiled to himself, pleased at his conviction. In their earlier meeting, Emily had been right about one thing: the flu had proved much too tame this season.

He hurried into the building and up to the meeting room

where Doctor Monroe Fink waited for him. Fink, a man without scruples and a dear friend, had worked alongside Andrew to build CDM Pharmaceuticals since the company's inception.

The gaunt man had thick salt-and-pepper hair and wore wide-rimmed glasses; though only thirty-six, anyone would have guessed Fink to be in his late fifties if they'd only passed on the street.

Monroe worked in the Research and Development division of the company, though most of his research happened strictly off the books. Andrew kept all the documents at home on his private servers and away from any prying eyes. CDM had suffered through two audits in the last three years, and the last thing he needed was a nosy government employee combing through sensitive materials.

That research, though, would prove instrumental in the coming days.

"You seem distracted," Fink said.

"Hmm?" Andrew asked, spinning in his seat to face the doc.

This conference room, unlike the one he'd rented to impress his investors, felt too small, too bright, and lacked any windows or natural lighting. He considered the two conference rooms to be the stark contrasts of his life: this room represented his past. The other his future.

"The meeting didn't go well?"

"No. I don't want to talk about it."

"That bad? Well, then, I have some good news for you. I sent the samples this morning for bird-flu strain one-three-seven. They are on their way around the country to the targeted locations we specified previously. Fifteen samples in all with an expected attrition rate of six days."

"You're certain they can't get traced back to us? This is extremely important, Monroe. If they even point a finger at us, it could all come crashing down."

"The ground-zero points all got chosen with care. The epidemic will prove terrifying but non-volatile."

"What do you mean?"

"I mean that the patients will all die before the virus has a chance to spread. I chose strategic locations to maximize both news coverage and confusion while minimizing the chances of a large-scale outbreak."

"How long is the incubation period?"

74

"Ten hours. Death within five days."

"Likelihood?"

"Fifty-eight percent. However, with its low volatility rating, it is non-contagious hours after incubation."

"So, nothing like our other pathogen?"

Monroe shook his head. "The exact opposite. Strain one-one-seven is incredibly contagious but also quite mild. Many people have become infected with it already, yet there has not been a single reported case. It will reach peak coverage in three weeks."

"Excellent, just in time for our next shipment of vaccines to go out. The timing is perfect."

"Almost perfect. We've had a slight delay in those shipments."

"What?"

"Nothing serious. I didn't expect them to test this batch so thoroughly."

"Test?" Andrew panicked. "You said they would only test the first batch."

"Relax." Monroe patted the air with his hands. "It's fine. They don't test for the biomaterial, and they've given us a perfect rating. The delay means an extra week before we can cover the entire country."

Andrew breathed a sigh of relief. "Great. Now, what about that special sample I asked you for? Did you manage to do it at such short notice?"

Fink hesitated. Then he said, "Are you sure about this? If we don't want any attention on us, then this seems like an unnecessary risk."

Andrew argued, "This *has* to happen. I'll not do all of this for my company only to have it stolen out from under me."

"Stolen, how?"

"She is planning a coup."

Monroe frowned. "Perhaps there are other ways—"

"This *has* to happen, Monroe," Andrew said. "Is the sample ready or not?"

"It's ready," Monroe said, sliding a bottle of antibacterial gel out of his pocket. He held it gingerly, keeping it away from his skin. Thick plastic wrap covered it. "Keep the lid on tight until you're ready to use it. Just make sure she applies it liberally to her hands."

"Gel?"

"I considered using lotion to spread the virus, but some people get specific about scents, and I worried that she might decline. Just make sure not to get any on your hands, or we might have a new problem."

"I thought I'd had the inoculation?"

"You did," Monroe said, then he added, "in theory."

Andrew blew out a low breath and slid the bottle into his pocket. "Is everything else in order? What about our other asset? Can we eliminate it yet?"

"Not yet. We haven't replicated the genetic structure as efficiently as intended, so we still need to harvest directly from the source."

"What about the genetic therapy?"

"It is point three percent effective and targets no demographics in particular."

"Point three percent? Why so low? I thought you said this would make us money."

"Low is good. Point three percent is considerably higher than originally intended and a side-effect of the genetic rewiring that takes place. We're talking thousands of cases in the first few weeks. Anything more would risk immediate exposure and a much harsher investigation."

"What symptoms does the first strain produce?"

"Itching, sore throat, and a minor temperature elevation. In most patients, it lasts two to three weeks but remains virtually undetectable. Most people won't seek treatment beyond vaccination."

"We should have made it more than a nuisance."

"Stronger treatment would have diminished the virus's effectiveness. We want people to feel afraid of acquiring the flu, but when they have strain B, we don't want them to need treatment. Ideally, everyone will get the vaccine, and no one will take Tamiflu."

"You're right. It's just been a frustrating day."

"We can hold off—"

"No, it's time."

Monroe sat in silence for a long moment. "They will know this was a deliberate attack. Our targets are too specific, and the overall intent too narrow to be random. We will have to answer a lot of questions."

76

"They will have no proof."

"Not here."

Andrew knew what the doctor implied. "The research is safe."

"Is it? If the FBI comes with a warrant—"

"They won't have any cause. *Nothing* points at us."

"Maybe you should destroy it."

"If anyone starts asking too many questions, I will. Right now, though, that research is worth billions of dollars. Regulators will come to us with questions, find nothing, and then move along. We have nothing to worry about."

Monroe hesitated and then nodded. "No, of course. Nothing to concern us."

"The new batch of flu shots will ship out in two weeks, and our plan will go into motion. For now, we just want to scare people and remind them that they want to get their shots: a little fear is healthy."

Andrew leaned back in his chair and let out a deep sigh. They had sped up their timetable, and this came earlier than he'd hoped to begin his plan, but all the pieces were lined up and ready to go. He would have preferred waiting another week-and-a-half before unleashing the deadly strand of flu Monroe had concocted, but he needed to take care of Emily now before she could do any more damage.

Andrew hated having to change his plans because of Emily, but it relieved him to think that soon she would be out of his way.

And in the most poetic way possible.

In perfect honesty, he barely understood much of what Dr. Fink planned. Much of it sounded like gobbledygook and math. In fact, they hadn't dreamed of the plan until they'd found their asset. It had come like a lightning bolt sent from heaven to make their wildest dreams possible.

From there, the plan had become the brain-child of Dr. Fink. This would make them a fortune with almost no risk. Just a whole hell of a lot of profit.

Andrew's part of the plan was to keep the board of investors in line and make sure the company went public in time to capitalize on their massive spike in value. If they remained a private equity company when their drug quadrupled in value, it would wreck their finances and lead to a hostile takeover from another business.

77

He wouldn't let that happen. So long as the company went wide before the epidemic, they would get rich.

"None of our competitors' drugs are effective?"

"We tailored Camlodien to this specific genetic defect. Our market competitors have only thirty percent effectiveness against it."

The door to the office opened. Andrew turned toward it in frustration. "This is a closed meeting."

Timidly, Fen Wu stuck her head inside. "S-sir," she said. "Emily Perkins has arrived. She asked for you."

"Excellent. Inform her that I will be with her momentarily."

Fen nodded and disappeared. He waited until she went out of earshot and the door had closed before turning back to the doctor.

"Emily is here early," Monroe said, glancing at his watch. "Is she trying to catch you off-guard?"

"Most likely," Andrew said. "After today, though, I feel fairly certain I'll have the upper hand. How much longer until our asset will no longer be necessary?"

"Once we can replicate the mutation independently and without contamination, the asset will no longer be necessary. A few weeks at most."

"Make it days, Monroe. We're on the clock here."

"I'll do my best."

"He is the only thing that links us back to the mutation directly," Andrew said. "I'll be thrilled once we get rid of him."

"As will I. We can step up our testing and extraction," Monroe said. "I'll see what I can do."

"Good," Andrew rose to his feet. He shook Monroe's hand and headed for the exit. "Keep me appraised of any developments."

"Yes, sir."

Andrew paused. "I might need your assistance for this meeting. Don't wander too far."

Andrew headed out of the conference room and back into the main facility. CDM Pharmaceuticals consisted mostly of a single room with high ceilings and lots of tables. The tan-painted walls looked aesthetically pleasing.

After the disastrous morning meeting, Andrew had grown depressed, but now he had regained the spring in his step. Everything seemed back on track, his plan set in motion, and he would get a little revenge while he was at it.

The lab floor felt more like a stuffy office space than a scientific facility. He hated the disorganization of it, but Monroe thrived in the chaotic setting. Employees in lab coats were scattered everywhere, though none of them paid him much mind.

Most of the staff remained blissfully unaware of Dr. Monroe's work or what really went on in his R&D division of the company. They kept busy working on new formulations of medications that would, probably, never amount to anything.

That was fine, though. CDM Pharmaceuticals only needed to strike gold once.

Across the office, he spotted Emily standing in the entryway near the elevators. It surprised Andrew to see that George Tiplin stood next to her.

She must have brought him along, most likely wanting to have an ally with her during this tour. It annoyed him that she hadn't asked his permission, but he quashed the feelings: he saw no sense in getting petty about it just now.

Chapter 8
Houston, Texas

1

Quickly, Andrew made his way across the open floor and waved at the man and woman.

"Emily! George! I'm so glad you could make it."

"Emily asked me to accompany her," George said, a little sheepish. He looked much like a prom date caught dancing with another boy. "I hope you don't mind."

Andrew pasted on a dazzling smile. "Of course not. The more, the merrier."

"This is the office?" Emily's tone expressed her disaffection. "Seems a little ... spartan. Is that the intention of the décor?"

"We only moved from our old facility a few months ago. This space is developing some much-needed personality, but slowly."

"Well, then, let's get on with the tour," Emily said. "Shouldn't take long."

"Not long at all," Andrew said with a smile, brushing off the insult. "Follow me."

He guided them around the office area, pointing out the various stations and projects that the researchers worked on. With casual introductions, Andrew ensured that Emily shook a lot of hands. She seemed like the type that didn't much care for physical contact, and if he got lucky, she would ask for some disinfecting gel unprovoked.

"We've organized our teams into pods of five or six researchers each. For some projects, we might have three independent pods working together toward a common goal, and for others, one pod might prove sufficient to handle the entire work stream."

"Why pods?"

"It makes the transition from one project to another considerably smoother. Each individual researcher might be unfamiliar with their new project when we shift them around, but they will get accustomed to working together as a team. It helps to personalize the experience and reduce drag."

"Interesting."

"That group over there is dedicated to our largest project—the gene therapy trials. We've developed a practical form of CRISPR gene editing, which requires little specialization or overhead, thereby making it cost-effective."

"Cost effective?"

"Hundreds instead of thousands," he said with a shrug.

"What is its efficacy?" Emily asked.

"Over eighty percent," Andrew said. "Though some people see an almost perfect recidivism rate after one visit."

"Why is that? I have heard that gene therapy treatment is an uphill slog. Everything I've read suggests that it is more like splashing paint on a wall than an arrow at a target."

"Everyone is different. One person might respond well to newly implanted genes, whereas another might reject them outright and require many repeat procedures. We don't know what to expect until the patient walks through our doors."

Emily pressed on, "What mechanism do you use for delivery of the proteins?"

"Hang on," George said, speaking up for the first time and glancing back and forth between the two of them. "Can we take a step back for a second? I hate to admit this, but I have no clue what CRISPR even is."

"Ah," Andrew said, laughing gently. "My apologies. In fact, allow me to bring the perfect person into this conversation."

He waved over at Dr. Monroe, who stood on the opposite side of the room with a clipboard in hand. It took a few tries to get the man's attention, and then Andrew gestured for him to come over. Monroe walked across the room and then nodded at the two investors.

"George, this is Dr. Monroe Fink, our lead scientist. Monroe, would you be so kind as to explain CRISPR for George here? You can do a much better job of it than I can."

"From the horse's mouth," George said. "I like it."

"Absolutely," Monroe said, adjusting his glasses further up his nose. "Where to start. Okay, well, CRISPR is an acronym. It refers to Clustered Regularly Interspaced Short Palindromic Repeats, which exist in all different DNA sequences."

George frowned. "That doesn't really help."

"True, but it does give us a grounding point from which to launch the discussion. Basically, CRISPR refers to a common repeated pattern that we can recognize inside almost all genetic code. Since we already know the pattern, we can use specialized proteins called CAS9 proteins to search for that pattern inside just about any living creature and find a specific chromosomal sequence. Depending on how we program those CAS9 proteins, we can find such chromosomes and mark them, read them, or in our case, remove them."

"Think of it this way," Andrew said, "we have little heat-seeking proteins carrying a pair of DNA scissors. We give them a mug-shot of exactly what piece of DNA to search for, and they go and snip it."

"Correct me if I'm wrong, but that would mean you're simply cutting out bad DNA, right? How does that fix people who have bad DNA already? Doesn't it repair itself to the same bad RNA?"

"The other half of our process is putting in the good DNA. This, actually, is the easy part."

"Easy?" George still looked baffled.

"When a specific sequence of DNA gets removed, a repair is attempted automatically. The mechanism for such repair will root out a replacement from any RNA nearby, and once it finds one that fits, it will insert it into the missing hole. Then, it zips the strand back up and, voila, your DNA is fixed. All we have to do is have our replacement ready and nearby to hijack the process your body does already."

"So, you inject new DNA into the bloodstream with the fixed sequence, let your little heat-seeking missiles loose, and as the body attempts repairs, you hope it grabs the new DNA instead of the old broken DNA?" George said, sounding much like the aggressive Emily.

"A concise summary," Monroe said, nodding

"What if it grabs the bad DNA instead? What do you do then?"

Andrew shrugged. "More treatments."

83

George smiled. "Means more money, doesn't it? That's all there is to it?"

"It isn't as clean or perfect as that, but yes, that covers the general process," Monroe said. "Some people respond excellently to our replacement DNA, and others require more finesse and work to trick their genes into accepting the replacements. Once the sequence is in place, though, it will, generally, replicate correctly across all future strands. We've raised our long-term success rate to over eighty percent."

"Incredible."

"And cheap," Andrew said. "Compared to previous genetic modification techniques, our cost is pennies on the dollar. If we can roll out therapy for Alzheimer's or Hemophiliac patients, then it won't take long before we can roll out fixes for many other genetic defects as well. Our trials have gone remarkably well."

"The world isn't ready for something like this," Emily said. "You keep talking about your trials, but you've only given half-honesty, haven't you? These are *animal* trials, not human, I assume."

"The overall process and efficacy remain the same," Doctor Monroe said. "If we can prove the treatment safe and effective in animals, then we can move on to—"

"It won't get approved for use in the United States on human patients anytime soon," Emily said, arms crossed. "If ever. You're talking about using CRISPR to change the very *meaning* of what it is to be human."

"We're talking about fixing genetic defects and saving lives," Monroe said.

"Those defects form a part of who we are. You can make all this sound pretty and simple, but it isn't. What happens when someone doesn't want to fix a genetic defect but, instead, make an unnecessary improvement? A parent who decides their child should have higher IQ or grow six inches taller?"

"That isn't what we are discussing with—"

"But it's possible, isn't it? The mere fact that your *science* makes it possible to modify embryos and create super humans is why the people of this country will stop you. It's an ethical nightmare."

"What do you mean?" George asked.

Emily frowned. "Andrew and his lackey have spent a fortune on scientific breakthroughs that may well end up being for

84

naught."

Monroe bristled, "The world will, eventually, accept this science, and if the *people* of the United States are too *stupid* to ..."

Andrew put a steadying hand on Monroe's shoulder to stop the flustered Doctor. This project was his baby, and he rarely allowed other people to attack it so fervently.

"Please reserve your judgment until you allow me to show you one last thing," Andrew said softly. "Come along."

Without waiting for a response, Andrew turned and strode across the lab toward the dog kennel.

This lay at the heart and soul of his operation: he had chosen dogs as test subjects because they garnered a more favorable response from outsiders and visitors than rats or other animals might.

That said, dogs proved annoying creatures; the kennel had to stay closed off behind soundproofed walls so that the constant barking and crying from the hounds didn't interrupt the work of his staff.

Along the way, he reached into his pocket and fished out the antibacterial gel. He faked a motion as though pouring some onto his hands, using his body to hide the fact that the lid remained on. Then he rubbed his hands together, stopping to face the others.

"Here," Andrew said, handing the bottle to Emily. "Please, use some of this before entering the kennel. It must remain a secured and bacteria free environment."

"I have some of my own."

Doctor Monroe lied, "This is specialized. Thirty percent more effective than normal gel. We must insist for the safety of our patients."

"Can I get some of that?" George asked, holding out his hand toward Emily.

Emily opened the container, but Monroe acted faster. He slid another bottle out of his pocket, flipped open the top, and squirted some into George's outstretched hand.

George rubbed in the gel, and Emily squirted some of the blue gel onto her palms. Andrew watched with morbid fascination as she spread and rubbed it over her skin before turning back to face the kennel.

"You never answered my question," Emily said, shaking her hands to dry the gel. "How do you administer the proteins? Viral

85

or non-viral?"

Andrew joined Monroe in lying, "Non-viral, of course. We considered short-lived viral strains for in-vivo administration but opted for non-viral targeting methods instead. The risk of cross-contamination seemed too great."

"So, this laboratory hasn't even researched viral applications of CRISPR?"

Andrew lied again, "None. Other facilities might specialize in such administrative methods, but our way proves considerably safer, if slightly less efficacious."

"Good. That's the first bit of positive news I've heard all day."

Andrew ignored her and opened the door to the kennel. Immediately, the sound of intense barking from many excited dogs assaulted them. George tensed up in fear, and Andrew fought down an urge to laugh at the fat and balding man.

"The patients in our clinical trials reside here."

"Seems a bit inhumane, doesn't it?" Emily asked.

"I assure you, the dogs receive the best possible care. Daily walks, expensive food, and companionship from our highly-trained staff. That isn't the point, though."

"What is?"

Andrew walked over to one of the closest cages. Inside, an enormous Great Dane stood panting, staring up at them with big eyes.

"This is Lexi," Andrew said. "She's fifteen years old."

"I thought Great Danes didn't live past ten?" George said.

"They don't. Nor does she have Hip Dysplasia, at least not any longer. It is a common trait in her breed."

"You were able to fix her genetic defect?" Emily asked.

"Yes," Andrew said. "We not only fixed her genetic defect, but we also rewrote her genetic code to correct similar defects in her species."

"What do you mean?"

"With Dr. Monroe's research, we've created not only a genetic fix for Lexi but also a solution for Great Danes that will, eventually, make Hip Dysplasia a thing of the past in her breed. It will take many generations of breeding and selection for her newly-improved genetics to propagate throughout the Great-Dane line, but we could, hypothetically, remove the disease entirely by fixing a few key dogs in a similar way throughout the gene pool."

86

George and Emily stared at him in stunned silence. It took a minute for the information to seep in, and Andrew savored the quiet.

"What would this mean for humans?" George asked.

"Using a similar technique, we could strengthen all of humanity's resistance against Monogenetic Disorders such as Cystic Fibrosis, Sickle Cell, and Tay Sach's Disease in only a few generations. We could even, potentially, weaken multifactorial inheritance disorders such as diabetes, heart disease, and alcoholism by strengthening certain genetic lines. We could battle chromosomal disorders, including Down Syndrome. With this research, we can make it possible for humans to live longer and fuller lives."

Emily shook her head. "The government won't—"

"It doesn't matter what the government will and won't allow," Andrew said. "It matters only what the people want. Will you be the one that tells a family we won't cure their infant daughter's cancer because some bleeding-heart liberal feels it is 'wrong'? You call it unethical to use our technology, but I say it is immoral not to. When ranked against the human lives it can save, your ethical objections feel pretty weak."

"It doesn't matter. Such science remains years away from human trials anyway."

"It is here," Andrew said. "Whether you like it or not, we could begin such trials now. And we aren't the only lab working on something like this. It *will* be the future, and the question is: does CDM Pharmaceuticals want to get on the ground floor of this genetic revolution, or would we prefer playing catch-up ten years from now after some other lab—or nation—has changed the world?"

George appeared keen. "What are you asking of us?"

"For you to share in my vision. To continue our research and become a world leader in new technology, we need resources, which means we have to take the company global."

"Incredible," Emily muttered, shaking her head. "That you will stand here and make that argument on technology that you know isn't market ready. Without human trials, it stays years away. Man up, Andrew. Stop making baseless claims and admit the truth: right now, the only thing we have to pitch to possible future investors is Camlodien, isn't it?"

"It will be enough," Andrew said. "Camlodien gives us an

87

incredibly valuable first step in our plan and is new to the market. In a few months, we will overtake Warfarin and Heparin and become the go-to medication for dealing with blood clots."

"I hope you're right," George said. He reached down and into the cage to pat Lexi on the head. "It's a big risk."

"Too big," Emily said. "You're ambitious, Andrew. I'll give you that. But you're also arrogant and a liar. I won't support you in driving our company into the ground."

Andrew pursed his lips. "You mean *my* company."

"For now."

With that, Emily turned and stormed away from Andrew, heading for the exit. Halfway there, she tossed the bottle of blue antibacterial gel into a trash can and kept going. The men watched her disappear.

"Sorry, Andy," George said with an apologetic shrug. "Sometimes, things just don't go in your favor. I like you, and I would have backed you, but this isn't the same world I grew up in."

"What are you saying?"

"I'm saying that *she* is the future. We've just got to deal with it and fall into step."

"You think she'll take my company from me?"

"If I could stop her, I would. But the board loves her, and she's got the credentials to make them rich. I didn't tell you this before, but it's four weeks until the board votes. I believe she'll move it up if she can. I love what you've done here and would stand with you ... but ..."

Andrew fumed inside, but outwardly, he nodded. "I understand. Thank you for warning me. It's good to know I've still got some friends on the board."

"You're a good kid," George said. "I'm sure you'll do fine."

Then he headed off to follow Emily. Andrew watched them leave the lab, a small smile curling his lips. If he'd felt unsure about whether to give Emily the blue bottle of gel before, he sure as hell felt happy with his decision now.

"I should have let George use the gel, too," Andrew said. "Whiny little piss ant that he is."

"Too great a risk," Monroe said, stepping up next to him. "The commonality of patients would point directly to us, and we certainly don't need *those* questions. I suspect we will have unpleasant questions either way, but no sense in adding insult to injury."

"Point taken," Andrew said with a sigh. "But it doesn't mean I didn't want it to happen. Make sure you dispose of that bottle before someone goes digging through the trash. I don't want anyone tracing some sick bum back to us either."

"They couldn't. By the time anyone tested the bottle, all traces of the virus would have gone."

"Better safe than sorry."

"Of course," Monroe said. After a hesitation, he added, "You do realize that we haven't even come *close* to those kinds of breakthroughs you mentioned, right? Everything you said in there remains theoretical at best, and maybe only hypothetical. We haven't managed to replace a stable strand of DNA apart from our asset's, and that happened on a complete fluke. The idea of modifying the entire Great-Dane species is twenty or thirty years away, if ever."

Andrew glanced back at Lexi—in actual fact, a three-year-old Great Dane, and one of the newest arrivals to the kennel. She hadn't even undergone any of the trials yet, so she remained one of the few who still appeared healthy and vibrant.

With a grin, he said, "I know that, but *they* don't."

Chapter 9
Freeport, Texas

1

Lyle rented a hotel room using a fake identity and then helped get Malcolm up to it. Thoroughly exhausted, the man could barely walk after the long drive, and Lyle realized that most of his quiet bravado about the wounds came from his unwillingness to complain.

The terrible injuries had left his bandages soaked with blood. His eyes appeared unfocused. Lyle couldn't imagine the pain Malcolm must be going through, and if he underwent similar duress himself, he wouldn't stay tough about it. Everyone would feel his pain.

They laid him on the bed, and then Kate replaced his bandages. Lyle closed all the curtains and hooked up his equipment. For his first step, he wiped everything clean and set up his defensive triggers in case something went wrong. They would all self-destruct, first using magnets to destroy the hard drives, and then melting the silicone.

Kate thought it too much security, but Lyle had spent a lot of time studying forensic computing. He wouldn't take any risks where his rig was involved. Lyle had custom built a highly secure network integrated with some of the newest encryption-cracking software on the market. It had cost a fortune and countless hours to build, but it made him almost impossible to locate or track.

His portable laptop setup didn't have nearly as much power, but he bounced most of his connections back here to do the heavy lifting.

In addition, Lyle had access to several catastrophic-level safeguards, including two different global networks for mobilizing DDOS attacks and a suite of attack programs. Those would trace back to him easily but could do some severe damage if he ever had to put them into action.

Lyle had just finished getting his gear in line when he received a ping from one of his search algorithms. At first, he thought that it had updated some information about Wallace Blake and their current job, but quickly, he realized it came from his other search.

The deep-web skim he'd run about Malcolm to try and figure out what, exactly, had happened to him back in Delaware had returned a packet with quite a bit more relational information than he'd expected.

He clicked it open, skimmed the first few data points, and then his eyes went wide. He turned in his chair and stared at Kate. *"You ..."*

"What?" Kate asked.

Malcolm leaned up on the bed, glancing at him quizzically.

Lyle checked himself. "Uh ... do *you* want me to go get some ice? Might help take down his swelling."

"Sure," Kate said. "I left the keys on the counter."

Lyle spun, locked his computer, and grabbed the ice bucket. He rushed out of the room, closed the door behind him, and then sucked in a few deep breaths. Then he rubbed his hands across his face and made a moaning noise in utter frustration.

"Are you all right, mister?" a little girl asked.

Lyle glanced up. A pair of young kids, a boy and a girl, stared up at him with concerned expressions. Dressed in bathing suits, they must be on their way to the pool.

Lyle realized he was blocking the hallway and stepped out of the way.

"Yeah," he said. "I'm fine, thanks."

"The ice is over that way," the little girl said, pointing back down the hallway. "Don't be upset. If you don't know how to find it, we can show you."

Lyle smiled. "No, that will be all right. I appreciate the offer, though. You know how frustrating it can be trying to find the ice machine, right?"

She nodded solemnly. She and her brother continued past him and down the hallway.

Lyle had always wanted to have kids, and until two years ago, he had assumed that was the trajectory of his life. Build his career, find a wife, and have some kids.

Now, though, he didn't feel so sure.

He headed down the hallway to get the ice, trying to come to terms with the information he had seen. He had known Kate had lied to him, but this proved much worse than he'd imagined.

As he filled up the bucket, he felt a presence sidle into the little cubby behind him. He glanced back. Kate stood just behind him, staring. A curious expression settled on her face, tinged with worry. "Need any help?"

He spun to face her, wagging an accusatory finger in her face. "It was you, wasn't it?"

She tilted her head to the side, and then her eyes went wide. She grabbed his arm and dragged him back to a far corner of the little cubby, making sure no one was around before speaking. "How did you find out?"

"I searched the area around Delaware for anyone active in the last few weeks who might have had involvement with Malcolm, and *you* popped up."

"Peter said all records got wiped." She cursed under her breath. "There shouldn't be anything linking me to Delaware."

"Almost everything got deleted, but I found backups that hadn't yet been purged from the servers. You lied to me. You told me you went to Brazil."

"No, you *assumed* I went to Brazil because that was where you tracked me to."

"You knew I had the tracker on you. It's a lie of omission at best."

"I asked you not to dig into this."

"Why the hell wouldn't I? It's not like I would get the truth from you."

"In any case, it wasn't supposed to become a big deal. An old contact called in a favor. I couldn't say no."

"Why didn't you tell me about the job?"

"I didn't want to get you involved. These aren't good people, and I wanted to protect you from it."

"You mean you didn't trust me," he said. "I could have helped. I could have kept all of this from happening at all, but you didn't even trust me enough to let me know what was going on."

"I didn't tell you about it because I didn't want *them* to know about you."

"Why not?"

93

"These are unsavory people, Lyle. This is the exact past I want to escape from."

"One hell of a start."

She winced. His words had cut her deep. "Don't remind me."

"Does Malcolm know?"

Her eyes went wide. "God, no. He has no clue. I don't ... I don't know how to tell him. I didn't even know he was involved until ..."

"Until you murdered his team?"

"That wasn't me." She grabbed his arm. "You have to believe me. I had nothing to do with that."

"Then what happened?"

"It was supposed to be a simple job. We had info that people would destroy cargo, and we got hired to stop that. No one should have got hurt. I had the shipment moved and used the boat as a decoy. Our job was to keep the crew safe and act like everything was normal."

"So, what happened?"

"Things went sideways. They didn't tell me about the plan to kill Malcolm. They used me. I didn't even know Malcolm led the other team until he fell in the water and nearly drowned."

"So, what? This is guilt, then? You feel bad for almost getting your friend killed, so you saved his life?"

"If you had *any* idea who Malcolm was, you would know that I had no other choice."

"What about the rest of the guys you worked with? I'd bet they didn't take it too well."

Kate looked at the floor. "You'd bet right. Jeff died. I shot him. The other two are in the wind."

"I can track them—"

"I know you can. I didn't want to tell you because I didn't want you involved. This is my mess, and it's my responsibility to fix it."

"Bullshit."

"What?"

"We're a *team,* Kate. A team. It's our mess, not yours, and not mine. Admit it: not telling me wasn't to protect me, it was to protect *you.*"

"What?"

"You're afraid to trust me because you don't trust anyone. I love you, Kate, and you still won't treat me like an equal."

94

Her eyes widened when he spoke. Had he just overstepped? He'd never used the 'L' word, or anything too close to it. The heat of the moment had gotten the better of him.

Would she say it back?

Doubtful.

The silence deepened. His face turned red. Finally, Kate cleared her throat. Part of him felt relieved that she just wanted to move past it and pretend like it had never happened.

An even larger part felt crushed.

Kate spoke, "I didn't want you involved."

"Well, I'm involved now."

"Yeah, but you have to stay careful. If you set off any red flags and show your involvement, they will come after you too."

"I don't care," he said. "You wouldn't have told me if I hadn't found out, would you?"

"I would have. I swear. I just ... we needed to finish this job before we could have this conversation."

"This job?"

"It was part of the deal."

"The deal?" he said, confused. Then it hit him. "Wallace was the one who hired your friends. The ones you betrayed."

"He negotiated everything through Peter, and Peter passed both jobs along to Jeff. They needed someone else to help plan the job, though, so they called me."

"And then you killed Jeff."

"The other two disappeared and left me holding the bag. The first job was, technically, a success, and then Johnson wanted someone to finish the second one."

"So, what then? You screwed up the first job, then why take on the second one? It wasn't yours to begin with."

"That was Peter's price."

"Price for what?"

Kate bit her lip.

It took Lyle a second, and then his heart sank. "You burned Malcolm, didn't you?"

"I didn't have a choice. He was going to start digging, and my name would have come up eventually. I needed time to figure it all out. I couldn't just let him die, but if he *knew* that I formed part of the team that killed his friends, he would have come after me."

"Understandable," Lyle said. "I'm not far from that right

95

now either. You aren't a trusting person, and I'm sick of it. You act like I'm a child, but we're *partners*. Or, at least, I thought we were."

"We are—"

"No, we aren't. If you keep tiptoeing around and hiding things from me, then this isn't an equal relationship. Hell, it isn't even a relationship at all, is it? You either have to trust me with everything, or I'm out."

"I *do* trust you."

He shook his head. "It's all or nothing. No more sneaking around behind my back. Either share everything with me, or I walk. What'll it be?"

For a second, she hesitated, and then blew out a breath of air. "This isn't really my thing … trusting people, you know. I just didn't want to put you at risk."

"That isn't your decision to make. We're partners, so we're in this together."

She nodded. "Right. Sorry. I've made a real mess of things, and it wasn't fair to you."

"No more secrets."

"None. I promise."

"You should tell *him* the truth, too," Lyle said. "The longer you go without admitting what happened to Malcolm, the worse it will be when he finds out."

"He doesn't need to find out," she said. "He'll only stay with us for a couple more days until he gets back on his feet, and then things will go back to normal."

"He won't stop looking for the people who murdered his team."

"No," Kate said, "but when you give him the list of names of who screwed him, I don't need to be on it, right?"

A pleading look dulled her eyes. Lyle scratched his chin and sighed. "All right, then. Let's go solve your mess."

2

When they made it back into the room, they found Malcolm passed out on the bed. Lyle remained furious with Kate for lying to him, but part of him could understand and sympathize. After everything she'd gone through, he doubted he could trust anyone either.

Hopefully, she would take the "no more lies" edict seriously, though, but he made up his mind that if she didn't, he would get out. He'd given up two years of his life to her already, and if things didn't change, he wouldn't give any more.

With any luck, it wouldn't come to that.

"Two hours and then we have to move," Kate said, softly, checking on Malcolm. She had reapplied his bandages, and he slept peacefully.

"I'll do what I can now and finish the rest later," Lyle said. "Now that I know what I'm looking for, I shouldn't find it hard to put something together. You should tell him, though."

"I will after this job finishes."

Lyle went to work, typing frantically into the system to draw up all the information he could about what Kate had told him. She gave him a list of names of the other people involved, and tracking them down didn't prove difficult. They all tried to hide, but it did little good when someone like Lyle knew where to look.

She had told him the truth; they seemed an unsavory bunch of miscreants. Each of them had criminal records that spanned gigabytes of data. Murder sat at the top of the list, and Lyle could hardly believe that Kate had worked with these people.

Geoffrey Tripp, or Jeff, had died, but the other two—Frank Portman and Roger White—remained very much alive. Worse still, they hadn't settled too far away. Their last sighting put them at about two hundred miles from this hotel, though he felt unsure of where they headed.

He couldn't rule out here as a possibility.

Though he should have looked up more information about their current job, it seemed more important to keep Kate safe. He needed to discover what Roger and Frank wanted and if they still searched for Kate.

Lyle deleted all the digital evidence he could find that linked Kate to the Delaware attack, added additional evidence that would put her in Brazil as expected, and then created a dossier for Malcolm that would point him squarely at the two men who had murdered his friends.

After printing the dossier, he stuck it in a folder and set it on the bed next to Malcolm.

Kate glanced at him in surprise. "Is it finished?"

"As finished as it will ever be," Lyle said. "Your digital

fingerprint has gone, and he has everything he needs to find Roger and Frank. I can't force the other two men to stay quiet if he finds them, though."

"It's enough," she said, a relieved smile spreading across her face. "I don't think they will get a chance to say much at all when Malcolm finds them. Thank you."

"Don't thank me. That's what partners are for. Next time, just make sure to keep me in the loop."

"I will. Promise."

"Good."

She glanced at her watch. "We need to get moving. I had hoped to scout the area before the truck arrived and get a feel for the place."

"I'll come along," Lyle said. "We shouldn't need any remote backup, and I could use some fresh air."

"Fresh air? Since when do you want fresh air?"

"All the time."

"You just don't want to be here when he wakes up, do you?"

"Hell no. The guy scares me."

"Really, he's just a giant teddy bear," Kate said.

Lyle frowned. "You didn't *have* to describe him like that."

Kate chuckled. "Of course not. I just like watching you squirm. Come on."

Chapter 10
Freeport, Texas

1

Several times, Kate and Lyle drove up and down the road where the truck would travel, trying to locate the perfect place to stop the vehicle and steal the package. Kate clenched the steering wheel and frowned the entire time.

"What's up?" Lyle asked.

Kate shook her head. "This won't work at all."

"What do you mean?"

"Too much through-traffic. All it takes is one bystander to get a call out to the police and wreck our afternoon."

"I could block outbound calls," Lyle said. "Hack in and shut down the coverage."

"That's it?"

"Yep," he said. "Actually, I would need to hit a couple of towers to stop all calls from getting out. And I would have to widen the net for people moving into another coverage area because they are in, you know, cars. Plus, I would have to ..."

Kate sighed. "Can you block all of them or not? Also, what about CB radios?"

"That's trickier. We would need a localized jammer. A powerful one, too, if you want to hit a wide enough area to matter."

Kate drummed her fingers on the wheel. "That would raise more red flags."

"Yeah. I know. So, how do you really know Malcolm?" The question burst out.

"He's like a brother," Kate said. "We go way back. We worked some of our earliest jobs together, and he took care of me and helped me learn the ropes. He taught me everything I know."

"You two were never ..."

"Romantic? No, though he did date my sister for a few years."

"The one in jail?"

"Yeah, Helen. They got serious, too, but then they broke it off."

"Why?"

"She thought I'd died."

"Oh," Lyle said.

"That was when she first started looking for me and got involved with JanCorp. She stopped talking to Malcolm, and I guess they drifted apart."

"Is Helen talking to you yet?"

"Nope. Still hasn't forgiven me. She only has a few months left in prison, though, before she's eligible for early parole."

"That's great," Lyle said. A moment passed. "Do you want me to ...?"

"No, she's fine. She asked us not to get involved."

"Ah. Okay."

A moment passed as she made another U-turn and headed back in the other direction. Idly, Lyle tapped on his computer and waited. Kate didn't desire his input at this moment. He would just keep his mouth shut and let Kate do her thing.

"We need a way to get them off the road and—"

"So, were you, like, involved romantically with anyone?" Lyle asked. This question also just burst out.

"We're having this conversation then, are we?"

"I felt curious whether you've ever had a serious relationship before. You know, like someone you loved."

"No," Kate said. "No serious relationships. Always too busy with work, and it never happened."

"Like never happened, or *never* happened?"

"Those are the same thing."

"You have to listen to the inflection."

"It never happened, Lyle. Nothing serious."

"Oh, okay."

A moment passed.

"Promiscuous sex, though," she said, slowly, a wry grin spreading on her lips. "I've had a *lot* of that. And I mean, a lot. There was one guy that—"

"Okay, okay, I get it." Lyle raised his hands. "Point made."

"You sure you don't want to hear about all the men I've slept with?"

Lyle frowned down at the map. "Turn left here," he said.

"Why?"

"Just turn. I've got an idea."

2

Lyle stood at the intersection of Hardy and Wayfair Avenue, wearing an orange road-crew vest and hardhat. He had a sign with him that said "slow" on one side and "stop" on the other. For now, he waited, resting the sign on the ground and watching out for their target to drive into sight.

Their dangerous target. Armed and dangerous. He lifted the walkie-talkie to his mouth, which they had stolen out of the road-crew truck, and clicked the button. The static dissipated.

"Are you sure I don't need a gun?"

"Why would you need one?" Kate said on the other end of the walkie-talkie.

"They have guns, don't they?"

"If this goes well, they won't get a chance to use them."

"What if I have to shoot someone?"

"You won't."

"Yeah, but what if I *do?*"

"I think we're all safer if you don't have a weapon."

"I've trained a lot with mine," he said. "I have, like, ninety-three percent accuracy."

"Then where's your gun?"

Lyle hesitated. "I forgot it."

"If you needed a weapon, you should have brought one."

"You have backups."

"That's right, I have *my* backups. Not for giving out to people who forget their own."

"When this is over, I'm getting another."

"So you can forget that one too? I'll make you a deal: I'll buy you a backup pistol after you take a gun-safety course."

"I know how to use one."

"Yeah, but I wouldn't call you 'safe,' exactly."

"You mean like a professional military training safety course?"

"No, like the one you drag your kid to so they know which end the bullets come out of."

"Ha, ha, real funny."

"I bet a kid wouldn't have forgotten his gun."

"Once we've done this job, we'll have a sit down and—"

Lyle's phone buzzed, which meant the truck had reached half a mile up the road from his position. He glanced at the image on his phone, made sure it was the right truck, and then grabbed a stack of cones.

"Inbound," he said.

"ETA?"

"I don't know. How do I estimate ETA for something like this? A few minutes? Thirty seconds? Hang on."

Lyle stuck the walkie-talkie back into his belt and then rushed out into the road, setting the cones out to block both lanes heading east. Then, he grabbed a barrel and dragged it over as well, setting it in the truck's path to block its progress.

Finally, he grabbed his sign and stepped out into the road as well. He flipped it to the side that said "stop" and held up his hand. The truck flew around a turn in the road.

They came at speed, a lot faster than the road limit, and thus far, they hadn't even touched the brakes.

"They'll stop," Lyle muttered, holding up his hand.

The truck barreled toward him, looming larger by the second. He held up his sign in clear view, waving.

"They'll stop."

The truck kept coming, and it occurred to him that they might just keep going right on through. It reached eighty or so meters away and didn't slow at all. He fought the urge to dive out of the way and forced himself to stay calm.

"Oh crap, oh crap, oh crap."

Finally, only a few dozen meters away, the driver hit the brakes. Lyle scrunched his face up as it dragged to a stop just a few feet in front of him, engine sputtering.

The driver rolled down the window. "What the hell?"

"Road's closed," he shouted back, willing his body to stop shaking. He strode around to the driver's door. "Didn't you see the signs?"

"Road looks fine to me."

"Nasty accident up ahead. All four lanes blocked. Detour only takes you a couple of miles around. It'll cost you five minutes at the most. Better than getting stuck in traffic all day, right?"

Lyle pointed off down the side road, a one-lane alley that headed through the trees and out of sight. Up ahead on that road, Kate waited, and all he had to do was send them down that path.

The guy glanced down that road and chewed over the idea, staring at Lyle.

"How long will the road stay closed?"

"A few hours at least. If you like, I can call a patrol car back, and you can talk to the cops who closed it."

"No, not necessary. Five minutes, you said?"

"Maybe less."

"All right."

The guy put the truck in reverse, backed up a little, and headed off down the side road. Lyle let out a shuddering sigh once they'd gone.

Adrenaline coursed through his veins, and his hands shook.

"The chickens are coming to roost," he said into the walkie-talkie.

"What? What the hell does that mean?"

"I mean, they took the bait and are on their way."

"Then why didn't you just say that?"

"I don't know. Didn't seem as dramatic."

"Oh, so it didn't fit you? Get your ass over here."

"I'll be there in a couple of minutes."

"All the fun will have finished by then."

"That's my goal," he said. "I don't have a gun, remember?"

He waited until the truck drove out of sight and then dragged the orange cones and barrel back out of the way. More traffic arrived. He'd cleared just in time. Lyle waved a couple of cars through and then took off the vest, tossing it into the back of the stolen truck.

They had picked up the truck from a nearby house. The worker who operated it on behalf of the state had gone on family vacation and wouldn't come back for another few days. Luckily, he had left the keys at home.

Lyle climbed in and drove off down the road after the truck. Lyle could hardly believe the drivers had fallen for his plan, and he felt mightily impressed with himself.

He rounded a turn and saw the truck idling up ahead. The left-side door hung open, and the driver had fallen out. He lay on the roadway, unconscious, pistol on the ground next to him. Lyle pulled to a stop next to the vehicle. The other guard sat motionless in the cab, a dart sticking out of his neck.

Kate's rented Chevy Cruze sat turned sideways across the road, blocking the path forward. Lyle glanced around but didn't spot Kate anywhere nearby. Just the two unconscious men.

"Kate?" he asked, turning off the engine and climbing out of the truck. "Where are you?"

He explored around, and the hairs on the back of his neck rose. Something didn't feel right. Too quiet. Had something happened to her? Maybe they had a third guard that Kate and he hadn't known about.

The stopped truck kept rumbling, idling in the center of the dirt road.

"Where'd you go?" Lyle called out.

He hadn't heard any gunshots, so he hoped that Kate was okay. If he found her wounded out here, he didn't know what he would do. One of the many reasons he didn't like working out in the field like this. He moved slowly, circling the truck and searching.

Nothing. The entire area seemed empty. He thought to pick up the discarded gun but changed his mind. Kate was right: he didn't want to use it, not really. What if she was hurt, though, and there was something dangerous out here?

Like a monster. Or aliens.

Stop it, imagination.

Still, he might need *something* to defend himself if he didn't find Kate. What had happened to her? Had something gone wrong with the plan?

Was she all right?

"This isn't funny. I'm starting to get a little freaked—"

"Boo!"

She leapt from around the side of the vehicle, huddled between the truck and trailer. Lyle screamed, falling onto his butt on the hard dirt, and Kate burst out laughing.

"See?" she said through bouts of hysteria. "That's why you don't get a gun."

"Not funny," he said, scrambling to his feet and brushing himself off. His face flushed crimson. "Not funny at all."

"No, hilarious!"

"You almost gave me a heart attack with your shenanigans."

"Oh, lighten up; you're fine," she said. "Besides, you love my shenanigans."

"Sometimes," Lyle said. "Not right now, but sometimes. The guards are out?"

"For a couple of hours, at least. I'll hit them with another dart before we leave for extra safety. Good job sending them this way. I worried they might just run you over and keep going."

"What? You thought that might happen?"

Kate shrugged. "That's what I would have done. If they were protecting important cargo, I figured they would too."

"Why didn't you say anything?"

"You seemed so confident, and it *was* a decent plan. If I told you they might just kill you and keep going, you might not have sold the bluff."

"Oh, wow, lucky me."

"It worked, didn't it? We'll take the win."

"Yeah," Lyle said. "A win."

"See? I told you this job would be easy. A cakewalk that pays a fortune and makes me even with Peter. We never had anything to worry about."

Begrudgingly, Lyle nodded. "Yeah. This wasn't too bad, and the guy wants to pay us two hundred thousand. I guess you had it right."

"I'm *always* right," Kate said. "Now, let's go see what this mysterious cargo is and get it back to Wallace for our payday."

"Bet it's drugs."

"Probably."

They walked around the side of the truck to the sliding door. Lyle flipped the latch on the bottom, which held it closed.

"Would you like to do the honors?" he said.

Kate grinned. "I thought you would never ask." Then she reached up, grabbed the handle, and pushed the roll-up door out of the way. Light filtered into the mostly empty back of the moving truck. It took Lyle's eyes a minute to adjust, and then he made out the contents inside.

His stomach flipped.

"Uh-oh," Kate muttered next to him. "I didn't expect that."

"What did you just say about this job going easy?"

Kate didn't respond. In the back of the truck sat a large, bunched up blanket, and on that blanket sat the important cargo they needed to deliver to Wallace Blake:

A little boy.

Chapter 11
Houston, Texas

1

Even inoculated, wearing latex gloves and a mask, and reassured by Monroe that the flu strain they had exposed Emily Perkins to no longer remained contagious, Andrew Carmichael still felt reluctant to walk into the sick woman's home.

He wouldn't have come here, in fact, except that his desire to gloat outweighed his sense of self-preservation. Just seeing the look on her face when he explained that *he* had done this to her would give enough of a reward to outweigh the minor risk. From all reports over the last few days, the virus had ravaged her system and left her too ill to leave her bed.

Andrew rang the doorbell of Emily's cozy two-story home and then took a step back, folding his arms solemnly in front of him, waiting. He assumed a live-in nurse would have come to look after her now. Emily lived in a suburban district just outside Houston.

A few moments passed, and then the door opened. A woman stood there in an impressive white power suit with enormous dangling earrings and entirely too much makeup. He'd expected a nurse and didn't recognize this woman.

"Hello? Can I help you?"

"Hi. My name is Andrew Carmichael. I work with Emily and know her from CDM Pharmaceuticals. I wanted to come visit and see how my dear friend is doing. I heard that she'd got sick and hoped I might bring her flowers to cheer her up."

"Yes, of course, come right in."

The woman stepped out of the way, letting Andrew pass. He pulled the mask up to cover his mouth and nose and then strode into the house.

The white-power-suit woman said, "The nurse explained that such precautions are not necessary. Emily no longer poses a threat."

"Oh? It's only been a few days. The sickness must have passed quite rapidly."

"Extremely. They said the onset took only hours, though she didn't mention feeling ill. It hit her suddenly and aggressively."

"Difficult to believe. She seemed so healthy a few days ago."

"The doctors can't explain it."

"I thought they said the flu was mild this time of year?"

"That's what I heard as well. I suppose such news reports get their information wrong more often than not."

"That's true. I'll keep the mask, though, if you don't mind. I prefer to take no chances. Especially with such a virulent strain."

"I understand. You can leave the flowers on the table. I will prune them before taking them to her bedside."

She gestured toward a large wooden table on the far side of the room, covered in myriad colorful flowers, baskets, and miscellaneous gifts from what appeared to be many well-wishers.

Andrew had never known Emily to have so many friends. None of them were here now, though, which reinforced his feeling about death: a lot of people might have loved Emily and wished for her to get better, but the actual process of dying would prove a lonely experience for her. The large and empty house had an air that made it feel like they were mourning her loss already.

Why bother with friends, then, if when the one time they were truly needed they had more important things to do?

He had only dosed her thirty-six hours ago. Monroe had said the virus would act quickly, and indeed, he hadn't exaggerated. The situation had developed so fast, it made Andrew's head spin.

He set his small bundle of meager flowers on the table beside the others and turned back to the woman.

"I apologize, but I don't think we've met."

"Forgive me, where are my manners. I'm Gertrude Pennington, Emily's sister."

"I didn't know she had any siblings."

"She likes to act as if she doesn't. We didn't get along well while growing up. Months have passed since we last spoke."

"She called you when she fell ill?"

"The nurse did this morning. I'm her closest living relative and the only one who could come on such short notice. I brought my children and husband with me to care for her."

He could see her hesitation.

Andrew smiled at her. "Take your time."

"I thought it would give us a chance to reconnect, you know? Show her that we cared and that we should put the past behind us. We didn't think ... we had no idea it would be this bad, though."

"No. How could you have?"

"I'm sorry for prattling on. I shouldn't be telling you all of this. You probably don't know her that well."

"Well enough. It's quite all right. I understand the pain of loss and am sure you're glad to be here with her."

"It's just felt so difficult. The doctors don't hold much optimism about her chances of pulling through. The flu kills thousands of people a year. Did you know that? I had always thought of it as a nuisance, but it really is deadly."

"They think she might die?"

"They didn't ... I'm sorry, I thought I would feel up to talking about this, but I fear now isn't the time."

"It's quite all right. Can I see her?"

"Of course. I'll warn you, though, she can't speak much. Her throat has swollen, making it painful for her to breathe."

"That's okay. I just wanted to stop in and say hello."

Gertrude nodded and led him to a stairwell in the main entryway of the building. It wound up to the second floor and creaked underfoot.

"What about your children, if I might ask?"

"They've gone to stay with my husband at a hotel. I had hoped to go sight-seeing with them a little while we visited, but things degraded rather quickly. I had thought to send them home, but ..."

Andrew waited.

Gertrude said, "No sense in paying for extra flights for the funeral, right?"

"My condolences."

She sniffed and rubbed at her nose vigorously. "In any case, right now, we're waiting and praying that things will turn around. The doctor said there is a chance, and the next few hours will prove critical. Emily might survive several more days either way, but this is the time when it matters most."

"Someone mentioned that more cases like this have hit all around the country. Did the doctors say anything about that?"

"A fluke, the doctor told me, and completely unexpected. Five cases in the last day. Apparently, the CDC is scrambling to make sense of it. Already, three news outlets have called here to ask for information on Em's condition. Thank God we didn't take her to the hospital."

"I wouldn't wish such a sideshow upon anyone. I'm terribly sorry about all of this."

"Don't be. It isn't your fault."

Andrew smiled under the mask, pleased with the irony.

They arrived at the master suite. The oak door stood closed, and Gertrude paused in front of it. "The smell is ..."

"It's quite all right."

She opened the door, and even through the mask, Andrew could smell the sickly-sweet scent of death wafting out to greet him. The dimmed room felt humid. A king-sized bed occupied the center. Tucked into that bed, diminutive and frail, lay Emily Perkins.

Or, what remained of her.

Her face looked sunken and clammy, and her eyes barely seemed able to focus. Her body seemed to be falling apart; organs failing as the sickness crept through her. She had curled into a ball under the covers and made little raspy noises with each inhalation.

Beside him, Gertrude shuffled. She took a steadying breath and walked into the room.

"Emily, a friend of yours from work has come to see you." Gertrude turned to Andrew. "I'm sorry, I've forgotten your name?"

"Andrew," he said. "Andrew Carmichael."

Emily perked up at the name, fear flashing across her face in the pale light. Gertrude didn't seem to notice; instead, she moved to a table to turn on a small light. The pace of Emily's breathing picked up when she tried to speak, but she could produce only slight raspy noises.

"It's horrible to see her like this." Gertrude covered her face with her arm to ward off the smell.

"I agree," Andrew said. "Would you mind if I had a few moments with her alone?"

"Of course not. I'll be right downstairs if you need me."

"Thank you."

Gertrude exited the room, closing the door behind her. Andrew waited until she had gone and then made his way over to the bedside. Emily cowered away from him, but that was fine. He picked up a glass of water with a straw in it from a nearby table and held it out to her.

"Drink?"

She struggled to crawl in the opposite direction across the bed. Her body didn't have enough strength—the muscles lacking oxygen. Her limbs shook under the pressure.

"Wait ... you don't ... you can't possibly think that *I* had something to do with this, do you?" he asked, oozing sarcasm.

Her head snapped over to look at him, a furious expression on her face. For the first time since stepping into the room, he saw something of the powerful woman she had once been.

Once, only a few days earlier.

"Good instincts, then," he said with a smile. Andrew spoke softly, resting on the edge of the bed and folding his hands in his lap. Comfortable, he shifted to face her. "Monroe estimates you only have a few hours left, but it could drag on with all the treatment you're receiving. You went in for help sooner than I'd expected, but it won't matter. The dose and strain we administered work rapidly. You are our patient zero, I fear. How is the pain? Terrible?"

The doctors had hooked her up to an IV bag. Andrew grabbed it. A smaller bag of morphine hooked up to it as well, along with a few other antiviral medications, which Monroe had assured him would prove ineffective against this strain.

The highly-paid doctors had thrown every possible solution at her, and the side-effects of that drug cocktail had made things much worse. Constant diarrhea, vomiting, dehydration, and nausea had become her existence in this moment.

Andrew savored it.

"I suppose you feel pretty upset right about now, and part of you probably wonders what you did to deserve this. That's the thing though: life isn't about what we *deserve*. We don't *get* what we deserve, we must take it. Had you followed my lead, I would have made you richer than you could ever have imagined, and over time, I would have given you anything you wanted for supporting me."

She opened her mouth, but again, she could make nothing

more than those wet rasping noises. It made his skin crawl, but he forced down his displeasure. He lowered his mask.

"You went another route, though, didn't you? You didn't like the secrets or the games, and instead, you wanted to turn the tables against me. You wanted to turn my family and friends against *me*. This company is all I have, and make no mistake, I have no intention of parting with it. Do you want to know why you've ended up here?"

Emily reached a hand up toward him. He caught it in his gloved hand before she could touch any exposed skin. She felt wet and clammy.

"You're not contagious. You're here because you made yourself an enemy, and enemies must get dealt with. This virus has no sophistication at all. It's a simple killing strain of the flu, barely contagious yet highly lethal. You'll die in a couple of hours."

Andrew sat on the edge of the mattress, still clutching Emily's arm. She looked so frail and weak, almost elderly. Part of him—a small part—felt sorry for her.

They lived in a vicious world, and only one person at a time could sit on top. If Emily had felt content on the ground, he could have had a positive future with her. They might have become friends, even. However, in her quest to dethrone him, the woman had put him in an untenable situation.

"When I started this company, I had *nothing*. I grew up with an alcoholic mother. My father was always working, but wasteful, and kept us in poverty. My mother hated all men, and I became the most natural target of her ire. Father's abuse children physically. With mothers, the physical abuse is as nothing compared to what she could do to me emotionally. She would beat and threaten me all the time, sure, but the casual neglect cut deeper. You can't tell people that, though. You can't tell anyone that your *mother* is the one who abused you or that it was emotional maltreatment.

"I only wanted to get away from them. I did decently at school, got a degree, and started this company. Then some *bitch* decides she wants to take all that away from me. *She* was born with a silver spoon in her mouth, handed everything in life. She bought her uncle's company with the money Daddy left her, but she wants to take everything from *me*."

He realized he had fallen into rambling and let out a sigh.

Just thinking about his childhood brought back rough memories he'd rather have kept buried. He never spoke about his family, and he found it quite therapeutic saying this to someone who could never repeat it.

"It's like having a pet," he muttered, brightly. "I never had a dog. Always wanted one, but felt too afraid to ask. After a while, I stopped caring, but I always imagined how *freeing* it must be to have a creature you can tell your deepest darkest secrets to without fear of reprisal. You're like a pet dog. Would you like to know *my* secrets?"

Emily jerked, trying to free her arm, and Andrew let her go. He didn't want her to develop any bruises, after all. She reached for the nightstand, and he spotted a bell tucked behind used tissues.

"Now, now, Emily," he said. "Is that any way to treat your guest?"

He stood and, quickly, circled the bed, grabbing the bell before her trembling hands could reach. He set it on a counter on the other side of the room.

As an afterthought, he glanced around, searching for any baby monitors or other devices. He should have asked Monroe for a wand or something he could have used to check the room for bugs. Did they do it like that in real life or just in the movies? He had no clue.

Not spotting anything, he resumed his seated position next to Emily on the bed. When he continued, he spoke softly so that nobody could overhear them.

"Want to hear a *real* secret? You can be one of only six people alive who knows about our true plans. Well, six for now. I suppose we'll drop back down to five again soon enough, but oh well." Andrew chuckled.

When he'd composed himself once more, he said, "When we first began the CRISPR trials, *nothing* worked. We tried everything we could think of, but it just wouldn't stick. We couldn't deliver the proteins effectively, and the project turned into a complete and undeniable failure.

"Actually, we'd reached the point that we felt ready to give up and scrap the whole thing, but then something miraculous happened. A stroke of luck, or fate. Whatever you want to call it. A man came to me with an intractable problem and begged me to help solve it. His son's blood clotted much more than it should have.

"The boy had a severe and rare case of Factor V Leiden Thrombophilia. I didn't even know what the hell that was at the time, and it certainly wasn't something we'd researched. The man just knew us as one of the few local facilities performing genetic trials and felt desperate for *anything* to save his son, even something incredibly illegal.

"The thing about the kid's condition is that most people who have it never develop a blood clot. In simple terms, it means they have increased risk of getting one. Usually, they don't even know that they have the condition. This kid, however, developed clots all the time. The doctors gave him a few years to live. If the condition didn't kill him, then the drugs they pumped him full of would."

Emily shivered.

Andrew reached over and grabbed her shoulder, steadying her. His touch only made her tremble more.

"Relax, the story gets interesting here. We couldn't help his kid, but the man had deep pockets, and we needed money. So, we grabbed a couple of drifters and ran tests on them. Neither of them had the Factor V, so we used our CRISPR strains on them, trying to find a way to fix the boy by reverse engineering their DNA into his. Petri dishes and dreams.

"We tried everything we could think of, but in all of our trials, the child's broken DNA kept rewriting that from the drifters. Desperate, we tried merging the kid's DNA with one of the test subjects' directly, and guess what? It overwrote *that*, too. Then, Monroe had an idea. We tested the same thing on the other drifter's DNA and got the exact same result."

Andrew stood.

"The *exact* same result. One in a million chance, and a complete freak of nature. It shouldn't work like that. DNA doesn't work like that, but it did.

"That's when our strategy took a U-turn. We had tried using CRISPR to make the kid healthy, but could we use it to make someone else sick?

"We tried it on the drifters. It worked, only in reverse of our original plan. Both men ended up with the same genetic condition as the boy.

"The point is, we'd thought about the entire problem the wrong way. While we ran tests on the sick child, we developed a custom drug to treat *his* extremely rare strain of this genetic condition. A custom drug for *one* particular genetic defect. We brought it to market and called it Camlodien. It's a passable blood thinner, but against this kid's disease, it became a game changer. The problem is, not many people have this disease, let alone the boy's mutation of it."

Andrew planted his hands into his pockets. "Not yet, at least."

A knock sounded at the door. Annoyed, Andrew glanced up just as Gertrude came back into the room. She held a cordless handset to her ear and placed her hand over the microphone.

"Yes?" Andrew said.

"Sorry," she said, tilting her head at him. "It's for you."

He'd left his phone on silent mode and hadn't checked it since arriving. Monroe remained the only person who knew he had come to Emily's home right now, so it must be urgent for him to search Andrew out like this.

Perturbed, Andrew slid his cell out of his pocket. The display showed seven missed calls and a dozen messages.

"Tell Monroe I will call him back," he said. "Thank you."

Gertrude nodded and disappeared from the room, closing the door again. Andrew waited a second and then punched in Monroe's number. He stepped away from the bed.

Monroe answered on the second ring.

"What is it?" Andrew asked without preamble. "What is so urgent that you felt the need to interrupt—?"

"We have a huge problem."

2

Only a few minutes later, Andrew flew down the road, careening along the highway toward his office. Blood and adrenaline coursed through his veins, and desperately, he wished that nothing Monroe had told him in Emily's room could hold any truth.

Monroe waited on the other end of the open line.

Over the car's Bluetooth, Andrew said, "How can he have gone?" He felt furious and out of sorts. "We locked him up out of sight. No one even knew he was there."

"A transfer report got filed for the asset—"

"Just tell me where the hell he went!" Andrew fumed. "How the hell did you let this happen?"

"The system is automated, and Madison filing a report didn't throw up any red flags for me to review personally. I never dreamed she would do something like this."

"Well, she did. Recall the truck. Get him back to the labs."

"I tried. They ... they haven't answered."

"Then get a team out there to find them. I don't care how much it costs, get *someone* out there to track that kid and bring him home."

"I'm trying. The last team we hired ended up dead with one of them burned, so people don't want to work with us right now."

"Pay double."

"I'm offering triple, but don't worry; I'll find someone."

"You better had and in the next couple of minutes. We can't lose Jason. Not right now."

"The tracker isn't in his arm anymore. That's how we didn't know he had left the facility. It shows him still in his bedroom. She must have dug it out before sending him. I stopped in to check on him, and that's how I found out what had happened."

"You've got to be kidding me. Where were his guards?"

"They were the transport crew. We'll find him," Monroe said. "But there's more."

"What do you mean?"

"Wallace did this. He's working with her from the outside. She did this for him."

"No, that can't be. How did she even know about him?"

"He must have tracked her down. I checked her messages and emails, and she's corresponded with him a lot for the last few months. We're decrypting the messages now, but I would bet just about anything that he orchestrated this."

Andrew cursed, slamming his fist against the steering wheel. He weaved erratically through the traffic, narrowly squeezing between two cars and flying through a red light. Vehicles honked all around him, but he didn't care.

"I should have dealt with him *months* ago."

"We thought the illusion of stability would keep him in line. He's stayed quiet up until now."

"He must have realized we had no intentions of giving him his son back."

"I think ... I think he also shipped the Camlodien to

Delaware illegally. The crates they stole from our facility. The one our team failed to destroy."

"How much did he get?"

"Enough for a lifetime supply for his son," Dr. Monroe said.

Andrew's hands shook. He had heard about someone stealing a shipment of his medication a few weeks ago—a couple of crates' worth. They had gotten it out of the city, but getting it into the US would prove a lot harder. At the time, he'd believed that some corporate espionage set-up had paid a team to take it. CDM had paid a group to destroy the cargo before it landed on American soil and someone could reverse engineer it, but they had failed.

It mattered little, though. Any company stealing their medication would have a monstrous time beating them to a patent or market. And, even if they did manage to reverse engineer the drug, CDM still held patent rights, which Andrew could claim by initial proof-of-concept diagrams and formulas from months ago. The point was, losing that shipment had hurt, but he saw no sense in crying over spilt milk.

When two weeks had passed, Andrew had thought that was the end of it. After a long pause, while he ruminated, he said, "They used it as a distraction. The entire shipment was a decoy, and Wallace actually wanted his son. We thought the theft came down to corporate warfare, but he wanted to put us off-guard and get the drugs to take care of his boy away from us."

"Precisely the conclusion I came to," Monroe said.

"We can't afford any more distractions. I don't care what it takes, Monroe. Find Jason."

"Yes, sir."

Andrew fell silent for a moment. "You know what? On second thought, don't hire another team. I have a better idea."

"What?"

"Call the police."

Chapter 12
Houston, Texas

1

Lost in thought, Frank Portman chewed on his cigar. He hadn't lit it, and the tobacco had become a mess in his mouth, but he barely even noticed. He sat thinking about everything that had happened back in Delaware, and all the events that had brought him out here. Someone had murdered his friend and dumped him in the ocean, and he couldn't get that thought out of his mind.

He wanted to kill Kate Allison more than anything else in the world.

"That the guy's car?"

Frank hardly registered the words, still lost in his thoughts. Kate Allison had made a run for it after leaving Delaware, and she'd taken Malcolm with her. So far, Frank hadn't had any luck in tracking her down. She'd come to Houston, but he knew little else. He wanted to know what she was doing here.

They sat parked outside of CDM Pharmaceuticals right now, the company that had hired Malcolm to destroy their cargo. This company's freight, Frank had learned in the last couple of days, didn't make a whole lot of sense. Why would the company want to destroy its own stuff?

"Hey, Frank? Is that the guy's car?"

Most of the last few days didn't make sense, and things had spiraled out of his control. The job went smoothly. He and Roger had taken out Jensen and Amy as expected, but when they went to regroup with the team, they found out that Jeff had been betrayed. Kate had killed him and dumped his body. Worse, Malcolm still lived.

Loose ends from hell.

"Hey!"

A jab landed on his shoulder. On instinct, he reached over and caught the finger, twisting it painfully and eliciting a shout of surprise from his partner. Frank blinked, ripped from his thoughts, and let go of Roger's hand.

"Ouch."

"My bad," Frank muttered, rubbing his face. "I got distracted."

"Clearly. I asked, is that the car?"

Roger pointed. Frank looked. A car pulled into the lot. It was, indeed, the vehicle they were searching for, though it moved semi-erratically just now.

"Yeah, that's him. That's the guy."

"Andrew Carmichael, right? He's the one we want to talk to?"

Frank didn't answer. Instead, he slipped the chewed cigar into his jacket pocket, opened the door, and stepped out into the sunshine. A warm breeze blew past as he walked toward Andrew's car. It parked in one of the private places near the front door, and a tall man climbed out.

"Andrew Carmichael?" Frank called out, ten feet away.

The man turned, a quizzical look on his face. Handsome, he had chiseled features and dark eyes.

"Yes?"

"We need to talk."

"I'm in a hurry, so you'll have to schedule something with ..."

Frank kept walking toward him, using his hand to brush his coat away from his side. The movement revealed the grip of a Glock tucked into his waistband. Andrew trailed off when he spotted the weapon.

"What the hell is going on?"

"We just want to talk."

Frank stopped a few feet away from Andrew, and Roger moved off to the left, blocking Andrew's exit if he tried to run.

Andrew scowled. "Then talk."

"Not here. This should take place somewhere private."

"Away from the cameras, you mean?" Andrew glanced up at the six or so trained on the lot. "I don't think so."

"At most, those cameras only mean I won't work in Houston for a few months. If you think you're safe, pretty boy, think again."

Andrew hesitated. "What is this about?"

120

"Does the name Malcolm Caldwell ring a bell?" Frank saw recognition in the man's eyes.

After a moment, Andrew turned and walked toward the building. "You're right. This is better done in private. Follow me."

Roger and Frank fell into step beside Andrew while he led them into the foyer. He swiped a key card at the front desk and took them to an elevator. Once inside, he hit the button for the third floor.

"It's obvious that you know him—"

"Not here," Andrew said, glancing up at the corner of the elevator, which had a tiny camera tucked in there, well hidden. "My office."

"We can talk. Security cameras can't, legally, transmit sound."

"No," Andrew said. "Not legally."

Frank fell silent, following the man's lead. They exited the elevator and traveled down a hallway to an ornate office. A receptionist rose to her feet when they entered, but Andrew breezed right past her.

"No calls."

"You have a meeting at—"

He ignored her and kept going. Frank and Roger followed him into the office, and he shut the door, locking it behind them.

Wordlessly, he moved over to a liquor cabinet and poured himself a tall glass of scotch. He didn't offer either of the other men any, taking a long sip before heading over to his desk.

"Please," he said, waving his hand at two seats on the other side of the table.

"We'll stand," Frank said, folding his arms over his chest. "Malcolm Caldwell."

"I hired him to do a job. Destroy some errant cargo. Last I heard, he failed and disappeared."

"Last you heard?"

Andrew waved his hand. "Not important. I have bigger problems."

"No, I don't think you do," Frank said, flashing the gun again. "We need to know if he's contacted you again since the job went down."

"Of course not. He took the advance money and is long gone, probably out of the country. The cargo still arrived as expected."

"It was your cargo."

"Originally. We had some internal sabotage, and someone shipped it without permission. We assumed a rival and an isolated incident, but we got it wrong."

"Wrong, how?"

"It doesn't matter. The point is, Malcolm failed in his mission, and I lost a lot of money on that venture. If I had any idea where he'd gone, I would tell you because it seems like you gents don't much care for him either."

Frank sized Andrew up and decided that he believed him. He walked over to the liquor cabinet and turned the bottles to read the labels. Pointless, as he didn't recognize any of the brands, preferring well liquor, but he didn't let on.

"That's top shelf," Andrew said. "Help yourself."

Frank shrugged. "It all pisses out the same."

Andrew said, "You don't know where Malcolm went?"

"No. Today is your lucky day because now you know *why* your job failed. We got hired to keep that shit safe."

Andrew sputtered out his drink and then set the tumbler on the table in front of him. "What?"

"Our job was to make sure the cargo arrived safely, and we had warning that someone would try to destroy it."

They had even known it would be Malcolm coming to destroy the cargo, a key fact they had omitted from their briefings with Kate. She wasn't part of the team, and it had been a need-to-know operation.

"Who hired you?"

"Wallace Blake."

Roger tensed when Frank spoke the name, flashing his partner a surprised look. Frank didn't care, though—giving up the client didn't matter much to him right now since Wallace's job had got his friend killed.

"I assumed," Andrew said, sighing and rubbing his forehead. "He's caused me endless grief these last few days."

"Can you get in touch with Malcolm?"

"No. I'm sorry. Would that I could, but none of my contacts have worked, and he hasn't reached out. I don't anticipate he will, either."

"A dead end, then," Frank said. He slid the cigar out of his pocket and stuck it back in his mouth. "Wasted trip."

Andrew hesitated. "Maybe not entirely. Whatever Wallace paid you to protect his cargo, I'll triple it."

122

"What's the job?"

Andrew smiled.

2

"You think we'll find her here?" Roger asked. Though they had left Andrew just an hour before, this seemed like a different world entirely. Luxury and wealth in private homes that cost the same as a small island surrounded them.

"I hope so," Frank Portman said, scratching his chin as they drove up to the gate of Wallace Blake's estate. He doubted it though—finding Kate wouldn't be that easy. If she suspected they'd come after her, she would hide out of sight.

They would find her, though. After everything that went down in Delaware, Frank had thought of nothing else except putting a bullet in her pretty little face and leaving her in a ditch somewhere.

He'd never liked Kate Allison and had remained firmly against bringing her onto the job when Jeff Tripp had suggested it. Jeff had insisted, though, wanting a good strategist on board to keep the cargo safe. Kate made them promise no one would get hurt, and Jeff said he could handle her when she found out they had double-crossed her.

Dumb bastard had gotten himself killed.

"You think Wallace will let us in?" Roger asked.

"I know he will. We worked for him, didn't we?"

"Jeff set up the contact. We never met the guy."

"Just follow my lead." Frank rolled down his window, but before he could hit the call button, the screen flashed to life. A bald man with a goatee appeared on screen. Undoubtedly, a manservant or butler.

"Can I help you?"

"Yes. We need to meet with Wallace Blake."

"Mr. Blake isn't entertaining visitors right now, but if you would call back at a later time—"

Frank lied, "We work with Kate Allison. She sent us here to meet with Wallace."

On the screen, the man frowned, and then the monitor went dark.

"We should get out of here," Roger said. "Our cover is blown."

"No chance," Frank said. "We will get inside one way or another. Probably, he's just talking to his boss."

"How do you know Kate came here?"

"I'm sure she came by to get paid. Most likely, she took the whole cut for herself."

"You think she would do that?"

"I know she would. You think Kate will give us a penny after what went down? The woman murdered our boss and left us with our dicks in our hands. I'd bet anything she's planning to murder us, too. Did you see the guy's expression when I said her name? For certain, she came here."

"We did kill everyone, and Jeff tried to kill Malcolm."

"So what if he did? I've itched to put a bullet in that bastard, too. Kate wasn't in charge of the run, and if she had a problem with what went down, she should have brought it up with us."

"All I'm saying is, if I were in her shoes, I would feel pretty pissed too."

"But you aren't. I told you we would get paid either way. You with me?"

Roger blew out a breath. "Fine."

The screen flickered back to life, and the butler reappeared. "Do you have an update regarding acquiring the package?"

"What pa—?"

Frank grabbed Roger's wrist, silencing him. "Yeah, we have an update about the package, but we need to talk to Wallace directly. For his ears only."

The man fell silent for a moment. Finally, he sighed. "I told him honesty was preferable. Your boss's concerns are understandable. Come inside."

The gate buzzed and then opened. The screen went dark once more.

"What package?" Roger asked.

Frank shrugged, grinning. "Damned if I know."

They headed up the drive to the estate, and it took several minutes to reach the home of Wallace Blake. Everything looked expensive, from the lawn art to the many fountains. They parked in front of the front steps, and the butler stood waiting for them.

"Let's go."

Frank and Roger climbed out of the car and headed up the

steps. A bored-looking valet sat off to the side, reading a paper.

"Leave the car, I know," the valet said, still staring down at his paper.

Roger and Frank exchanged confused shrugs and then went inside.

"Welcome. Master Wallace awaits you in the study."

The butler gestured, and the two men headed into a doorway off to the right. They entered a large and decorative room. A man with a long brown robe stood up to greet them, visibly annoyed.

"I was in the middle of changing for my reunion and travels. Why did you come here? Have you acquired the package?"

Frank didn't answer except to draw his gun and aim it at Wallace. Roger followed suit, turning his weapon to face the butler.

Wallace's eyes went wide, and he took a few steps backward.

"No change," Frank said. "Where is Kate Allison?"

"You don't work with her?"

"That bitch? Not a chance. I will kill her, though, once you tell me where she is."

"I have no idea."

"Don't lie to me."

"I won't. She came by earlier, we spoke, and she left."

"You'd *better* know more than that."

"I swear that's all I can tell you."

"We have her license-plate number," the butler said.

"Anshelm, no," Wallace said, taking a step toward the servant.

Frank took a step sideways, cutting him off and regaining his attention. "Where do you think you're going?"

"Don't tell them anything."

The butler turned to Frank. "If I give you the license plate number of Ms. Allison's vehicle, will you let Master Wallace live?"

"Absolutely. You have my word."

"Our valet has it. We record all licenses at time of arrival."

"Out front?"

"Yes."

"Perfect." Frank swiveled and fired two shots at the butler, one in the chest and the other in the head. His skull fragmented with the impact of the high-caliber rounds.

Then Frank turned back to Wallace, who had his hands up

125

defensively—wild-eyed and petrified.

"I would have killed you for free," Frank said and then fired three shots into Wallace Blake's chest.

Roger ran to the front door, and after a second, another gunshot sounded.

Frank walked over to stand over Wallace. Dead, the man's eyes had glazed over and looked empty. To make sure, he put two more bullets into the brain.

Done, he went out front and found Roger standing there. A few dozen feet up the driveway lay the valet. The poor kid had tried to make a run for it before Roger shot him in the back.

"A lot of the yard crew got away."

"Who cares?"

Roger chewed his lip. "I'm just saying, loose ends and—"

"Get the plate number. We can track down Kate and find out where she's staying. Let's get a move on before someone calls the police."

This time, Roger didn't object, heading over to the valet station and combing through the records. Frank closed his eyes and breathed deeply, taking in the fresh air and sunlight. He felt great—better than he had in a long time.

Chapter 13
Beaumont, Texas

1

Malcolm Caldwell couldn't remember the last time he had felt so terrible physically, not to mention his mental anguish. His entire body ached with each breath he took, and merely stumbling to the bathroom sapped his strength.

When he awoke from his nap, he lay alone in the hotel room with all the lights off and the curtains drawn closed. It was the middle of the afternoon, so he figured Kate and Lyle had gone out handling the job for which they'd driven down here to Texas.

Honestly, he shouldn't have made the trip. Not that he could have argued that point with Kate, but they ought to have known better. He remained in no condition to travel, but right now, he didn't have any good alternatives. The people he worked for had burned him and left him out in the cold, and until he could sort out everything that had happened to him, he needed all the help he could get.

When Malcolm made it back to the bed from the restroom, he noticed a manila folder lying on the edge of the mattress. It had the words 'read me' scribbled on the front. Inside, he found information detailing the attack against him and his team in Delaware.

The information surprised Malcolm. Not that Lyle had come up with something, but that he had delivered the information so readily. Lyle seemed like an excellent hacker and an even better person. He talked too much, but that was all right. Malcolm had gotten used to hackers having quirks, and it didn't bother him anymore. Jensen had his own problems, but he'd also been a dear friend.

Plus, Lyle had somehow managed to win Kate over, which

Malcolm had thought an impossible feat. Kate worked alone and refused to trust anyone, yet she seemed to give credence to him.

Malcolm poured himself a glass of tap water and then leafed through the pages in the dossier, glancing at the mug-shots of the people who had murdered his team. Jeff Tripp came first, marked deceased, and he recognized the other two on his team as well. Frank and Roger, two of the most pathetic human beings he'd ever met.

Malcolm had worked with Roger, though more than ten years ago. Mercenaries and cold-blooded killers, all of whom worked for a shady military agency known as JanCorp.

JanCorp had tried to recruit Malcolm several times in his career. Each time, he had refused. Malcolm didn't mind taking on risky jobs and defending himself when needed, but he wouldn't take blood-money for assassinating civilian targets. Only the shadiest of street thugs and ex-military personnel worked for JanCorp.

Now that Malcolm had the information he needed, it seemed time to start calling in favors and track down the names. Most probably, Lyle could do that for him in a heartbeat, but he had taken advantage of Kate and Lyle's hospitality for too long already.

Still, something about the dossier didn't feel right. He couldn't remember, exactly, what had happened back on that boat, but he felt as if something was missing. None of these guys had smarts enough to pull off a job like that, much less without Jensen getting word of it.

Someone else had to have gotten involved. That person must have done a great job of covering his or her tracks if Lyle hadn't located a trace of them, but without a doubt, they too would pay before this was through.

Since he'd gotten burned, his resources would prove limited, but he still had enough people he trusted, which kept him confident he could earn the revenge he sought. Again, he glanced at the mug-shots of the three men who had ruined his entire life in a night.

They would pay for what they'd done to him and his team.

2

"What the hell, Kate?" Lyle asked, locked in place, as they stared into the back of the moving van. "Why is a *kid* in the truck?"

"I don't know."

"Is he the package?"

"I don't know."

"Are we kidnappers now? Or, maybe, human traffickers?"

"Lyle, I have no idea," she snapped, climbing up into the back of the vehicle.

The kid shifted uncomfortably, making gasping noises and scrambling deeper into the back. Kate held up her hands and made shushing noises.

"It's okay," she said. "We won't hurt you."

"This is insane," Lyle muttered, pacing back and forth behind the truck. "Utterly and completely bonkers."

She ignored him. "What's your name?" she asked the kid. "Do you know where you are?"

He didn't respond except to glance between the two of them with wild eyes. Kate moved a little deeper into the vehicle, but the kid kept crawling away.

"We won't hurt you." Kate stopped about ten feet in front of him and kneeled. "Can you tell us your name?"

"Ja ... Jason," the boy muttered, pulling his legs up to his chin and wrapping his arms around them.

"Do you know your last name?"

This time, the lad didn't respond.

Kate glanced over her shoulder. "Did you get that?"

"On it," Lyle said, and then he rushed over to the car and grabbed his laptop.

Kate watched him disappear and then turned back to face the kid. "Do you ... feel all right?"

Kate didn't know a lot about children, so she felt unsure of what to say. He didn't appear malnourished or mistreated, but clearly, he felt afraid. Out of sorts might have been a better description, she decided.

"Where ... where are you taking me?" he asked. "Why am I in this truck?"

"We didn't put you here," Kate said. "The other two men did that."

"They always stood outside my door. Where are they?"

"Sleeping," Kate said. "And they will wake up with one hell of a headache."

129

"Kate," Lyle called out. "We've got a problem."

"Wait here," she said to Jason. Then she dropped to the ground. Lyle stood there with his laptop resting on the trunk.

"So, the kid's name is Jason Blake."

"What?" Kate stared. "Blake, as in Wallace Blake? What are you talking about?"

"One and the same. Wallace Blake's son. Our client."

"No, that can't be. You told me his son was away at boarding school."

"He was. Is. There *is* a kid named Jason Blake registered at a boarding school in upstate New York. He is, in fact, in class right now, and I have the camera feeds to prove it."

"So, then who is this?"

"Best guess? *This* is Jason Blake. The kid posing as him at school is the fake, and it looks like the imposter's photos and identity got swapped a few years ago when he enrolled in boarding school. When I search farther back into family photos, that boy looks nothing like the real Jason Blake. This one does."

Kate shook her head. "You're telling me that Wallace hired us to kidnap his own son?"

"Yeah," Lyle said. "It looks that way. The bigger question is why the hell is there a kid posing as his son back in school? Why the hell would Wallace do that?"

"I don't know," Kate said. "Let's go ask him."

"And get paid."

"Yeah." Kate nodded. "That too."

Lyle folded up the laptop and tossed it into the backseat of the car. Kate felt stymied and more than a little frustrated at this latest development and also more than a bit pissed off at Peter for setting her up on this job.

Had she known that the package meant a child, she would have turned it down on principle. Kids stayed off-limits, and whatever sick game their client wanted to play, she would have no part of it.

It seemed too late to drop out now, though, and she had backed herself into a corner. Kate couldn't afford to fail this mission and risk Malcolm finding out what she had done.

That just meant she had to break her rules this once and take the kid back to his father, and then she could get some *real* answers about what on earth was going on and why—

"What's that sound?" Lyle startled.

Kate glanced at him in confusion for a second, and then she heard it, too.

Her eyes went wide.

"A helicopter."

"Uh-oh."

"Start the car," she said, rushing over to the truck.

"What? Why?"

She didn't answer; instead, she leapt into the bed of the vehicle and ran over to the boy. He curled up defensively when she approached.

"I promise I won't hurt you, but we need to move. Now."

The kid weighed his options. Kate waited, giving him time they didn't have. Finally, Jason lifted himself from the blanket. She wanted nothing more than to grab him and drag him along but feared that would just slow things down even more.

"Hurry. Follow me."

She jumped out of the back of the vehicle and then helped Jason climb down to the dirt road below. In the sunlight, she could see him a lot better. Small, he could maybe be eight or nine years old, and he had curly brown hair and big blue eyes.

Lyle had the car running and drove it over next to them. Kate opened the door for Jason and then climbed into the back seat next to him. The helicopter drew near, and without overhead tree cover, would have had a clear view of them already.

"Drive."

"Where?"

"Anywhere but here."

Lyle put the car into gear and took off down the access road. The tires kicked up a cloud of dust behind them. Through it, Kate caught a glimpse of the helicopter, overhead and off to the right. Sirens blared in the distance, coming in their direction. Before long, the area would swarm with police.

Her phone buzzed, but she didn't bother to check it. Lyle's did too, and he slipped it out of his pocket.

"Eyes on the road," she said. "Turn left up here."

He made the turn and then glanced down at the cell.

"Oh, it's just an amber alert. I hate when I get those and think it's an important message, you know? I mean, you never actually *see* the kidnappers, right?"

"Focus, Lyle."

Still looking at his phone, he did a double-take. "Oh no ... is

131

that ...?"

They exited the tree line and onto an open two-lane highway. The helicopter came into view, hovering maybe a few hundred feet above them.

Off to the right, about half a mile away, a beach butted up against the Gulf of Mexico.

A megaphone amplified voice came from the helicopter, but they couldn't make out any of the words.

"Not good," Lyle muttered, slamming on the gas pedal and weaving around traffic. "This is *not* good."

"Stay calm," Kate said, reaching over the seat and grabbing his arm to steady him. "Just keep going. We've still got a minute before any police cars catch up. Turn right up here."

"Where are we going?"

"Toward the water."

"What? Why?"

"Just drive."

Lyle's knuckles turned white on the steering wheel. Any second now, he would go into full-on panic mode. The road ran not too far from the Gulf, though, and they didn't have too far to go.

"We should have just left the kid," Lyle muttered to himself, wiping sweat from his brow. He swerved around the slow-moving traffic with erratic motions. "I can't believe we're doing this."

Kate said nothing. She reached into a bag at her feet and drew out her tranquilizer gun again—she had no intention of using live ammunition against any police officers, though she doubted they would have the same qualms if push came to shove.

Always wanting to stay prepared, she had brought plenty of darts but hoped she wouldn't have to fire a single shot.

"Left," she said, "then another right. Pull into the parking garage up ahead and then get out. In the basement, you'll find a tunnel that connects to another building with a keypad on the door."

"How do you know that?"

"I used this safe house a long time ago. Should be empty. The old key code was six-one-four-three, but I don't think it'll work anymore. It's been too long."

"Then how do we get inside?"

"Improvise," Kate said. "I'm sure a little keypad won't stop

132

you."

"What will you do?"

"Keep the police busy for a while. Once you get inside, call Malcolm and tell him to pick us up. He'll need to get a new rental because this one is compromised."

"Malcolm said he would stay out of this."

"He's in it now."

"Okay."

"Once this is over, I'll meet you in the bunker, and we can wait for Malcolm. There's the turn, just up ahead. Once we get inside and out of sight, move fast so I can get out of there."

He nodded, swerving into the parking garage. Sirens blared in the distance as the police closed in on them, but at least the helicopter wouldn't have a clear line of sight anymore.

Adrenaline coursed through her veins, and Kate worked to keep her nerves steady. She lived for this, surrounded by excitement and action. None of this had gone as planned, and she had to go up against the police, but that wasn't the point.

The point was that she felt alive.

Lyle turned a corner in the garage and put the car into park, and then they piled out into the empty space. Kate helped Jason out of the backseat and then gestured toward the stairwell about twenty feet to their right.

"Basement, hallway, keypad. Got it?"

"Got it," Lyle said. "Stay careful."

"Don't worry about me," Kate said. "I'll be fine."

She climbed into the passenger seat, threw the car into gear, and took off out toward the side exit of the parking garage. The gate was down, but that didn't matter at all. She broke through it, wood shards flying everywhere.

The police had drawn close now, as had the helicopter, but she didn't worry. She had an exit plan in mind—something she'd mapped out for just such an occasion.

They wouldn't see this coming.

3

Lyle half-dragged and half-carried Jason down the steps. The kid tried to keep up but seemed somewhat disoriented by everything going on. If Lyle had to guess, the two men had drugged Jason, who looked lethargic and could barely keep his eyes open as they moved.

The police sirens sounded from all around them, and Lyle fought down his panic. They reached the bottom of the stairwell and found a door. He opened it and saw the tunnel Kate had mentioned. A few overhead incandescent light bulbs lit the path, which slippery moss and mold covered. It didn't look as if anyone had come down here in ages.

They rushed through the tunnel, with Lyle dragging Jason along. Tires squealed in the parking garage. Perhaps from one of the police cars pursuing them. Most, he figured, would have chased after Kate, but a few might stay behind and check the garage.

At the far end of the tunnel, they reached a thick iron door. Next to it, on the wall, hung a standard keypad lock with unlit buttons. It had power, which surprised him. He punched in the code Kate had given him.

It blinked red.

Lyle cursed, scanning over the little box. It appeared simple with safety screws and internal wiring—something from a long time ago. And though he could hack into it dozens of ways, he didn't have a lot of time.

"Why couldn't it be a keycard lock?" he muttered, pulling out his tools.

With a number lock, he would need to gain access to the electrical interface to try multiple combinations, but this one didn't have an external interface. Quickly, he took off the safety screws and then removed the faceplate, exposing the internal wires.

No matter how well designed a security system, it still needed to have power to work. Even with a battery backup, the controls could get overridden manually by bypassing the original system and taking control of the electronics.

Lyle took a steadying breath and focused, picking through the wires to figure out which ones bridged essential connections. Most of them proved useless for his needs, which meant all he had to do was find the right bypass wires and splice them together.

He found the first one easy enough and snipped it, peeling off the external covering.

A loud banging sounded behind him. A glance back showed

134

that the tunnel door remained closed. The door up above, however, had just slammed shut.

That meant someone had entered the stairwell.

"Crap, crap, crap, crap," Lyle muttered, feeling his way through the wires.

Footsteps echoed in the stairwell as the intruder drew closer. Lyle blinked sweat out of his eyes and then grabbed the second wire he needed to splice. He snipped it, peeled off the covering, and then touched the two wires together.

The lock snapped, allowing the door to swing open.

"Yes," he hissed. "Grab that door. Keep it open."

Jason grabbed the handle, keeping it from sliding closed.

Lyle used the pliers to rebind the other wires. A click sounded when the mechanism locked once more. Then he put the faceplate back on, hiding the wires. He didn't have time to put the safety screws back in, but the plate should prove enough to deter a casual inspection.

Finally, he grabbed Jason, and they dashed inside only a second before the stairwell door behind them opened. The room lay in darkness. Lyle closed the door behind him as gently as possible.

They had made it.

"Phew," he breathed. "Safe."

A gun cocked behind him.

"Just who the hell are you?"

4

Kate drove like a lunatic through the sparse traffic, weaving in and around cars and up onto the median to create some distance between her and the cars in pursuit. Three of them chased her, with a lot more on the way.

The helicopter still flew above her position, and sirens approached from the city, so it wouldn't take long for them to get out in front of her and cut her off.

Already, she'd managed to swerve past two police cars without trouble, and they hadn't done much to try and keep up. The traffic remained fairly congested at this time of day, and the police wouldn't want to risk civilian lives—nor the child they thought she'd kidnapped—to catch her. They could outlast her.

Right now, their goal focused on lulling her into a false sense of security, tightening the noose until she had nowhere left to run.

Luckily, they assumed her escape plan involved roads.

Kate needed time and a distraction, something that would keep the police busy while she made her real getaway. The coastline appeared up ahead, and she pressed down on the gas pedal, swerving off the road and heading straight for the edge of the land.

Relieved, she spotted the private dock she'd picked out on the map earlier. A decorative white picket fence blocked her path onto the lawn of one of the coastal properties, but she blasted straight through it.

One thing she had learned in her time with JanCorp was to over-prepare for every situation. Past experiences told her that the jobs which seemed easiest would go sideways the fastest.

Never had she had a job go *this* far sideways, though.

While she drove toward a long wooden dock that jutted out over the water, she rolled down all the car windows. Not that wide, the jetty would only give her tires a few inches of coverage on either side. She couldn't afford to miss.

Though old, the wood looked sturdy, and Kate hoped it would support the rental vehicle's weight. The property appeared empty right now, and it had one boat docked along the right-hand side, but it would be out of her way.

"All-righty then," she muttered to herself, flying at the dock at eighty miles an hour. "Here goes nothing."

She reached the jetty, tires bouncing across the rough wood as she flew along it. Everything happened all at once. The dock ran for about seventy feet—a distance she covered in no time at all.

And then, suddenly, the car left the wooden planking.

It barreled off the end and flew out toward the water, ten feet below. Kate leaned back in her seat, closed her eyes, and counted.

She made it to four before the nose of the car hit.

The airbag felt like the worst of it, slamming her in the face when the stopped momentum rocked her forward. Even expecting it, the motion made her dizzy. She reached down and unclipped the seat belt, freeing herself from its grasp as the car sank into the sea.

The water poured in the open window, filling the car up

quickly. She waited until the vehicle had submerged fully and only her head remained above the inside water level, and then she took a deep breath and went under.

Kate scrambled across to the passenger side and out through the open window. With a hard kick, she pushed off the side of the car and then swam as hard as she could away from the submerged vehicle, staying close to the bottom of the shallow sand shelf.

The water, though clear, offered enough depth to give her the confidence that no one could see her from up above. If anything, her pursuers would expect her to exit via the driver's side window and be watching in the wrong place.

She could hold her breath for a long time, a skill learned from her high school and college swim-teams, and she put that ability to good use. Kate swam the length of multiple pools, lungs burning, before coming up for air, and only long enough to get another breath and go down again.

For several long minutes, she continued that pattern, pausing several hundred meters away, just long enough to make sure the helicopter hadn't followed.

It hadn't. In the distance, it hovered over the submerged car while police vehicles pulled in around the dock. The chopper would scan the surrounding area and look for any signs of life from either her or the kid they assumed she had with her.

Once more, Kate turned and continued swimming, putting even more distance between her and the pursuit. Once she grew confident she'd created enough separation from the downed car, she scrambled over to the shoreline and exited the gulf.

Soaked and exhausted, she couldn't afford to wait around and catch her breath. Once more police arrived on scene, they would continue widening their net, and she couldn't get trapped in it. She needed to keep moving.

The water had felt colder than she'd expected, and she found herself shivering as she walked. She raced along, outside a residential area with a lot of expensive houses near the waterfront. Carefully, she crept through the neighborhood, watching for any dog-walkers or kids playing outside, and finally found an unattended vehicle in the driveway of one of the homes.

The door wasn't locked.

Kate climbed into the driver's seat and opened the bay under the steering wheel. It took her only a few minutes to hotwire the ignition.

The SUV sputtered to life, and she went on her way. Headed north and then west, she put as much distance between her and the submerged car as possible before redirecting to the hideout where Lyle waited for her. She hadn't gone to the safe house in years and hoped it remained operational.

Her sodden clothes clung to her skin, and she needed a good power nap, but she had to admit that she felt great. That getaway had seemed fun and exciting. Kate had discovered nothing like the rush she got when a plan went wrong.

However, something nagged at her. Why had the pickup gone so wrong in the first place? Why had Wallace Blake put out an amber alert on his own son after he'd asked them to kidnap the kid, and especially after withholding the information that the boy was their package to begin with?

Another set-up?

Something didn't add up. The time had arrived to go talk to the kid's father and get some answers.

Chapter 14
Freeport, Texas

1

"I won't ask you again," the man said, pressing the end of the gun between Lyle's shoulder blades. Lyle's knees wobbled in fear. *Kate said this place was empty, so what the hell is going on?*
The man asked, "Who are you?"

"Lyle Goldman."

"What are you doing here? Who do you have with you?"

"His name is Jason. Kate Allison sent us here. She said the place should be empty."

"It isn't."

"Clearly."

"Why are the police after you? Where is Kate?"

"She took the car and left us here to distract the police. Quite frankly, I have no idea where she went or if she is even okay. They came after us because ..."

"Because what? Spit it out."

"Because we kidnapped the kid here," Lyle said, pointing down at Jason. He gulped. "I mean, technically, we didn't kidnap him ... I think his father hired us to get him back from ..."

"I'm not a big fan of people who kidnap children," the man said, ominously.

"Neither are we. Had I known what the job entailed, I never would have agreed to it. I mean, his father set this up, and he didn't tell us ... it's complicated."

A long minute passed, and then, finally, the metal tip of the gun drew away from Lyle's back. Another click sounded when the man un-cocked the firearm.

"Then un-complicate it."

Lyle kept his hands up and continued facing away, not

139

wanting to tempt fate. "Full story?"

"Full story."

"A man named Wallace Blake hired us to steal a package."

"You and Kate?"

"Yeah. Kate and me. Only, the package turned out to be this kid, and he is the son of the guy who gave us the job. Then, before we knew it, someone called the police and sent them after us. Wallace must have called an amber alert."

"You got played."

"Sure looks that way."

The guy shifted. "Kid, has this man been mean to you?"

Lyle tensed up, having no clue what the kid would say. Technically, they had forced him into the car and driven away, so he didn't know how it would go.

"No," Jason said, after some thought. He grabbed Lyle's arm. "You've seen my father? You know where he is?"

"Home," Lyle said. "Your home, I'd guess." To the man with the gun, he said, "Can I turn around now?"

"Yeah," the guy said. "No funny business."

"You mean like no jokes?"

"You itching to get shot?"

"Not today."

Lyle turned. A guy in his late fifties stood in front of him. The man had salt-and-pepper hair and a beard that hung down to the middle of his chest, giving him a rugged and world-weary look. He wore a pair of overalls and carried a 9mm pistol in one hand and a wrench in the other.

"Name's Colton."

"I'm Lyle. Nice to meet you."

"You got a ride coming to pick you up?"

"I'm supposed to call someone to come get us, and until then, we'd hoped to hide out here."

"All right. You can wait up in the office for your lift. Hungry?"

"Starving," Lyle said.

"I wasn't talking to you."

"Yeah," Jason said. "I feel kind of dizzy, and I'm tired, but I think I'm hungry too."

"I've got some snacks upstairs. Come on up, and I'll get you situated."

"Thanks," Lyle said. "I appreciate it."

"Not you. You go fix my damn keypad."

2

By the time Lyle made it upstairs after fixing the keypad, Jason had started on his second single-serve package of potato chips and almost finished with his coke. Lyle had tried calling Kate but hadn't gotten a response. Malcolm, on the other hand, had answered quickly. He was on his way with an ETA of about an hour.

Colton sat at the desk in the old office building, which had no windows and walls a lot thicker than Lyle would have expected. Colton eyed Lyle suspiciously when he walked into the room. "Fixed?"

"Like new," Lyle said. "I re-ran the wiring so it wouldn't be as easy to break in next time. Now, if you splice the action, it'll force the lock to stay closed instead of releasing."

"Want me to thank you?"

Lyle shrugged. "Not shooting me gives thanks enough. Our ride is on the way."

"And Kate?"

"No word."

"All right."

"Fine."

"Good."

Jason took a sip of his coke and then let out a yelp, rubbing his armpit. Colton jumped up from his chair and rushed over to the boy.

"You all right, son?"

Jason gasped, glancing up at them with the expression of a deer caught in the headlights. He looked skittish, and Lyle wondered what could have happened to make him so jumpy.

"I'm fine," Jason said, jerking his hand away with another wince.

Colton said, "No, you aren't. What's going on?"

"It's nothing. It just hurts sometimes and—"

"Show me."

Jason hesitated, but he withered under Colton's glare. Slowly, he raised up his shirt. A few inches under his armpit, a short tube stuck out of his side with about half-an-inch exposed.

It was capped off and wrapped in tape to keep it in place. The area around it looked red and uncomfortable.

Lyle's mouth dropped open. "What the hell is that?"

Colton didn't answer for a minute. He studied the tube, frowning. "A central venous catheter."

"Am I supposed to know what that is?"

"It's a line hospitals use when administering drugs over a long time or continually drawing blood from a patient. Only, this one isn't in the right place."

"What do you mean?"

"Usually, they put it in the leg or the neck."

"Why put it there, then?"

"To hide it."

"Looks uncomfortable," Lyle said. "Can we pull it out?"

"It's probably a few feet long and wrapped inside his body to reach a good vein," Colton said. "We pull that out, and the kid will bleed like a sieve. He'll be dead in minutes with all the internal damage it would do."

"How do you know so much about this?"

"My mom had one for chemo. They're a bitch to keep clean."

"You think the kid has cancer?" Lyle asked.

"Why the hell are you asking me? *You* stole him."

"We didn't *know* it was a child," Lyle said. "At least those bandages look fresh."

Colton stood in silence for a long moment, staring at the exposed area. Then he said, "We need to remove the bandages."

"What? Why?"

"I see something else there, and it's probably what's bothering the boy. You take the bandages off. I'll go find a med kit to rewrap the area."

Colton didn't wait for a response; instead, he disappeared out of the room and up a flight of stairs. Lyle watched him go and then turned back to face Jason.

"You okay?" he asked.

Jason didn't respond except to turn his face away.

"Great, just great," Lyle muttered. He lifted Jason's shirt and eased the tape loose. The kid made a sucking noise with his teeth each time Lyle pulled on it. "People always say to yank these off quickly because it hurts less, but that's not true. It hurts *faster,* which means you recover faster, but it'll hurt no matter what I do."

142

Jason didn't reply. Gently, Lyle worked the tape loose and took it off the catheter line. Attached to the tape was a small plastic box, which had pressed into Jason's side just under the tubing.

"... the hell?" Lyle muttered, working the box loose.

In his hand, he held a USB drive—a small one about the size of his thumb. Lyle looked it over, frowning and then stuck it into his pocket. He had no idea what it was, but he also didn't know how much he trusted Colton. Jason still faced away and didn't seem to notice.

A few minutes later, Colton returned with a med kit.

"Find anything?"

"Nope," Lyle said. "The tape had lumped up. The area looks sore."

Colton pulled fresh tape and alcohol swabs out of the pack. Then he cleaned the area around the catheter and bound it with tape.

"You sure you didn't find anything?"

Lyle noticed what Colton had: the slight indentations where the plastic box had pressed into Jason's skin.

"The tape folded in on itself," Lyle said. "Looks like someone did it in a hurry."

"You need to get this catheter out of him, but you'll have to get to a hospital and some serious professionals to do that. For now, keep it clean and bandage it every couple of hours."

"Will do."

Just then, a knock sounded at the front door of the building. Colton stood up, drawing his gun from his belt, and edged across the room to the door. He glanced through a peephole and then relaxed, throwing it open.

Kate stood there, dripping wet and panting. Lyle let out a sigh of relief and rushed over to her. He got to her before she could object, wrapping her in a tight hug.

He hadn't admitted to himself how worried he'd felt about her until she stood there in front of him. "Thank God."

"I'm fine," she said, extricating herself from his hug. "Where's Malcolm?"

"Not here yet," Lyle said. "He's on his way, though. How did you get away?"

"I crashed into the gulf."

"What?"

143

"Intentionally. They'll have to get the car out of the water before they realize we aren't in it. It won't buy us a lot of time but should give us enough. They came without much prep. There better not be a next time."

"What the hell went wrong?"

"I have no clue," Kate said. "We need to have a conversation with Jason's father and figure this out."

"All right."

Kate turned to Colton. "Thanks for letting them stay here. I thought the place was abandoned."

"It was. I'm not assigned, just on leave. You guys can't mean the Malcolm I think you mean? Caldwell?"

"The same."

"He's blacklisted, Kate. You need to stay as far from him as you can. They'll come for him, and when they find him, you and your boy scout here shouldn't get caught in the crossfire."

"Boy scout?" Lyle narrowed his eyes. "You mean me?"

Colton ignored him. "I would hate to see you get hurt. After everything that happened with your sister, I don't want to see you getting yourself into even more trouble. Not for Malcolm"

"I'll be fine," Kate said. "Don't worry. I can take care of myself."

"I'm aware."

Lyle got a ping on his phone. He glanced down at it. "It's Malcolm. Says he's nearby."

"Tell him to meet us up the road three blocks to the east. The authorities have barricaded the parking garage, and the area is swarming with police. We'll have to use the tunnels and get out of the way."

"Tunnels?"

Kate ignored him, moving back downstairs to the basement. The two men and the boy followed her. She went over to a large cabinet and dragged it away from the wall, revealing a hole leading into a tunnel. "Got a flashlight we can borrow?"

Colton opened one of the cabinet doors and retrieved what she wanted. He offered it to her, but then he held it back for a second. "Be careful, Kate. I'm serious."

"I will."

"I know you trust Malcolm, but I'm telling you to keep your eyes open. That guy is dangerous."

"I know."

144

"No, you don't. You knew him from a long time ago. He's changed."

She nodded. "So have I."

"That's what I'm afraid of."

"I'll keep careful."

Reluctantly, Colton handed her the flashlight. Kate gestured for Lyle to follow and then headed into the tunnel. Lyle guided Jason inside, and they went deeper underground.

The manmade hole cut through the earth with wooden beams holding it up. Some sections had begun to collapse, and none of it seemed particularly safe.

After what felt like forever—but was probably less than ten minutes—they made it through to the other side and came out into the basement of another building. This one looked older, more rotted and less cared for.

"That was fun," Lyle muttered. "Let's never do it again."

They made their cautious way upstairs and back into the sunlight. They stood about five blocks from the parking garage. Police covered the area, but not many this far out. Right now, they performed due-diligence sweeps, covering their bases in case the kid happened to be in the area.

After a few minutes, Kate and Lyle reunited with Malcolm in the new rental vehicle. Kate and Jason huddled in the backseat while Lyle climbed in up front. Malcolm still appeared in a lot of pain but didn't mention it.

"Where to?" Malcolm asked.

"Take us back to Wallace Blake's estate," Kate said. "That man has got some explaining to do."

3

Before they even made it to the drive of the expensive estate where Jason's father lived, they guessed that something had gone awry. More police cars patrolled the area, as well as several ambulances. Something terrible had gone down, and it hadn't happened that long ago.

Jason had fallen asleep, leaning against Kate in the backseat, and they didn't wake him. The kid was exhausted and out of sorts from everything that had gone on, and Lyle didn't want to tell him that his father might be dead.

Malcolm stopped the car some distance up the road from the house just as an ambulance pulled away. "Morgue," Malcolm said. "If they were going to the hospital they'd run the lights."

"What the hell happened?" Lyle asked, speaking softly.

Malcolm frowned. "Someone got to him. He's dead."

"Why would someone kill Wallace?"

"I don't know," Kate said. "But we need to find out."

"Yeah, I'll look into it and ... hang on, did you grab my laptop?" Lyle asked.

"What?"

"From the car. Did you bring it?"

"You didn't take it with you?"

"When I jumped out of the car in the parking garage? No. I was a tad busy," he said. "I hadn't expected to have the cops chasing me and didn't think to get it."

"I didn't grab it, either. Looks like it's at the bottom of the gulf."

"Crap."

"Can they trace it back to you?"

"No. It'll take them weeks to break through the encryption, and if they even remove the hard drive, it'll overwrite itself. Everything on the device points to other firewalls. That will keep me safe. Still, it was an expensive computer."

"You can buy another one."

"Buy? Not a chance. I have to build it from scratch."

"Is that all you're worried about right now? Having to put in a little extra work?"

"No," Lyle said. He held up the flash drive. "I need some way to read this."

"What is it?"

"I don't know. It was with the kid, hidden in his bandages. I figure whatever is on it might give us some clues about all this."

"All right then," Kate said, turning to Malcolm. "Back to the hotel."

With a nod, Malcolm put the car back into gear. Lyle stared through the window at Wallace's estate, wondering what had happened. The man they thought had set them up was dead.

They needed answers.

Chapter 15
Beaumont, Texas

1

It took a few hours of driving to make it back to their hotel. The police had set up various checkpoints around the city, but Lyle hacked into the local department and pulled up a map of all closed roads, which made it easy to route them around to avoid detection.

Hacking on his phone, though, brought a nightmare. The stupid keypad wasn't optimized for what he wanted to do, and it took a lot longer than he would have liked. He felt exhausted, too, with the adrenaline wearing off, and all he wanted was to collapse into bed and pass out.

He doubted he would get that chance anytime soon. Not with an amber alert out on Jason and so many other problems heading their way. Who had set off the alert? Most likely not the kid's father. But then, who?

The people who'd had the boy to begin with?

Still hurting, Malcolm drove for a while, but eventually, Kate took over, and he slipped into the back seat. The trip out had cost him a lot of energy.

As soon as they made it inside the hotel room and locked the door, he fell onto one of the beds and fast asleep.

"We should get him some painkillers," Lyle said.

"I offered. He's not interested."

"Still, the guy is in a lot of pain—"

"Let me know what you find," Kate said. "We don't have a lot of time, and I need something."

"Maybe we should rest first—"

"We don't have that luxury," she said.

From the look in her eyes, Lyle could tell that she felt

worried. Rarely had he seen her like this, and it increased his concern.

Kate carried Jason, who remained groggy from his nap in the car. She laid him on the other bed and slipped him under the covers. The kid fell back to sleep in seconds.

"All right. I'll dig around and see what comes up," Lyle said.

Kate nodded. "I'll come back in a bit."

"Where are you going?"

"Around the block. I want to get a feel for the neighborhood in case we need an escape plan. I saw a laundry chute earlier, and it might give us something we can use. Is your computer secure?"

"Mostly."

"Make it so. If we need to get out of here in a hurry, we won't be able to take it with us."

"You're talking about abandoning thirty-thousand dollars' worth of tech."

"Better than dying or going to prison."

"True. The amber alert is still out," Lyle said. "They have a couple of pictures of us, but blurry, so no one should recognize us."

"That's good. How long does an amber alert last?"

Lyle shrugged. "Usually a few hours before things wind down. It's difficult and costly to mobilize so many resources, and if they don't recover the child right away, they end it and assign it as a missing person. That could take hours, or it could take days."

"Okay."

Then Lyle said, "We can't assume this is a normal alert, though."

"What do you mean?"

"The alert went into effect before we even *had* the boy. Someone wanted to send the police after us and get this kid back. Not only that, but they murdered Jason's father within hours of the alert going out. Whoever is pulling these strings has power, and that means they have deep pockets."

"Deep enough to keep the amber alert alive?"

"Deep enough to make sure the police locate us. This isn't good, Kate. A guy hires us to kidnap his child in the shadiest way possible and then winds up dead?"

"I know. You told me this was a bad idea."

"No point in gloating, though. Not right now, at least. We have to assume someone is still searching for Jason, and they

148

won't stop until they find him."

Kate nodded. "I know."

"Maybe ..." Lyle bit his lip.

"Maybe what?"

"Perhaps we should abandon the kid. Set him loose for the police to find."

"That thought had crossed my mind," Kate said. "It surprises me that you came up with it too."

"What do you mean?"

"Nothing. Never mind. Probably, we will need to dump the kid, but first, we need to know what's going on. Do your best to figure out why whoever wants him so badly. I'll come back soon."

"All right."

Kate slipped out through the doorway and into the hotel hallway. Lyle turned his attention to the memory stick he'd found beneath the kid's bandages. It looked like a new device, but cheap, as if picked up at a corner store. That was deceiving, though, and once he plugged it in, he saw that it held many gigabytes of data.

They hadn't even encrypted it, so he had full access to the files as soon as he connected it. Documents and memos filled it to the brim. Lyle pored over them, hoping to make sense of what they were and understand why they would have hidden the USB drive with the kid.

Business reports, board meeting minutes, the first twenty minutes of searching seemed full of benign and useless information. It looked like a lot of second-hand accounting.

Lyle found himself yawning and struggling to keep his eyes open. Behind him, he could hear the heavy breathing of Malcolm and Jason as they slept in the pair of queen beds, and just the sounds of their breathing made him drowsy.

It had turned into a bust. Useless information, and a lot of it. Regardless, Lyle kept skimming through the files.

"Come on, there has to be *something* juicy on here."

Lyle's wish came true only a few minutes later.

In stunned silence, he sat in his chair reading through a document in the middle of the list—a second-hand account from someone who had participated in a meeting a few weeks earlier. The person who'd written up the document had taken meticulous notes.

He barely even noticed when Kate slipped back into the

room, too caught up in what he read. Absorbed, Lyle went through other files, searching for any corroborating evidence. A lot of second-hand accounts and notes, but nothing definitive.

No proof.

Kate hovered over his shoulder.

"This is insane," Lyle said.

"What did you find?" Kate asked.

"Nothing good."

"What do you mean?"

"Genetics."

"Genetics? Like DNA?"

"Yeah. This kid has crazy genetics, and the company has weaponized them."

"What do you mean? Weaponized them how?"

"They plan to spread his rare genetic defect all around the world."

"What? That's not possible," Kate said, shaking her head. "Rewriting genetics on a global scale? No way."

"An hour ago, I would have agreed with you wholeheartedly. The science isn't near this level, let alone legal. This, though, if it's true ..."

"Sounds far-fetched."

"Then why go to such lengths to include the information? The notes are exquisitely detailed. Whoever wrote these documents believed it was possible. Not just possible, but happening."

"How are they doing it?"

"They've distributed the carrier virus around parts of the country, which is the first part of their plan. From the numbers mentioned, I would guess about forty percent of the United States population has the bug. Maybe even us."

"I don't feel sick."

"You wouldn't. It's engineered to be highly contagious and long lasting but with almost no symptoms."

"So, that's to spread the genetic defect?"

"No, that's to spread the CRISPR proteins that target a particular genetic sequence. Basically, the virus is in your body right now, wreaking havoc on your genes. The flu shot is the more important part, designed to spread the contaminated DNA and rewrite the original. They estimate about a point-three percent initial application rate."

150

"Which means millions of people."

"Yeah, and that could be a drastically low estimate. Their numbers don't look right. The person who sent these documents estimates the application rate could go upwards of tenfold that estimate."

"So, what are you saying?"

"This kid forms a part of CDM Pharmaceutical's effort to undermine our entire medical system and introduce DNA rewriting on a massive scale. It gets worse."

"What could be worse than that?"

"Cases where the rewriting doesn't work. CRISPR targets a specific genetic strand, but it isn't perfect. Not even close. On that kind of a scale, it could do an unfathomable amount of accidental damage without even trying."

"How?"

"DNA getting corrupted and broken happens all the time. Every few seconds, something breaks in your genetics, and your body must repair it. Cancer is the literal effect of such a circumstance when your body fails to replace a broken or missing strand correctly. In your lifetime, such occurrences happen millions of times, but never at this speed. The company is, possibly, doing years' worth of genetic damage to everyone's DNA in just days."

"And we have proof?"

Lyle hesitated. "Not exactly."

"What do you have?"

"These files show second-hand copies, not originals and not proof. The scientist who compiled them attended the meeting when this got discussed, but she or he couldn't get access to any necessary proof. They tell a horrifying story, but it would never hold up in court."

"Why not?"

"Illegal search and seizure, for one thing. Also, they are hearsay, not physical proof. A few documents reference an offline server where the proof is stored, but the author of this doesn't know where. If we took this public, it wouldn't be hard to make this look like a fake."

"What does that matter? We should still tell people about this. If CDM Pharmaceuticals is rewriting human DNA, people deserve to know."

"I agree, but if we release the information like *this*, then they could bury it under countless gag orders. We have no credibility with the public. We give it a news outlet, and they'll worry about running it for fear of getting sued for libel and slander. The places that would run a story like this with such circumspect evidence don't get taken seriously."

"So, you're telling me that what we have is worthless?"

"More or less," Lyle said. "I can distribute it and get it out into the world, but it'll have about the same change potential as fake news and click-bait. The authorities will spend more time and energy trying to track us down than they would checking out the claims."

Kate sighed. "All right. So, what do we do?"

"With this? Nothing."

"Then we're back to square one. We still need to figure out what to do with the kid and get out of the state until things settle. With his father murdered, it makes our lives a lot more dangerous, and since we can do nothing—"

"Actually," Lyle said, "there *is* something we can do. You just won't like it."

Chapter 16
Beaumont, Texas

1

After a short drive, Kate arrived at the home of Emily Perkins. She lived about twenty minutes away from the hotel in a cozy house in a suburban district. The street was bustling, but Emily's home looked quiet and empty with a ghostlike feel to it.

She would find no life here, Kate realized. Only death.

"I should have brought some latex gloves with me," she muttered. "When you said she might be close to death, you didn't exaggerate."

"You won't need them," Lyle said, speaking through the earpiece in her left ear.

"You told me that earlier."

"And I meant it. Emily is no longer contagious. She hasn't been for days."

"That's supposed to reassure me?"

"I'm not the one who made that diagnosis. Her doctors did."

"And you feel confident they know a lot about human engineered viral infections?"

"They know a lot about contagions," Lyle said. "And they consulted with the CDC, which does know a lot about engineered strains. You should be safe."

"You said *should* that time. So, which is it? I *should* be safe, or there is a one hundred percent certainty I *will* be safe?"

"Nothing is one hundred percent certain."

"See what I mean? You are not good at offering hope."

"Would you prefer that I lie and say you will *definitely* be safe when I couldn't possibly know for certain?"

"Yes. Or, better yet, go yourself next time."

"I'm not great at winning people over and getting them to

trust me."

"And I am?"

"You're better at it than me. Just use your glowing personality."

Kate sighed. "Why can't you just hack into her device remotely?"

"I tried," Lyle said.

"And it proved too much for you? The great Lyle, hacker extraordinaire? We finally found something you can't hack?"

"It isn't that I *can't* hack it. It's just that it would take too long."

"Admit it, you can't hack it."

"I can hack *anything*," he said harshly, and then he added the caveat, "with enough time. That's the thing about hacking. It's a lot slower than in television shows or movies. A lot of things that take weeks in real life, the silver screen depicts to take only minutes."

"Could you imagine if they showed it in real time? Just sweaty and antisocial men and women sitting and quietly typing into a computer for hours. Who would watch that?"

"I don't ascribe to that base prejudice. I am neither sweaty nor antisocial. Of course, I also don't ascribe to the one where all the hackers are beautiful, either. Why can't TV be more like reality?"

"Have you met you?"

"Hmm. Point taken."

"Anyway, you've told me this before," Kate said.

"Have I?"

"You sound like an old man, telling the same stories repeatedly. Should I bring some soft foods back with me so that they don't hurt your teeth?"

"You love my stories."

"Do I?"

"Yep. In any case, I'm more help to you from here," Lyle said. "Over the phone."

"While I do the heavy lifting?"

"Yeah. I had enough excitement when we kidnapped the kid."

"Stop talking."

"Why? Because I said we kidnapped a kid? Don't worry; the line is secure. It has end-to-end custom encryption and would take a top-of-the-line computer ten years to decrypt a few

154

sentences of our conversations."

"I know. I'm just sick of listening to you. Why am I here, Lyle? What does this woman know that you need me here to discover?"

"She sits on the board of directors for CDM Pharmaceuticals."

"And you think her flu diagnosis wasn't natural?"

"If my hunch is correct, then she stepped on the wrong toes sometime in the last couple of days. If that's the case, and someone is trying to kill her, then my guess is she has an ax to grind and might be willing to help us out."

"Help us how?"

"Access. We need original documents, which means we need access credentials to get on the server mentioned in the notes. Emily should have some sort of access I can piggyback off to get into the company's servers. Then, once we have the documents and proof we need, we can distribute them and stop CDM's plan."

"Sounds easy enough."

"Just plug the USB device I gave you into her computer, and I'll do the rest. Should only take a couple of minutes."

"Got it."

Kate walked up the front steps to Emily Perkins' house and knocked on the front door with soft taps. After a moment, a woman opened it. She didn't look sick, though she did seem exhausted and out of sorts.

The woman stared at Kate with a puzzled look. "Hello, can I help you?"

"Hi, are you Emily Perkins?"

The woman shook her head. "I'm Gertrude. Emily is my sister."

"This is her home, though?"

The woman nodded. "How can I help you?"

"I had hoped to speak with Emily."

"I'm sorry, but she doesn't feel at all well right now. I believe she'd rather not have any visitors."

"It will only take a minute," Kate said.

Gertrude thought it over for a second and then shook her head. "I'm sorry, but no. She's resting right now and has an appointment with Doctor Palani in a few hours. I'd rather not wake her just now."

"Tell her that—"

155

Lyle started to speak in her earpiece, but Kate didn't wait to let him finish his thought. Instead, she slipped her gun free of her hip holster and held it casually in front of her, out of sight of any neighbors but visible to Gertrude.

The woman's eyes went wide, and she took a half-step backward.

"What are you ...?"

"Please, show me to your sister," Kate said.

"You don't have to do this."

"I don't want to, either. Nevertheless, I would appreciate your cooperation."

Gertrude seemed to weigh her options before gulping and stepping out of Kate's way. Kate strode into the house, pushing the door shut behind her. "Your phone, please."

She held out her hand. Reluctantly, Gertrude handed over her cell phone. Kate slipped it into her pocket and then gestured with the gun, pointing further into the building.

"Please, take me to your sister."

"She is seriously ill."

"I'm aware," Kate said. "I've had a long day, though, and feel exhausted, so let's skip all of the preamble."

Gertrude hesitated a second longer and then went toward the staircase to the second floor. Kate followed, sliding her gun away. She'd only needed it to get Gertrude's attention, and it wouldn't be necessary any longer.

She hoped.

"There are better ways to do this," Lyle said through her earpiece. "You don't need to scare the poor woman half to death."

"I know I don't *have* to," Kate muttered.

Gertrude glanced over her shoulder, but she didn't say anything.

Silent, she led Kate to a room on the second floor, but she didn't open the door.

"She's in there?"

"Yes. But she's incredibly sick and *highly* contagious."

"No, she isn't," Kate said. "She hasn't been for days. Open it. Go in first."

"When did we become the bad guys?" Lyle asked.

Kate ignored him. She followed Gertrude into the dimly lit and uncomfortably warm room. The air inside smelled stuffy, and a humidifier in the corner pumped out camphor and

156

eucalyptus-scented air.

On the king-sized bed lay Emily Perkins, tiny and frail as she curled up near the pillows. Her breath came in short raspy gasps, and her face was a mask of agony as she struggled to sleep.

When the door opened, her eyelids lifted, but she seemed incapable of focusing on anything around her. Gertrude walked over to the bed and sat down next to her, gently brushing the hair out of her face.

"Hey, sis," she whispered, voice wavering slightly. "A friend has come to speak with you."

She emphasized the word 'friend,' staring pointedly at Kate. Emily blinked, shifting her head to the side. Her mouth hung open, and she looked completely out of it. Kate walked to the end of the bed and folded her arms.

"Emily Perkins," she said. "I'm not a friend, but I'm here because we have a mutual enemy. Andrew Carmichael."

Saying the name elicited a strong reaction. Emily's eyes focused, and she forced her body up higher on the pillows. Her arms shook, but Kate could tell she paid attention now. Her eyes asked Kate to continue.

"Andrew Carmichael?" Gertrude asked. "One of Emily's work associates? He came here a few days ago to visit her."

Kate kept her attention on Emily. "Andrew made you sick, using a modified strand of swine flu. A doctor named Monroe Fink developed it. Do you know him?"

Gertrude stood, narrowing her eyes. She took an angry step toward Kate. "You can't simply barge in here casting accusations—"

Emily reached out, catching Gertrude's hand before her sister could continue forward. Gertrude glanced down at her in confusion. Her face fell. "Oh. Oh, God. You knew?"

Emily nodded, staring up at her sister.

"Oh, God," Gertrude said, holding her hand up to her mouth and turning to Kate. "And I let him in here? I'm so sorry. What can I do? Is there a vaccine or something we can give her to ...?"

Gently, Kate shook her head.

Lyle sighed and said, "I searched it, but found no mention of it in the notes. An inoculation does exist, but it will become entirely ineffective once the symptoms have set in."

Kate lied to Gertrude, "Maybe. Actually, that's part of why I came here."

157

"What? What do you mean?"

Kate turned back to Emily. "I need a way to look at Andrew's server. My colleague and I found mention of a private one? We hoped we could use your credentials to get in. Do you have a device from that company that we could borrow?"

Emily let go of her sister's wrist and pointed at her bag in the corner of the room. Gertrude fetched it. Emily opened the top and pointed at a tablet inside. Gertrude slid it out and handed it to her sister.

Emily held a shaky finger on a scanner on the bottom bio-reader, and the machine flared to life.

She held it up to Kate.

"Thank you," Kate said, sliding the stick Lyle had given her out of her pocket. She examined the device, flipping it over, but didn't see any empty ports where the device might fit. "Uh ... it won't fit?"

Gertrude tilted her head in confusion, but Kate hadn't spoken to her. She'd addressed Lyle.

"Those little adapters I gave you," he said.

"The adapters?"

"Yeah, the little black bag I gave you when I left."

"Oh, that? I left it with you."

A pause. "You put them on the bed? Remember how I said you might need those?"

"Optimal word being 'might.'"

He sighed. Kate turned back to Emily. "You wouldn't happen to have ...?"

Already, Emily dug through her handbag, and then she pulled out a three-inch-long adapter cable. Gertrude handed it to Kate, who plugged in the device.

"Ah," Lyle said a second later. "Jackpot."

A moment passed. "So ... how long will this take?"

"I have to access the root servers. Shouldn't take long. I'm in already. Just searching for proof."

Kate stood in the middle of the room, feeling awkward. She set the tablet on the bed, careful to keep it connected. Then she exchanged glances with Emily and Gertrude.

"Sorry," Kate said. "About earlier. We don't have a lot of time, and ..."

Gertrude looked down at her sister. "I understand. I've never had anyone point a gun at me before, but I think I

158

understand. Don't worry. I won't tell the police or anything, not if you can help my sister."

"We'll do everything we can. You have my word."

Gertrude nodded. "I just ... I can't believe someone would do something like this to Emily. Andrew seemed like such a nice man when he came by."

"What he's doing is horrible, and—"

"We have a problem," Lyle said, suddenly.

Kate turned to Gertrude. "Hang on a second. I'll come right back."

Gertrude nodded, turning and kneeling next to the bed beside her sister. Emily seemed to lose focus again when exhaustion crept back in. Kate stepped out into the hallway, carefully shutting the door behind her.

"What do you mean?" Kate whispered. "You said this would get you access."

"It does get me access," Lyle said, "but the files aren't here."

"They aren't on the server?"

"Not *this* server. But I did find the fingerprints of another server."

"So, he has two? Why would he keep them separate?"

"Probably for this precise eventuality. The other server is air-gapped, but it does make frequent connections to this one to run backups. However, it hasn't connected in weeks."

"You can't access it?"

"It's air-gapped," Lyle said. "Which means it needs plugging in to an internet terminal directly for me to access it."

"Can't you install, like, a Trojan horse or something?"

"I could put malware on this network-facing server for when the next backup runs, but it won't do us any good. Based on their schedule, it won't connect for at least another month, which will be after the global distribution finishes."

"So, what then? That's it? Nothing else we can do?"

Lyle stayed silent on the other end of the line. Kate frowned. "Lyle, what are you thinking?"

"A guy like Andrew wouldn't allow that server out of his sight. Probably, he has it at his office or home."

"So?"

"So, we can still go get the originals—we just have to plug in directly."

"What? No way," Kate said, shaking her head. "Hell no."

159

"You haven't even heard my whole plan yet."

"I heard enough. I came here and got you the device, but we're not risking anything else. Stop thinking with your heart and think with your head."

"I am," Lyle said. "That's why this is worth the risk."

"What do you mean?"

Lyle took a deep breath. "If anything, this helps us. If we can get the files on Andrew's air-gapped server and transmit *those*, there will be no disputing where they came from and no way to hide the story. It will, effectively, give an admission of guilt."

"I thought you said the network was air-gapped. It wouldn't let the files out, would it?"

Lyle made a coughing noise. "Please. For me, it would be child's play. If I can get onto the root network from the inside, I can send the files anywhere in the world, along with routing numbers, IP addresses, and digital stamps to make it clear where the files were and that they are legit proof of a heinous crime."

"That's fine," Kate said. "But who will pay us to do this? Last I checked, if our client is dead, then it isn't likely we'll get paid for our effort, and that means two jobs we've lost out on. Precisely why I make the decisions about things like this. Why would we risk our lives for the files when we have more pressing problems already?"

"It's the right thing to do."

"My point exactly. You're thinking with your heart, not your brain."

"Then how about this … if we go through with my plan, we'll stabilize the world from a possibly catastrophic global disaster. They expect the flu-shot distribution to get up and running at full capacity in two weeks, and in certain parts of the country, have released the genetic restructuring virus already. Many people have gotten affected. We sit on the brink of a disaster, but what happens if we do nothing and let it reach the peak?"

Kate hesitated. "A lot of people will panic. Markets will collapse."

"Markets collapsing is bad for business. We should do this to protect our livelihoods."

"You make a lot of assumptions," Kate said. "None of this might happen. The virus might fail. The flu-shot might fail. You can't even prove the reality of these documents."

"Maybe not," Lyle said. "But what if they are real? What if

the virus and the shot work? Just because it may not work doesn't change the possibility that it might. We *need* to do this."

"You didn't even want to take this job."

"No, but this changes things. This is something we *must* do. I don't ask for a lot, Kate, but I won't back down from this. We need to stop Andrew."

"I'm in," Malcolm's voice said over the line.

"Malcolm? What the hell? You should be resting," Kate said.

"I'm done recuperating. I refuse to sit by when someone does something like this. Paid or not, Lyle's correct."

"We're not even sure if this is—"

"Let's hear his plan first, Kate. Lyle, what's your idea?"

"Simple. I break into the server and broadcast the information to major news outlets directly, along with all the proof we can find. With the original files and complete access, no one could dispute the claims, plus we have the kid. If we act fast, they'll have the ability to pull the flu shots from the market and quarantine and treat any sick people to keep the dangerous virus from spreading."

"Can you do any of that from here?"

"I need the server connected to the network, which means plugged in. I need to be there physically to do this."

"Then you need to get on site. How do we get you in there?"

"I haven't worked out all the details," Lyle said, "but I have some ideas. In any case, it's the only way."

"How do you know Andrew still has the data at all?" Malcolm asked.

"The information on this drive was documented meticulously. By all accounts, Andrew is the sort of person who won't risk losing any of the proof that he was behind it. He doesn't just want to do this, he wants credit. He is a narcissist and thinks one day he'll be hailed as a hero for this. We need to break into the company headquarters and—"

"Why do you assume it's at his company?" Malcolm asked.

Lyle hesitated. "That seems the likeliest place."

"Why not his home?" Kate asked.

"Could be," Lyle said. "And that makes sense if they worried that regulators might stop by the laboratories unannounced. Let me see what I can find."

Kate waited for a few minutes for him to speak again. She hated getting involved in this, but Lyle was right. They couldn't allow Andrew to get away with this. She paced down the hallway, waiting for him to find something.

"The layout of his home looks odd, mostly custom," Lyle said, finally. "If I were a betting man, I'd say that we'll find a hidden server in his wine cellar."

"Probably that's also where he hid the kid," Kate said.

"Possibly."

Malcolm said, "All right, so the files might well be located there. How do we get in?"

"Andrew is hosting a gala tomorrow night at his house. A fundraising event for charity. Five thousand dollars a plate with plenty of unclaimed reservations."

Kate said, "I can't believe I'm saying this, but okay. Seems doable. Two of us need to go in, though."

Lyle asked, "Why two?"

"I won't let you go in there alone. But where can we get ten thousand dollars?" Kate said. "The entire point of taking this job was because we *needed* money."

"I can handle that," a female voice said from behind Kate.

Kate spun, hand slipping to the pistol grip at her waist. She relaxed when she realized it was only Gertrude, standing in the doorway of her sister's room.

She had gotten so distracted by the conversation that she hadn't heard the door open. Nor did she know how much of the discussion the woman had heard.

"Sorry," she said, relaxing. "I didn't know you'd come out here."

"I can help with the money," Gertrude said. "If it will help you take down the man who did this to my sister, I will. It's the least I can do."

"We couldn't possibly ask—"

"Then don't," Gertrude said, shifting and looking back into the room at her dying sister. "Just make sure the son of a bitch who did this to Emily pays for it."

Chapter 17
Houston, Texas

1

"How has no one located them yet?" Andrew said.

"We're looking into it."

Andrew, back at the office with Monroe Fink, sat in a boardroom and felt sick to his stomach. Disheveled and disorganized, he found it difficult to get his thoughts in order.

Seated across from him, Monroe looked cool and calm in his white lab coat. Andrew wasn't supposed to come in today, but staying home and worrying had not been an option. He had thought the situation would resolve last night, and yet they had come no closer to finding Jason.

"How hard can it be? The amber alert remains active, doesn't it? Even though we called it in yesterday, every officer in the city should be out searching for them! Why haven't they found him?"

"It's active, but most resources have gotten re-tasked or canceled. The city has downgraded the alert."

"What? Why?"

"They are starting to ask questions."

"Questions?"

Dr. Fink hesitated. "*We* called in the amber alert for Jason on behalf of his father, but we can't follow up on it, not exactly. Wallace got murdered, a fact which raised a lot of red flags, and they are searching just as hard for us as for the child now."

Andrew shook his head. "A child got kidnapped."

"But it wasn't the first time this child got taken from his father," Monroe said. "Was it?"

Andrew rose and took a threatening step toward the doctor.

"Do you question my choices?"

"No, sir." Monroe stood as well and took a tiny step backward. "Not at all. I just think it might have been more prudent to keep the father alive until this situation resolved."

"Maybe. But if we had done that, he might have absconded with my property. In any case, we can do nothing about that right now. The only thing we *can* do is move forward. Find Jason and bring him back to me."

"We will. In the meantime, you have to go and get ready for the gala event tonight."

Andrew cursed, sitting back down at his desk. He had forgotten about the stupid event at his house. Due to his concern about his missing asset, he had barely slept through the night, and the last thing he wanted was to host a party.

However, he had scheduled the thing months earlier as a way for him to rub elbows with some of the city's elite, but right now, it seemed like the biggest waste of time possible.

"I should cancel it."

"Too late for that. The caterer called, and many of the preparations are complete. A lot of people are flying from out of state to attend."

"Fine, I'll make an appearance. Are you coming?"

"Yes. I will get there by the time it starts."

"Good."

"You'll need to stay there for at least a few hours. We can't shirk our responsibilities, Andrew. But don't worry; we will find the child and recover the stolen information."

"See to it."

2

Andrew twined his fingers through practiced motions, wrapping his tie in front of a full-length mirror in his private quarters. He trembled, though, and snagged the large end before he could draw it tight. It ended up way too short for his three-piece suit, forcing him to start over.

With a growl of frustration, he jerked the whole thing loose. This wasn't like him. He always stayed calm and collected in his business dealings and life—never out of sorts like this. Everything had been going perfectly, and now the entire

164

situation had devolved in front of his eyes. Andrew had no idea how to stop it.

It had all started with the missing kid. Jason had been the last of his concerns leading up to tonight. Not even a blip on his radar. As soon as Jason went missing, however, things fell apart. Andrew no longer had control of the events taking place, and he didn't feel comfortable with the situation at all.

The party would start in an hour, and already, the caterers worked at finalizing the food and decorations. It felt like an invasion of his household, his sanctuary, and he hated it. Normally, he enjoyed micromanaging the decorations, but right now, he couldn't imagine even trying to focus on something so trivial.

What could he do? Everything he had built hinged on keeping these secrets. He should have terminated Jason when he'd had the chance. Never had he dreamed Madison would betray him like this; he couldn't even find her after she had sent the kid away. She had gone into hiding.

Madison would get dealt with, he promised himself, the same way Wallace had.

Even the insinuation that he had involvement in what was about to happen around the world could ruin him. If Madison told anyone what she knew, or if someone could use Jason to link it all back to his company ...

He needed to recover the missing child.

A knock came at the door.

"Come in."

The door opened, and one of the caterers stepped into his private room—the snooping woman he'd met earlier, though he'd forgotten her name.

"The guests will arrive shortly."

"Of course they will. It is a party, after all."

"We have begun pouring the champagne and prepared the hors-d'oeuvres. Dinner will be served promptly at seven-thirty."

He glanced at his watch. "Can you bump that forward to seven?"

The woman hesitated. "We have scheduled—"

"I'm the one paying for this dinner, yes? It is my money paying for all of this food, so I should have a say in when it gets served."

"The original orders were explicit—"

165

"They were *my* orders."

"The invitations—"

"Oh, for God's sake, fine. Just keep it at seven-thirty. Jesus."

"Very good, sir."

"I'll come down shortly. If anyone arrives early, just offer them food and keep them busy until I get there."

"Of course. Do you ... um ... need help with your tie, sir?"

Andrew stopped moving, fingers still fumbling with the red and green cloth he was attempting to wind around his neck. With his most scathing expression, he turned his head to face the servant. "That will be all."

"Very good, sir."

The sheer idea that Andrew would need help fastening his tie was unthinkable, much less that he would need help from a servant. The impropriety of it all felt overwhelming.

It didn't help, of course, that Andrew's fingers didn't want to cooperate. Tonight formed a vital piece of his overall agenda. Monroe was right; it must go off without a hitch. He needed to regain his calm and cool attitude.

Finally, on the fourth try, Andrew managed to force his tie into passable order. Not perfect by any means, but it would pass inspection. He sucked in a deep breath, studying himself in the mirror.

Monroe had assured him that they would find Jason. That child had become the most magnificent gift Andrew ever could have asked for, but now he had turned into a nightmare. Andrew needed to resolve it, and he had faith in himself that he would. They would recover the child, and then his plan would get back in motion with only the one minor misstep.

"Well," he said to his doppelganger in the mirror. "Let's get this over with."

Chapter 18
Houston, Texas

1

"Do you plan to stare at yourself in the mirror all day, or can we get moving?"

"I'm just making sure my bowtie looks right."

"It's right," Kate said.

"It looks a little crooked," Lyle said, twisting it around his neck and frowning. "There, that's better."

"That's worse."

"What?"

"You look like a professor. Don't make it so perfect. Loosen it up a bit."

"Like this?"

Kate sighed. "Sure, yeah, whatever. Can we go now?"

He turned to face her. She had a robe thrown over her body and was fussing with her hair. "Yeah. We can go. Is the limo here?"

"Limo?"

"Yeah. To drive us to the party."

"You're enjoying this too much."

He shrugged. "I don't get out a lot. It's been a long time since I got to go to a fancy party like this."

"We're not, exactly, *going* to a fancy party. We aren't there to have fun. We have a job to do."

"I know. Just let me savor the moment."

Kate sighed, dropping the robe to the floor. Underneath, she had a shimmery blue dress. Lyle froze, mouth hanging open.

"What?" she asked. "What is it?"

"You ..."

"What? What about me?"

"You look incredible."

"If I look anything right now, it's annoyed."

"I've never seen you in a dress before. Or wearing makeup. I didn't even realize you knew *how* to apply makeup."

"Funny."

"No, I just mean—"

In his pocket, his phone buzzed. He slipped it out. "Ah. That's the limo company. Out front waiting."

"Then let's *go.*"

"Fine. Okay. All right. Just let me take a quick picture—"

He held the phone up, and she snatched it away with one quick movement, sliding it into her purse. "If you behave, you'll get it back."

He frowned at her but didn't respond. "Malcolm, will you be all right?"

"Yeah," Malcolm said, sitting on the bed with a bemused expression. "Jason and I will be fine here."

"Want to keep another kid here with you?" Kate asked.

"Funny," Lyle said.

Malcolm chuckled. "Nah, you're babysitting him tonight. Call me if you need anything."

"We won't," Kate said. "This will be easy."

Lyle's jaw dropped. "Why would you even *say* that?"

Kate waved away the concern and walked to the door. "Let's get this over with."

Lyle followed her. "At least knock on some wood before you get us all killed."

"We'll be fine."

Lyle stared at her. "God, I hope those aren't our last words."

2

"Stop that," Kate said, drawing Lyle out of his thoughts. They sat in the back of the limousine on their way to Andrew Carmichael's party. Dark outside, the sky had cloud cover, and Lyle wondered if it might rain.

Lyle had thought through their plan, running over all the details to see if he might have missed something. He had hacked into Andrew's security and gained control of their cameras, but what if they had backups offline? Any good security team would have backups in case they got hacked, but he hadn't found any.

Lyle glanced at Kate, "Stop what?"

"Scrunching up your pants like that. You'll end up with wrinkles."

Lyle glanced down at his hands. He'd squeezed the fabric of his pants with his hands, balling it up. As a young child, he'd developed this habit whenever he got nervous.

"My palms get sweaty."

"Then use your handkerchief."

"I have a handkerchief?"

"In your front pocket."

"I thought that was just for decoration."

"It is, but it's also usable."

"I don't think I should. When the guy put it in there, he did a lot of twisting and knotting to get it to look just right. If I take it out now, I'll never it back right."

Kate sighed and dug around in her purse. Her hand came out with a small container of tissue paper. She pulled a few loose and offered them to him. "Here."

He accepted and then just stared at the tissues. "I don't think these will—"

"For God's sake, just put them in your pocket and shut up. Keep your right hand in your pocket as well, and before you shake anyone's hand, wipe it off."

"Oh," he said, doing as she said. "What if the person's a lefty?"

"What's wrong with you? You've gone to parties like this before."

"Yeah, but always as a guest. Never as a ..."

"Criminal?"

He laughed, nervous. "Yeah, that. It's one thing to get invited to a party and just be there trying to make an impression on other guests, but it's a completely different thing to have to plan how you're going to commit a felony against the owner of the establishment."

"Multiple felonies," Kate said. "Like six, at least. But it doesn't matter. You just have to stay calm."

"How do you do it? How do you go into situations like this where *everyone* is your enemy, and if you get found out you could spend the rest of your life in jail?"

169

"It's the job."

"It's barely a job," Lyle said, snorting. "With your skills, you could do a million other *legal* things and make a good living."

"Maybe." Kate nodded. "But the thrill of it wouldn't be there. I grew up in this life, but it never really gets any easier. If you think I don't feel nervous, you're kidding yourself. I'm terrified, but that makes it fun. Sometimes, you have to do dangerous things."

"You mean getting chased by police for kidnapping a kid?"

"Yeah," Kate said, leaning back in her seat. "And years ago, it was a lot harder. I hated always having to look over my shoulder and worry about who might be coming for me. That's why I faked my death and tried to get out of the life."

"Yet, here you are, back in it. What changed?"

She fell silent for a long time. Would she even answer Lyle's question?

"You," she said, finally. "I met someone I could work with, who I didn't have to watch my back with. I never had a single doubt that you wouldn't be there for me. You are ... simple."

"Simple?"

"Uncomplicated."

"Thanks ... I think."

"I meant it as a compliment. People in my world are all Rottweilers or Terriers. Ready to bite your dick off if you let them. Golden retrievers don't end up in this life, and you wouldn't be here unless you had to be."

"You mean if my life hadn't gotten ruined."

Kate nodded. "It got taken from you, and you decided to make the best of it. That's brought a blessing for me because, finally, I found someone I can trust completely."

"Then why do you keep withholding things from me?"

"Old habits die hard." Kate faced away from him, staring out of the window. "And, if I'm honest, it's because I didn't know what to do with someone who would always have my back. It's not something I thought I deserved."

"You definitely deserve it."

"No," she said, softly. "If you knew more about me, about what I've done, you'd know that wasn't true."

"All I know is that when the people I thought cared about me ruined my life and tried to have me killed, you protected me. You saved my life."

"So, you think you owe me?"

Lyle shrugged. "Actually, in some cultures, the fact that you saved my life means *you* have a responsibility for *me* now. It's your job to keep me safe, like an obligation you're stuck with. I'm your obligation."

Kate chuckled. "It does seem that way sometimes. I mean, you *never* leave me alone."

"Hey, I let you have plenty of time—"

"And you're always chittering away in my ear. Just chit-chat non-stop. Like a squirrel."

"I resent that remark."

"You know, come to think of it, you *do* look an awful lot like—"

The divider window of the limousine rolled down a few inches. "We're arriving now."

"Okay, thank you," Lyle said. The driver rolled the window up again.

Instantly, the mood in the back of the car grew somber. All of Lyle's worries and hesitations came flooding back.

"Are you ready?" Kate asked.

"As ready as I'll ever be."

"Are you up for this? You don't have to go in there if you don't want to. You can just show me what to do, and I'll take care of it."

"The time it would take to walk you through what needs to happen is time we don't have."

"Okay."

Lyle took a steadying breath. "I'll be fine. How hard can it be?"

3

"This is the place?" Roger White asked. They pulled the car into a handicap spot up near the front door.

"This is their hotel," Frank Portman said, turning off the car and leaning back in his seat.

"You think Kate is here?"

"Hopefully," Frank said, pulling his pistol out of his shoulder holster and making sure he had a round chambered. "I wouldn't mind putting a bullet between the bitch's eyes."

171

"Me neither," Roger said. "But I'd settle for just finishing the job we started back in Delaware and putting Malcolm in the ground. For real this time."

They waited in the parking lot of the Four Seasons Hotel where Kate Allison stayed, looking for any sign of their prey. They had retrieved the license plate information from Wallace Blake's residence and used it to trace them back here.

It didn't look like anyone would come out to meet them, but that was no matter. They had no trouble going in after their enemies. Andrew wouldn't pay them to do this, but they could care less. In a few hours, the police would put the pieces together and realize that Roger and Frank had murdered Wallace, but by then, they would have been paid and left the country.

After this little visit, they would leave Malcolm and Kate dead in their wake.

"Ready?"

"Always." Roger nodded.

Together, the two men climbed out of their car and walked toward the lobby entrance. They didn't know which room Kate occupied, but they didn't worry about figuring it out. She was predictable like that.

Frank pushed open the front door and went directly toward the front desk.

The clerk, a smallish man with glasses and a sweater vest, smiled at him. "Can I help you?"

Frank slid his pistol free and rested it on the counter in plain sight. "Yes. I think you can."

The guy gasped and shifted away, holding up his hands defensively. "Look ... l-look, I don't want any trouble."

"Neither do we. That's why you're going to stand here next to me and have a nice chat while my associate takes care of some business in the back. Right?"

The lobby stood empty, which made a good start. Roger walked over to the front door and locked it. "Where do you keep your video servers?" he asked.

The guy stared at him, and then he pointed to a closed door behind the desk. "It's locked," he said, "but you'll find the passcode on a piece of tape under the handle."

Roger disappeared into the back office. Frank stood at the desk, tapping his pistol against the wood lightly, and smiled at the man. "Busy day?"

"Excuse me?"

"A lot of customers?"

"Not really. It's been a slow month."

"How is your insurance?"

"What?"

"Got it!" Roger said, reappearing. "They aren't recording anymore, and she's on the fourth floor. Malcolm is with her, plus some other guy and a kid."

"A kid?"

"Looks like."

"All right," Frank said. He turned back to the attendant. "Cloud backups?"

"What do you mean?"

"Does your system perform any cloud backups of video files?"

"Yes. Nightly."

"You're sure it isn't real time? Only nightly?"

"No. I mean yes, I'm sure. The system only does nightly backups before refreshing the entire system. It records motion and timestamps."

"How do we stop them?"

"Unplug the network cable, and the batch will fail."

"All right," Roger said, reading the name tag on the man's shirt. "But, Kyle, if I find out you've lied to me—"

"I haven't. I won't. I swear. I helped the company set the system up. If it fails the backup before the refresh happens, it overwrites anyway. I swear."

Frank nodded. "Excellent. Now, if you wouldn't mind, we need to see your guest list. Who, pray tell, is staying on the fourth floor?"

Chapter 19
Houston, Texas

1

"I hate this," Lyle whispered to Kate, clenching and unclenching the wadded-up tissue paper in his pocket. "Already, I've had to shake, like, fifty hands."

"You're telling me," Kate mumbled. "Every guy here wants to kiss my hand and look at me like I'm a piece of meat."

"A pork chop?"

"Hell no. I'm at least a good cut of steak. Prime Rib maybe, or a filet."

"Dry aged?"

"I will shoot you."

"This conversation went downhill fast," Malcolm said over the little buds in their ears. "Would you two remain on topic? You went there for a reason, after all."

"I need to slip away for a while to find his server," Lyle said. "Once I plug in the adapter, I'll have access to his files and can download anything we need."

Malcolm asked, "How long will that take?"

"Twenty minutes."

"All right. Find an opportunity and then make it happen."

The gala event was in full swing around them. Hundreds of well-dressed and pretentious individuals stood chatting and laughing around them. A band played classical music on the stage, and snacks and hors-d'oeuvres covered various tables lined up around the outer walls of the room. The caterers had situated other tables in an adjoining room for the dinner when it began; though, right now, none of the guests seemed even remotely interested in them.

"I need a drink," Lyle said.

Kate scowled at him. "Hell no."

"It will steady my nerves."

"That won't steady you. It will make you less competent."

"Yet more confident."

She crossed her arms. "You're not getting a drink. End of story."

Lyle sighed. "Fine. When do you think I should go search the house?"

Kate glanced around the room.

"What? What is it?" Lyle's eyes widened in alarm.

"He has security keeping an eye on things."

At her words, Lyle relaxed. "I took his cameras offline."

"But you can't hack the humans. I count at least twenty."

"Twenty? I only see four."

"You're counting the obvious ones. Most are in normal clothes trying to blend in. We need to make sure they don't pay attention to you. Slipping away from the party won't be easy."

"What do you recommend, then?"

"We'll need a distraction."

"What did you have in mind?"

"Not sure yet. We'll have to play it by ear. Let's wait a couple of minutes until dinner starts."

Lyle grew more anxious still. "We can't wait too long."

"I know. An opportunity might present itself."

They slipped back into the crowd, shaking hands and making pleasantries as they moved through the group. Gertrude had secured them reservations for the dinner, and they introduced themselves as her cousins visiting from out of state. Each conversation lasted only a couple seconds before moving on with mostly well-wishers wanting to say how sorry they were for Emily's condition.

"This feels like speed dating," Lyle said, after a while.

Kate grinned. "Oh? Is that something you've done a lot?"

Lyle blushed. "No, I mean, not that I wouldn't do it or have something against it or anything, it just seems like we keep getting funneled along to meet new people before we can have a real conversation."

"Rubbing elbows," Kate said. "Everybody wants to know everybody."

"There he is."

"Who?"

176

"Andrew," Lyle said.

Andrew Carmichael stood about twenty feet away from them, surrounded by party-goers. He laughed pleasantly while talking to an older man with gray hair, though they couldn't even guess at what the joke might have been.

Kate asked, "He's the guy?"

"Yep. He calls the shots."

"Looks like a smug asshole," Kate said.

"I know, right."

"Reminds me of you."

"Hey!"

"Kidding," Kate said. "Sort of. Want to go talk to him?"

Lyle shrugged. "Not particularly."

"You could say something clever like, 'hey, jackass, I'm about to bring you and your company down.'"

"That's clever?"

She shrugged. "Work in progress."

"Wouldn't telling him we're on to him defeat the entire purpose?"

"Probably. Doesn't mean you shouldn't do it."

Lyle cringed. "I think we're better off without him knowing we ever came here at all. We shouldn't bother talking to him."

"Looks like that may not be up to us. He's heading our way."

Lyle cursed under his breath, shifting to get a better view over Kate's shoulder. Sure enough, Andrew made his way across the room, coming directly toward them. An introduction, it seemed, couldn't be avoided.

"Hello," Andrew said, smiling and extending his hand. "I'm so glad you could make it tonight. I'm Andrew Carmichael."

Kate accepted his extended palm. "I'm Elizabeth Perkins."

"You wouldn't by chance happen to be related to Emily Perkins, would you?"

"My cousin," Kate said, smiling. Then her smile faded. "I arrived in town when she fell ill."

"I am tremendously sorry. Emily is a good friend and even better person. I feel terrible about what has befallen her."

"Thank you."

"And who might this be?" Andrew asked, turning toward Lyle.

"Ah," Kate said. "This is my date for the evening. Curtis Yelchin."

177

Lyle shook Andrew's hand, trying not to squeeze too hard.

"It's a great pleasure to make your acquaintance," Andrew said.

"Likewise," Lyle said, through gritted teeth.

"The firm sent Curtis over for the evening. Not exactly a top-notch offering, but what can you do with such short notice? I can't fault the service; they did their best."

Andrew chuckled, sizing Lyle up in a way that made his hair crawl. "No, of course not. In my opinion, they did swimmingly. Well, it was a pleasure meeting you both, but I must move along to make sure I manage to thank everyone for coming. A considerably larger guest list than anticipated."

Kate nodded and said, "No problem."

"I am quite pleased you came and would appreciate if you told your cousin that I said hello and wish her well."

"Absolutely."

"Nice meeting you, Elizabeth. And you as well, Curtis."

Lyle flashed a half-hearted smile, and then Andrew disappeared back into the crowd.

"Did you just introduce me as your prostitute?"

"Relax. You're my escort. You don't have to put out."

"We had the chance to make *any* identities we wanted. I couldn't have been your husband?"

"Do you see a ring on this finger?"

"Boyfriend, then."

"You think we're going steady?"

"You find this hilarious, don't you?"

Kate admitted, "A bit." Then her mirth subsided, "But it helps us a lot more than I ever would have imagined."

"How come?"

"Did you see the way he leered at you? I reckon our golden opportunity just presented itself."

Lyle opened his mouth to object, and then his eyes went wide. "Wait, what?"

2

"I can't believe you're making me do this."

"No one is making you do anything," Kate said, her voice

tinny through the earbud. "You can back out anytime you want."

"If I back out, I can't get to the server. And if I can't get to the server, I can't get the proof we need to bring down the company."

"I know."

"So, I *have* to do this."

Kate enquired, "Are you telling or asking?"

"I'm waiting for you to tell me we have no other way."

"Nope. This offers our best chance. You just have to flirt a bit."

"I'm not good at flirting. Even with the opposite sex."

Kate laughed. "Tell me about it."

"What was that?"

"Nothing. Look, it's easy. All you have to do is get him talking. Then, just laugh at his jokes and touch his arm. After a couple of minutes, tell him you don't feel well and need to rest because you think you drank too much. He'll insist you stay here and will take you somewhere private to lie down and recover."

"And then what?"

"Then, when he comes back to the party, you go find the server, plug your dongle in, and come back."

"Did you just say dongle?"

"Shut up."

"What happens if he doesn't want to leave when he takes me somewhere to rest?"

"Well, then, in that case, you'll have to plug your dongle into his port."

Lyle coughed. "*What*?"

Kate's amusement showed in her voice, "Oh, I have to explain it in non-computer terms? Well, when a man and a man are—"

"I don't think I want you to finish that sentence," Lyle said, shaking his head.

"No," Kate said. "Probably not. Just be confident and be yourself."

Lyle sought help, "Malcolm?"

"Don't ask me," Malcolm said over the comm. "I've had to seduce women before, but this is all you."

Lyle sighed, rubbing his face. "Fine. Jesus. I can't believe I'm agreeing to this, but okay."

"Don't worry; we'll be here to talk you through it. Go ahead

179

and walk over. He's about to wrap up a conversation with that woman, and it provides your perfect opening."

"Great."

Lyle dragged himself across the room toward where Andrew stood. Just before he arrived, Andrew flashed him a puzzled smile.

"Of course, Senator," Andrew continued his conversation, shaking the woman's hand again. "You'll have my full support for your next bid in the fall, and I would *love* to come to your daughter's wedding."

The woman nodded curtly at him, gave Lyle a passing glance, and then disappeared into the crowd. Andrew turned to face him. "Hello again. This is a pleasant surprise."

"Hi," Lyle said, awkwardly.

"Curtis, was it?"

Lyle stared at him.

"Nod," Kate said in his near. "That's your name, remember?"

Lyle jerked his head up and down once. "Yeah, Curtis. Good memory."

"At least one of you has one," Kate mumbled.

"I could never forget a face like yours," Andrew said.

"Oh," Kate said. "He's good."

Lyle cleared his throat. "I just wanted to come over and say hello again. So, uh, hello."

"I take it the arrangement isn't perfect for you either?"

"Excuse me?"

"With Elizabeth?"

"Oh. No, not exactly. It sort of got thrust upon me. I'm just doing my job, you know?"

"Nice, putting the word *thrust* in there," Kate said.

Andrew nodded. "I understand completely. You didn't seem like her type, anyway."

"True that," Kate whispered.

"That's not helping," Lyle mumbled.

"Sorry, what?" Andrew asked, confused.

Lyle froze. "Saying that out loud, I mean. You're right. It's just me, you know? I think she wanted me to come here to help her ... with her sister, you know? Since her sister is sick, and she wanted someone to talk to. But I don't think I'm much of a help. She didn't want to keep me around, so I ... left."

"Good save," Kate laughed.

180

"Ah, I see," Andrew said. "Her loss."

"Ask if he's here alone," Malcolm said.

Lyle now wished he'd taken the earbud out before coming over here.

"What about you?" Lyle asked. "No attractive woman on your arm this evening?"

"Stag tonight," Andrew said. "In all the excitement, I never even thought about it."

"You do seem quite busy."

"My work keeps me occupied enough. It's my passion."

"Always nice to have a passion."

"Snoozefest," Kate whispered.

Andrew said, "What about you? Is *this* your passion?'

Lyle shrugged. "This just pays the bills."

"Then what do you love? What does Curtis like to do when he isn't coming to fancy parties with stuck-up women?"

"Oh ... ouch," Kate said. "I'll show him stuck-up."

"Computers," Lyle blurted. "Software."

"Like development? Engineering? I dabbled in software engineering once upon a time. Studying algorithms in school made for one of the few highlights."

"Really?"

"Yeah, I had a particular interest in sorting algorithms for a while. I wrote a paper on John von Neumann back in the early days of my education. A fascinating man."

"He's brilliant. I always found heap and quick sort the fastest and most implementable algorithms despite what my professors said."

"But so much less stable."

Lyle laughed. "Quite true. Did you ever study RSA?"

"I never had much interest in the security aspect of computer science. It's fascinating, but I've always found the idea of perfect security redundant."

"Oh, I know. Client keys are easier to acquire than anyone could ever guess, and as any professional knows, a minor defect is a total flaw."

"Exactly. If people had the slightest clue how insecure the internet really was, it would terrify them."

Lyle nodded, in his element. "No system is un-hackable."

"You've got that right."

"Are you done geeking out?" Kate asked in his ear. "Love the flirting, but remember, you're supposed to feel sick."

Lyle wobbled a little bit, putting his hand on his forehead. "Oh, I don't feel so good."

Andrew reached out and caught his arm. "Are you okay?"

"I think I had a bit too much to drink," Lyle said. "It's nothing."

"Maybe we should get you some water."

"Maybe," Lyle said. "I should head home, though. I need to lie down."

"We haven't even served dinner yet," Andrew said, checking his watch. "It won't be for another half hour or so."

"That's quite all right."

"Nonsense, you paid for a plate, and you should get the dinner. My chef says it will taste exquisite."

"I didn't actually pay," Lyle said. "My date did."

"The point still stands. Please, come with me. I'll find you somewhere to rest until we can eat. Once you have food in you, you'll feel quite a bit better. And then, hopefully, we can finish this conversation." Andrew smiled lasciviously at him. "In private."

"That's too kind of you," Lyle said.

Andrew led him through the crowd.

"See?" Kate said. "So predictable."

Lyle used the momentary distraction while Andrew faced away to pop the earbud free and slip it into his pocket. He'd had enough of the peanut gallery and figured he could handle it himself from here.

He removed the throat mic as well so that they wouldn't overhear his conversations. Andrew led him out of the ballroom and up a flight of stairs to the second floor of the vast house. Based on the diagrams Lyle had seen, they were heading toward the master suite.

They went down the hall, where Andrew stopped in front of a door on the right-hand side.

"This is my personal bedroom," Andrew said. "I hope that's not too presumptuous?"

Lyle forced himself to smile and nod. "It's perfect. I only need to lie down for a few minutes."

"Excellent. I have to admit, this has brought a rather pleasant distraction from an otherwise terrible day."

Andrew swiped his thumb across a pad on the wall,

unlocking the door, and led Lyle inside. A beautiful room with high ceilings and ornate carpeting met his gaze. The enormous bed, which looked custom sized and quite a bit bigger than a king, had an overhead flowery canopy that left him stunned.

Andrew guided Lyle over and helped him sit on the mattress. "I appreciate this," Lyle said.

Andrew waved away the concern. "Think nothing of it. No guest of mine will suffer a lack of hospitality. Can I get you anything?"

"No. I'll lie down for a couple of minutes and then return to the party when I feel better."

All of a sudden, Andrew leaned in and kissed Lyle on the lips. Lyle nearly jerked back in surprise, eyes widening, but he forced himself not to move. Luckily, Andrew didn't try to use any tongue, and it lasted for just a few seconds. While they kissed, Andrew stroked Lyle's neck.

"I can't wait," Andrew whispered, finally separating from Lyle. He smiled at him, lust in his eyes.

Lyle forced himself to return the look. "Me too."

With that, Andrew adjusted his suit and headed back into the hall. Lyle sat there on the bed for a second until the door shut, and then wiped his mouth with the back of his hand.

"Jesus, why am I his type?"

He fished the earbud and mic out and popped them back into place.

"Lyle?" Kate said over the speaker. "Lyle, where the hell are you? What's going on?"

"Here," he said.

"Where did you go? I've been trying to reach you for two whole minutes."

"The master suite, apparently."

"Why did you take out your earpiece?"

"Just in case, so it wouldn't get spotted. I was right, too. He uh ... he kissed me."

"We have a problem," Kate said, apparently glossing over the admission.

"I know," Lyle said. "He has fingerprint scanners on many of the doors. I thought he might, but I hoped it was just a keypad. It will be harder to get to the server than I anticipated. Happily, I brought a kit, but it will still take a while to find a good fingerprint and clone it."

"That's not what I meant."

Lyle paused and then said, "What did you mean, then?"

This time, Malcolm spoke, "All the cameras just switched off."

"At the gala? You think someone has messed with the security system?"

"No," Malcolm said. "At the hotel. I think someone has come for Jason."

Chapter 20
Houston, Texas

1

Alone in Andrew's private quarters, Lyle took a moment to steady himself. He stood and paced across the enormous room, trying to think his way through Malcolm's predicament.

"You're at my computer?"

"Yeah. That's how I'm monitoring you guys."

"Hit the 'Window' and 'R' keys at the same time and then type 'CMD' and hit enter."

"Okay, then what?"

Rapidly, Lyle listed off a series of commands to type into the system. It would have been a million times easier—and faster—to do it on his own, but at least he had simplified the system enough that Malcolm could use it.

"That should pop up the cameras I installed. They shouldn't be offline."

"They aren't. I see them."

"All right, what do you see?"

A moment passed. "Two guys coming up the stairwell."

"That camera should be two floors down from you, so you've only got about forty seconds."

"They don't know which room we're in."

"We have to assume they do," Lyle said. "If they've made it this far, then probably, they know exactly where they need to go."

Malcolm sighed. "All right. I'll take it from here."

"You're still injured," Kate said. "Just take the kid and run. The exit plan I sent you."

"Too late for that," Malcolm said. "Don't worry. I'll be fine."

"Malcolm, just listen to me. Run."

"No, Kate. Finish your job and then come get me."

The line went dead. Kate cursed over the comms, "Stubborn jackass."

"What do we do?" Lyle asked.

"Finish the job."

"Like hell," Lyle said. "He needs help. You should go."

"I can't leave you."

"Yes, you can. I'm inside already, and it should be smooth sailing from here."

"What if you run into trouble?"

"Then I'll deal with it. Go."

Kate hesitated. "Okay. But, Lyle, stay careful."

"I will."

"I mean it. If you die, then I'll kill you."

2

"Stay back there in the corner," Malcolm said to Jason. "And keep your head down. Don't stand up or move from that spot until I say so. Got it?"

Terrified, Jason seemed on the verge of collapsing. He did nod, though, and move to where Malcolm had pointed.

"It will get loud in here, but if you do everything I say, things will work out fine."

His body still hurt, and pretty much every muscle ached from his recent brush with death, but he didn't have time to worry about that right now. Kate had it right—he was in no shape to stand his ground. And in even less shape to make a run for it, but at least here he had the advantage of forcing the intruders to come to him.

He had a pistol, though he'd loaded only two clips of ammunition. The cameras showed just two men, so it would have to be enough.

If he were completely honest, his condition wasn't the only reason he didn't want to make a run for it. He had recognized the two men in the stairwell: Roger and Frank. Two of the people who had murdered his team in Delaware and tried to kill him. If not for the fact that Jason occupied the room with him, he would have welcomed this attack with open arms.

A chance for revenge.

As it was, though, he had to worry about the possibility of a stray bullet catching the kid or a million other things going wrong. Had Frank and Roger come for the kid or for him? Did it matter that much?

"Okay, then," he muttered. "Let's get this over with."

A few more minutes of silence had passed before he heard someone messing with the front door of the hotel room. They took their sweet time, savoring what they must think a vast advantage. They had acquired a room key, and Malcolm heard the lock buzz.

Leant around the corner of the bathroom wall, he had stood waiting for that exact sound. Now, he lined up his shot to where he assumed they would be standing, and just before the door opened, he pulled the trigger.

Hopefully, it wouldn't be a maid.

With the lights of the room switched off, an instant flash of light blazed when his bullet ripped a hole in the flimsy wooden door.

Someone screamed. From the pitch of that yell, it hadn't come from a maid.

A second later, the door flung open. It caught on the locking hinge, but a swift kick knocked that loose. Malcolm fired again, but this time, no one stood in his line of fire.

Malcolm ducked out of sight just as the two assailants returned fire. One enemy on each side of the doorway. They shoved their weapons through the doorway and filled the room with bullets, shooting in a haphazard pattern to hit anything possible.

Malcolm slid low to the floor behind his partial wall while they fired. Shards of wood and plaster pelted him from every angle as the bullets tore the room apart. Both men used high-caliber rounds, the kind that could stop a charging bull. Just getting clipped with one could prove devastating.

Finally, the barrage stopped, leaving behind a ringing silence.

"Malcolm, is that you?" someone shouted from the hallway. It sounded like Frank.

He thought to stay silent, but he needed time to breathe and think. The last thing he wanted was for them to rush up on him. "Did you put the burn notice on me?"

"You think I have that kind of weight?"

Malcolm said, "You could have called in favors."

187

"I don't have any favors that big. Besides, you're nothing anyway. Why would I even waste the effort on you? Kate in there too?"

"Yes."

"Liar. How'd you know we were coming?"

"I'm just better at this than you."

"Yeah? We'll see about that."

Malcolm called, "Cops are on their way already."

"We still have plenty of time to kill you and get out of here."

"Then get on with it," Malcolm said, leaning back around the corner to watch the doorway.

He saw nothing, but he got ready to fire as soon as one of them showed any body part.

"I'm not in a hurry."

Malcolm read between the lines—he must have clipped Roger with his first shot, who now took time to patch himself up. That would buy Malcolm a couple of minutes, but eventually, they'd be ready to come in for a second round.

Malcolm wouldn't have the element of surprise the next time.

Chapter 21
Houston, Texas

1

Lyle listened at the door for a full minute before he opened it and stepped out into the hallway of Andrew's house. No sounds of the nearby party reached him, which meant they also wouldn't hear too much of him.

He rechecked his phone, glancing at the cameras he had hijacked before the party began. Lyle felt a lot more nervous than he had a few minutes ago before Kate left. But letting her go had seemed like the right thing to do for her, Malcolm, and Jason; however, that didn't help him relax at all.

The hallways stood empty. He didn't plan to turn off the cameras completely, but rather to use them to slip through the hallways undetected. Someone would monitor the cameras, and if the feed went dead, it would alert security.

He found a camera in the hallway off to his right. Quickly, he turned the camera so that the left-hand wall went out of frame. Cautious, he moved in that direction, skirting the wall and keeping an eye on the feed.

Lyle didn't like this at all. It felt worrisome enough when Kate went out and he just controlled the cameras, but now he worked completely alone. A more reasonable person would scrap the mission and get out of here.

It had all gone wrong, and Lyle had jumped in over his head. Unarmed and unprepared. Time remained for him to get back to the party, find an excuse to leave, and bail.

But Lyle couldn't do that. If he left now, they would never have a second chance to get what he needed. Every second they wasted, more people would get infected and sick, and once the next batch of flu vaccines got released to the public, it would all

189

be over.

No, he had to push through his fears and worries and get this job done no matter the cost.

Lyle moved past the overhead camera, readjusted its lens to face the hallway once more, and then crept further into the building.

The immensity of the place made it clear that Andrew had no need for money. What he did wasn't to pad his pockets. A man like him, his only interest lay in power and influence. He had a pathological need for importance, and wealth alone would never satisfy him. The guy wanted people to worship him as a hero.

Lyle had to admit that Andrew's similarities with the person he had been only a few years ago were hard to miss. He, too, used to have an obsession with his power, influence, and money. He'd worked as lead developer on a project implementing drone technology for major government contracts, and had become damn good at his job.

Then his company had sold him out, stolen his technology, and used it in a domestic terrorism plot. They had made Lyle the sacrificial lamb and turned him over to the FBI for blame.

In a matter of hours, he'd lost everything and would have spent the rest of his life in jail—or worse—if not for Kate Allison. She had saved him from the abyss and even helped foil the very terrorism plot for which they'd blamed him.

That life had finished, and he didn't miss it. He no longer recognized the man he'd almost become. Now, he lived as a fugitive from the law with no other recourse than to lurk in the shadows and stay out of sight.

If anything, though, getting scapegoated had turned into a blessing. To turn into Andrew would have brought a far worse fate.

Lyle adjusted another camera, slid along the wall, and then tested a door handle on his right-hand side. Locked. A physical lock, not a digital one. An electronic system would have taken him only a few seconds to bypass.

A physical one, though ...

Kate had given him a crash-course on how to pick locks, sure, but he'd never taken her seriously. After all, Kate went on sites like these to deal with threats, so why would he need such skills?

"Great," he mumbled, kneeling in front of the door and

pulling a lock-picking kit out of his pocket, glad that at least Kate had insisted he always bring it along, and it had come in handy many times.

It took about thirty tries and a lot of luck before Lyle finally managed to get the door open. Luckily, no patrolling guards came by and saw him there. The tumblers clicked into place, and the handle turned.

Lyle let out a hiss of triumph and eased open the door.

"I'm in," he said to no one in particular. Kate and Malcolm both remained off-line.

And, of course, he received no response.

Hopefully, Malcolm hadn't died. Lyle barely knew him, but in the last couple of days had gotten a good sense of Malcolm's character: loyal to a fault, practical, and with a conscience.

Worse, though, if Malcolm had died, then no one could protect Jason. Already, they might have killed or taken the boy.

Well, Lyle could do nothing about those problems right now. He couldn't even work out for definite what he could do about his own issues, except to stick to the original plan and get the information he'd come after.

Lyle stepped into Andrew's personal study. Would he find the server here or in the basement? Whichever, his route to the cellar took him past here.

The decorations here appeared elaborate and ostentatious. A large and ornate fireplace ran along the right wall, and the carpet and walls showed muted brown colors. An oak desk that must have cost a fortune rested on the far side of the room, and a couch sat along the left wall. Unlit, the fireplace seemed to run by gas.

No obvious signs of a server, but this would have made a good place to secure it if Andrew wanted to keep it close. Lyle didn't spot anything right away, but that just meant that he would have to do some physical sleuthing.

"If I were a server, where would I be?"

Lyle moved through the room, opening every cabinet or drawer big enough to hide one. Thankfully, the desk and cabinets stood unlocked (no more lock-picking), but most of them didn't have enough space in which to hide what he wanted.

Satisfied that the server didn't occupy the space, Lyle moved along the walls, rapping his knuckles gently against the wooden exterior and listening for any echo that might indicate a secret

191

hiding place—something he'd seen people do in movies, so he figured it must work.

So distracted in his work, he never heard the door behind him open and close.

"Don't move."

Lyle froze in place, knuckles poised next to a side wall. A sudden jolt of fear coursed through his system, kicking his fight-or-flight instincts into high gear. He struggled to stand perfectly still.

Uh-oh, uh-oh.

"Turn around."

Lyle turned slowly. A short man stood in front of him. Dressed in a three-piece suit, he wore a cloak slung over one shoulder. Lyle recognized him from photos as the Doctor who worked with Andrew Carmichael—Monroe Fink.

Right now, Doctor Fink stood only a few feet away, aiming a pistol at him.

Lyle gulped.

Monroe demanded, "Who the hell are you?"

2

Still around the corner and out of sight, Frank Portman called out to Malcolm, "If you give up now, we'll let you walk away from this. No one has to get hurt. We only want Kate."

Malcolm shifted, pain shooting up his spine from his awkward position on the floor. He'd torn open at least one of his wounds in the first salvo of the firefight, if not more, and blood ran down his side.

Or, maybe, one of the stray bullets had hit him. In any case, his blood pressure hadn't dropped fast enough or far enough to send him into shock, so it must only have grazed him at worst. It was difficult to tell and not worth checking right now. Experience had taught him that the flow of blood wouldn't turn dangerous for many minutes, and he didn't have time to patch himself up right now.

"You mean no one else has to get hurt," Malcolm shouted back. "How is your arm, Roger?"

A minute passed. Finally, Roger shouted, "You barely clipped it. How'd you know?"

"I told you. I'm better at this than you."

The long pause told Malcolm that he'd hit Roger somewhere other than his arm and given him more than just a clipping.

That brought mixed news. It minimized Roger's capability, but it also sped up their timetable. They wouldn't wait for long before they needed to get Roger to a real doctor and patch him up.

If only Malcolm's bullet had put him down for good.

"We don't want to kill you," Frank shouted.

"Like hell. You already tried in Delaware. You murdered my team, and Jeff tried to finish me. You failed then, and you will fail now."

"We didn't fail."

"Then why am I still alive?"

"Someone betrayed us."

Malcolm snorted a sarcastic chuckle. "That feels familiar."

"You should feel dead. If that bitch hadn't murdered Jeff and dragged you out of there, you would be floating on the bottom of the ocean by now."

A chill rushed up Malcolm's spine, along with a flash of memory. "Woman? Since when do you work with women?"

"We made an exception. She planned the whole thing, right down to killing your team."

"Who?" Malcolm asked, afraid he knew the answer already.

"Who do you think?"

"You're lying."

"Kate planned the whole goddamn thing."

"She saved my life."

"Cold feet. She also turned on us."

Malcolm didn't want it to be true. He wanted it to be a lie concocted to turn him against his friend.

But it wasn't.

Part of him had known this the entire time, but he'd refused to admit it. Now, though, he had no other way to deny it.

"Son of a bitch," he growled, leaning his head against the wall.

He had wondered why Kate had shown up out of the blue to save him. They had been friends, sure, and Kate was a loyal woman, but it had seemed an overreach. She just happened to have heard he'd got into trouble and came to rescue him?

It hadn't made sense. Still didn't.

193

She had betrayed him.

She had killed his friends.

His family.

Malcolm forced the thoughts away, focusing only on the situation at hand. Frank wanted to get in his head, and even though it had worked, Malcolm couldn't let it compromise his situation. Even with this hard truth, it didn't change what Frank and Roger had done to his team.

They still needed to pay.

"You didn't know, did you?" Frank shouted.

Off in the distance, the first faint echoes of a siren reached them. They would arrive in the next couple of minutes and surround the building. Malcolm didn't answer, instead shifting onto his knee to get a better vantage from around the corner. He held his pistol ready, waiting.

"Running out of time, Frank," he said. "Ready to give up?"

"I wonder what else that bitch didn't tell you. Are you willing to stick your neck out for her, or do you want to help us get revenge for what she did? The way I see it, we're on the same side."

"Cops are coming," Malcolm shouted. "This is your last chance to get the hell out of here."

"No way. We've still got a couple of minutes. Plenty of time. What'll it be, Malcolm? Want to help us pay Kate back for what she did?"

"She'll pay," Malcolm muttered. "But you'll pay first."

Suddenly, from off to his left, there came the sound of gunshots, fired from the next room over, right through the wall and aimed at where he crouched.

Roger must have slipped next door while Frank distracted him. They'd never wanted him to join them, but had distracted him to buy time. The first few rounds hit the wood above Malcolm's head, and then one slammed into his shoulder. It didn't hurt, at least not at first. Instead, he felt a heavy pressure on his arm, which knocked him sideways.

He dropped prone, cursing his distraction, and rolled toward the doorway. Roger needed to keep him off-guard while Frank came in through the front door. The real threat still came from the doorway. He ignored Roger and focused solely on the main entrance. Malcolm raised his gun, aiming with his good arm to where he imagined Roger would have hidden.

194

A second later when Frank popped around the corner and fired, he proved Malcolm right. Initially, Frank aimed where he thought Malcolm would sit and wait, assuming he would have lost a few seconds from Roger's attack.

His mistake.

Frank fired, recalibrated, and then aimed down at Malcolm's prone form in the hallway.

Too late. Malcolm fired first.

His first-round hit Frank in the chest, sending the man staggering away from the door. Frank pulled the trigger anyway, but his shot went wild.

Malcolm fired again, putting three more rounds into Frank's chest and then one in his head. Frank slumped to the ground on the opposite wall, in a sitting position, dead and crumpling sideways.

Malcolm's satisfaction came short-lived, as Roger continued shooting through the wall, using his initial bullet holes to sight in. Malcolm scrambled and rolled, moving around the corner of the wall and toward the room's front door.

More pressure hit his back-left leg. At least one more bullet, maybe two, had hit him. And then he wriggled out of sight. Finally, he made it out of Roger's sightline and forced himself to a sitting position.

Malcolm's hands shook, and blood covered him. He popped out his clip and slid in the other one, though it took two tries to pull the slide back with his blood greasing the grip.

"Not my day," he mumbled, leaning against the wall and sucking in a breath of air.

"I hit him!" Roger shouted. "He's down!"

Footsteps raced down the hallway out front, followed by a curse when Roger spotted Frank lying dead. Malcolm swung the gun over, aiming at about knee level, for where he assumed Roger would have stood behind the wall.

Malcolm drew in a steadying breath and listened for any sound of movement. Roger would try to close in, moving quietly.

Then he heard it. Only a faint noise as a shoe scuffed across carpet.

Malcolm adjusted his aim and pulled the trigger, firing through the wall at knee level. Roger screamed in surprise when the bullet crashed into his leg, and then he fell forward. The front half of his body landed in front of Malcolm in the doorway. Roger tried to react, to draw up his gun and shoot Malcolm.

He never got a chance. Malcolm fired off a series of shots, silencing the man forever. The last gunshot hung in the air, followed by a profound silence, punctuated by a steady ringing in his ears.

Malcolm just sat there, staring at Roger's lifeless corpse and listening to the sounds of police sirens closing in on the hotel. He had his vindication. Had taken care of the people who had murdered his team. But he didn't feel it.

The heavy admission that Kate had betrayed him smothered any relief or joy. Did she help him still? Or hinder? Did it come from guilt? From sadism? Did she enjoy watching him suffer?

A flurry of footsteps sounded outside the hotel room, jolting him back to reality. He had no idea how long he'd sat there bleeding, but realized a good amount of time must have passed. He had fallen unconscious. The sirens blared louder, just outside the building.

Malcolm raised the gun with his wobbly left arm to shoot whoever came up on him, but it slipped from his grip and collapsed to the ground a few feet away.

A second later and Kate stepped around the corner.

"Oh, God," she said, rushing up to him.

He tried to jerk away from her touch but had grown too weak. She looked him over, sizing up his wounds.

"We need to get you help," she said, rushing past him and further into the room. Frantically, she typed on Lyle's computer and then ran over to the closet. From there, she grabbed a bag of medical equipment and another duffel bag.

First, she brought the medical bag over to him and pulled out a container of liquid band-aid and a cauterizing iron. She plugged the iron into a wall socket and applied the liquid bandage, sealing his wounds and stopping the loss of blood. For the more considerable injuries, though, she used the iron.

"Hold still. This will hurt," she said. "A lot."

He turned his head to face her, staring directly into her eyes. "You couldn't possibly hurt me any worse."

Her face fell, and he saw genuine hurt in her eyes when she realized what he meant. "I never. I mean, if I had *known* ..."

Kate trailed off, shaking her head. "Never mind. You can hate me later. Right now, I need to get you out of here."

She pressed the iron to his flesh, and it sizzled and boiled.

196

He screamed but heard nothing. His poor condition meant that he didn't feel much of anything now, but it would hurt like hell later.

Kate said, "I left a distraction in the lobby, along with another one up here. Lyle's hard drives are getting wiped as we speak."

Malcolm didn't care. Kate went back into the room and brought out Jason. Ashen, the kid could barely keep his eyes open, but he didn't fight back or object.

"Come on," Kate said.

She pulled Malcolm to his feet, slinging his arm over her shoulders, and then wobbled down the hall. They made it to a laundry chute and then stopped.

"Don't worry," she said. "It's safe."

"Just leave me."

"Not a chance."

"I'll never forgive you."

She hesitated. "Neither will I. Now get your ass in there."

She pushed it open and helped Malcolm squeeze into the small gap. It proved a tight fit, and it would be uncomfortable on the way down. Ironically, his blood would serve as a lubricant to help him slide down the shaft.

He went in legs first, sliding down multiple flights to, finally, reach the bottom. At speed, he fell out of the shaft and landed in the back of a truck full of dirty sheets and towels. A few seconds after he'd rolled to the side, the boy came tumbling out of the shaft, landing in the plush blankets next to Malcolm, who dug into the material to pull Jason free.

A few seconds after that and Kate came tumbling into the pile as well. She hit, rolled to the side, and dropped to the ground outside the truck bed. Malcolm couldn't see anything, but he heard someone shout.

"Hey, you!"

A second later, something heavy collapsed to the pavement. Hopefully, Kate hadn't killed whoever had seen them.

Then came two explosions. The first at ground-floor level and the second from up above. Both sounded loud and shook the area, but it seemed concussive rather than dangerous.

Mostly for effect.

Kate yelled, "I'm getting us out of here." And then the door to the truck's cab slammed shut.

197

The truck rumbled to life. Gears ground when Kate shifted it into motion. Malcolm rolled to the side of the truck bed and glanced over. On the ground, a few dozen feet away, lay an unconscious cop, a dart sticking out of his neck. His police car sat at the other end of the alley, blocking that exit.

Up ahead, in the other direction, though, the way looked clear. Kate turned left into traffic, made another few turns, and continued driving away from the hotel. The twin distractions had kept the attention of the police, and right now, they hadn't managed to lock-down the area. No one chased them.

Malcolm lay in the plush blankets, staring up at the blue Texas sky.

Never had he felt as alone as he did right then.

Chapter 22
Houston, Texas

1

"I'm nobody," Lyle said, still holding up his hands in as unthreatening a manner as he could. He racked his brain to think of everything he had learned about Doctor Monroe, but right now, nothing would come to mind. "Your boss brought me up here. He told me to wait for him to come back."

"Like hell," Monroe said. "I saw you flirting with him downstairs. You might have him fooled, but not me. What agency do you work for? DEA? Homeland security?"

"I don't work for the government."

"Don't lie to me. I know you've come here working for someone. Who wants to bring us down? What do they know?"

"I'm telling you ..."

Monroe took a threatening step toward him, cocking the gun. "Don't test me."

Lyle didn't know what to do, so he told the truth, "I'm a wanted criminal," he said. "My name is Lyle Goldman, the FBI wants me. I don't work for the government."

"Should I recognize the name?"

That hurt Lyle. "A few years ago, I got charged with domestic terrorism. Though all a mistake, the FBI has kept after me ever since."

Monroe stared at him blankly. "Doesn't ring a bell."

"Drones? Bombs? Thousands of people almost died? Nothing?"

Monroe shook his head. "I don't believe you. You made it up."

"I need to talk to my agent."

"Why else would you come snooping around in here? You

want something. What, though?"

Lyle's hands shook. He wished Kate could help him. She was the brave one; she dealt with dangerous situations like this and would know what to do.

"You're right," Lyle said, shaking his head. "You caught me. I'm with homeland security."

Monroe blinked and shifted uncomfortably. "Prove it."

"I left my badge behind since I'm working undercover, but my team is here, too. All of them. Parked outside and waiting for my order to come in. They know my precise location and what I'm doing, so if you shoot me, you'll spend the rest of your life in jail."

Hesitation dulled and narrowed Monroe's eyes as the doctor considered Lyle's words.

Lyle took a tiny step toward the door. Should he make a run for it?

Monroe shook the gun. "I said, don't move."

"Look, if you let me go right now, I can talk to the prosecutor. We can go easy on you. Just let me walk out of here, and we can pretend this never happened."

An instant later, he realized that he had said something wrong.

The expression on Monroe's face shifted. "Liar."

Lyle racked his brain for what to do next, but his body didn't wait around to see what he thought up. Instead, he sprang into motion, ducking low and charging at Monroe. The weapon went off, but the bullet passed well above Lyle's head, thudding into the wall behind him. It seemed Monroe had little clue about how to use the gun.

He tackled Monroe around the waist, knocking the doctor to the floor and collapsing on top of him. The firearm fell loose, bouncing across the carpet to land a few dozen feet away from them.

Monroe scrambled, punching Lyle in the side and shoving him off. Lyle rolled to his feet and charged back in at the doctor, launching a series of furious blows at the man's face. Kate had trained him how to fight, and instinct took over.

Some landed but most didn't. Too panicked and full of adrenaline, Lyle didn't know how badly he hurt the doctor or not, but his opponent remained standing. Monroe got a few clean hits in on him, too, as the furious fight raged on.

It went on like that for what seemed forever as Lyle and Monroe Fink pounded away on each other. One moment Lyle had the upper hand, and the next, the doctor would seize an advantage.

If only Kate could see him now, engaged in a battle between two titans.

Finally, Lyle shoved Monroe to the ground and rushed across the room, snagging the dropped gun from the floor and raising it up. Monroe raced only a step behind him, but when Lyle pointed the weapon in his face, he stopped, raising his hands in submission.

"Okay, all right. You win."

"Back up," Lyle said, rubbing a hand across his face to see how much damage he had sustained. His entire body hurt, and his muscles ached for oxygen. He had a bloody lip. Maybe even a broken jaw.

Monroe backed off, still holding his hands in the air. Lyle slid his phone out and checked the security feeds.

The hallway outside looked clear. No one seemed to have heard the errant gunshot or fight.

Lyle thanked his lucky stars.

"The server. Andrew's server where he keeps all the files about CRISPR," he said. "Where is it?"

"What server?"

"Don't play with me, Monroe. I'm not in the mood. Where does Andrew keep his private server?"

Monroe hesitated. Lyle took a step toward him. "I won't ask again. Next time, I'll shoot you in the leg and see if you feel more cooperative."

"The wine cellar. In the basement."

"Lead me to it."

Monroe weighed his options and then nodded. "All right, follow me."

He led Lyle back into the hallway. "Hang on," Lyle said. He slid out his phone and scrolled through the cameras, shifting them all to look at the right-side wall. "Stay to the left."

Monroe did and then down a flight of stairs to the basement. They went through the kitchen and a pantry before coming to a locked door. Unlike the others, thick sheets of steel made up this door, and it had a heavy-duty lock in it.

"I can't open it," Monroe said. "Only Andrew can get in here."

"I can, too."

Lyle stepped up, sliding his fingerprint kit free and pulling out the mock he'd made of Andrew's print earlier. Lyle put the thin plastic sheet over his thumb and pressed it against the biometric scanner.

The entire time, he kept the gun trained on Monroe, waiting until the lock buzzed. The door popped open, and he beckoned with the barrel of the pistol for the doctor to continue.

"Move."

Monroe did, walking quickly down the stairs to the cellar. At one time, it might have acted as a wine cellar, but in recent years, Andrew had converted the space. Cold, dark, and damp, the basement lay hidden, and only the occasional overhead light fixture guided their way.

The doctor led Lyle through a maze of stone passages to a cavernous underground area about thirty degrees colder than the party hall above. Here, the only light came from a single overhead fixture that seemed almost blindingly bright.

To his left, a doorway led into another room. This one a complete opposite to the prison-like cellar. It gave the impression of a young boy's room, as though ripped from the pages of a Goosebumps story. Warm and inviting, it had blue walls, toys on the floor, and a computer desk on the right.

No windows, though.

"This is where you kept Jason?" Lyle said.

"Yes, we ran tests on him here."

"How could you do something like that to a child?"

Monroe pushed his glasses up on his nose. "Do you eat meat?"

"What?"

"How can you eat meat knowing that an animal got slaughtered for your meal? We never mistreated Jason. The light is UV, his food organic, and he had every possible treatment for his condition he could ever need. What else could we have done?"

Lyle wanted to argue further, but it would waste his breath. Instead, he turned and surveyed the rest of the room. In the far corner sat a Faraday cage, which surrounded a bank of computers. A generator stood near the cage, humming along.

"Gas-powered," Lyle said. "Completely self-contained. Smart."

"Necessary," a voice said from behind. "In case someone

tried to hack our server using the electrical grid. If anyone wants to steal from me, I want them right here, looking me in the face when they do it."

Lyle spun. Andrew Carmichael and two bodyguards stood there. Andrew didn't smile, and he looked downright scary.

Both guards trained their pistols on Lyle.

"Uh-oh."

2

"How did you know I would come down here?"

"I didn't." Andrew held up his cell phone. "Clever that you got past all my security, but anytime one of my biometric scanners gets utilized, I receive a text message. Most of the time it's redundant and annoying, but I think you'll agree it has paid off tonight."

"Ah. I didn't think of that."

"Lower your gun."

"I'll shoot the doctor."

"Go ahead," Andrew said.

"What?" Monroe asked, sounding shocked.

"Relax. He won't shoot you. He's bluffing."

"Like hell I won't."

"He doesn't want to die."

Lyle knew that as accurate, but he held the pistol trained on the doctor all the same. He had bitten off more than he could chew, and he couldn't imagine how he might get out of this situation alive.

"I have to say, I feel a little hurt," Andrew said. "I thought we had a connection."

"You thought wrong."

"So, who are you, really?"

"He's with homeland security," Monroe said.

"No, he isn't," Andrew said, still staring at Lyle. "I thought you seemed familiar, but it took me quite a while to place you. After all, over two years have elapsed since you betrayed your country."

"Finally, someone recognizes me."

"So, you admit to being a terrorist?"

"I got framed. Even if I hadn't, I don't come anywhere close

203

to your league."

"I'm a businessman. And right now I don't care much either way. All I know is you are somewhere you shouldn't be, and that poses a problem for me. The question now is, how do I deal with you?"

Andrew gestured forward with his hand, and the two bodyguards walked toward Lyle.

"What do you want us to do with him?"

"Find out why he came here. Then dispose of him. Make sure the tech's remove him from all the cameras and no one ever finds him. As far as anyone is concerned, he never came here at all. Monroe, come with me. We must return to the party. Many more hands to shake."

Lyle didn't know what to do. He still had the pistol in his hand, but they outnumbered him, and he had no preparation for a situation such as this.

Why had he let Kate leave?

He would die in this assholes' root cellar.

Monroe smiled at Lyle. "Well, it's been fun, but—"

"We know what you're doing," Lyle said. "We know everything. The virus, CRISPR, we know it all. We have proof. And we're releasing it to the public whether I make it out of here or not."

Andrew stiffened. "Wait," he said to the guards. He turned to Lyle. "What is it you *think* you know?"

"Everything. We have Jason. Already, we've run genetic tests to prove what you did to him. You murdered his father, and we know about the virus you've released. You can expect to spend the rest of your miserable life in jail."

"So, she sent the kid to you?" Andrew rubbed his chin. "I had thought he would go to his father. Just who the hell are you?"

"I've told you guys, like, three times. I'm Lyle mother-bleeping-Goldman."

Andrew stared at him. "Did you just say 'bleeping'?"

Lyle pressed on, "The point is, all the information about your little operation is on its way to the CDC, and you'll get arrested in hours."

A stunned expression settled on Andrew's face, but then it spread into a broad smile. "If that were true, why would you have come down here? You came after proof, which means you have only hearsay. All you have is a story. A clever fiction that you

204

would never prove. Not without what lies on that server. That's why you came down here."

"No, that's why *he* came down here," Lyle said, pointing over Andrew's shoulder down the empty hallway behind them.

This most critical bluff of his entire life came from a desperate ploy to buy him a few extra seconds. He prayed that they would turn away just long enough for him to perform one final last-ditch act.

It worked.

On instinct and distracted, everyone turned to see who Lyle had pointed at. The momentary pause gave Lyle all he needed to take one shot with his stolen gun.

He didn't fire at the guards, though, or at Andrew or the doctor.

Instead, he shot the light.

This deep underground, Lyle banked on the hope that without any overhead light the room would fall into utter blackness. With how bright that bulb glowed, it made it seem as if the room had multiple light sources, but Lyle felt confident the area held only the one.

And, better yet, it provided a static target. He didn't like shooting at things that moved.

Lyle aimed and pulled the trigger, but he didn't wait around to see if his gamble had paid off. Instead, he dropped to the ground and rolled to his right.

The light exploded, and a bright flash of sparks rained down on everyone. Then, thankfully, darkness plunged into the room.

The final ruse had worked.

His momentary distraction ended, and gunshots roared when the guards tried to shoot him. The echoes filled the room, but none of the bullets hit him.

Lyle allowed himself an internal fist-pump of happiness at his frantic plan panning out, and then he crawled toward a corner of the room. Someone shouted. The guards continued firing, using the light from their muzzles to try and locate him.

A bullet thudded into the ground only inches from his face. Shrapnel grazed him when bullets hit the ground.

The happiness evaporated.

Andrew yelled, "Stop firing, damn it!"

However, it took a full ten seconds for the guards to cease their shooting, and that only because they had run out of ammo.

205

"He's over there, in that corner!" Another male voice said.

Yet a third man spoke up, "I think I see him."

"Get out your flashlights," Andrew said.

A pause ensued.

"You didn't bring flashlights with you?" Disgust laced Andrew's tone.

"You just said to come with you."

"How do you not have a flashlight everywhere you go?"

"Normally, we carry one, but with the party, we—"

"I have a pocket knife," the other bodyguard said.

"What the hell good will a pocket knife do?" Andrew screamed, incredulous. "Someone, find him! Don't let him leave here alive."

Lyle crawled across the room, making as little noise as possible. His muscles ached, and he fought the urge to draw in a loud breath. His heart pounded in his ears. He might be seconds from dying.

The guards walked across the cellar floor, spreading apart—judging from the footsteps—and felt in the darkness trying to find him. Lyle dragged himself into another corner of the room, holding the gun at his chest, and faced back to the central area.

He did his best to figure out where the four people stood. Two of the men hadn't moved—most likely Andrew and Monroe—but the guards continued to search for him. The guards made a lot of noise. One of them bumped into a table.

"Ouch."

"Shut up," the other one said.

"Did you find him yet?"

"Not yet. You?"

"He couldn't have gone far."

"Maybe we hit him."

"You think he's dead?"

"Or dying."

"Maybe you should stop talking," Andrew said. "And *find* him."

Lyle's plan took him no further than this. It shocked him that he had made it this far. Now, he had run out of ideas.

Well, he realized, maybe he had one more idea.

Gingerly, he reached into his jacket pocket and slid out his phone—the only heavy object he had that might make enough noise when it bounced across the room.

He closed his eyes, taking a steadying breath. Then, clutching the gun to his chest with shaking hands, he tried to relax and focus.

Just like shooting at the range.

Not real people, just cardboard prey.

Just targets.

"I don't think he's on this side," one of the guards said.

"Do you think he crawled out of here?"

"Maybe. That's what I would have done."

"Let's check over there. That corner."

Their footsteps came in Lyle's direction.

Now or never.

He opened his eyes, forced his hands to steady, and then tossed the phone across the room to his left. He hurled the phone toward the last place he remembered seeing Andrew standing, hoping that he or Monroe hadn't moved much in the previous few seconds.

As he threw the cell, he raised his gun and clenched his teeth.

The phone hit the cellar floor and bounced, the motion causing the screen to flicker to life. The sudden bright light after over a minute of darkness jarred. It also had the effect he'd hoped for. Both guards turned and fired at the sudden sound and light.

Right at Andrew and Monroe.

"Hey!" Andrew shouted, diving away from their shots.

Monroe didn't have the same luck. One of the bullets clipped him, and with a shriek, he collapsed to the ground. Lyle ignored them, thought, and focused instead on where the guards stood.

He watched for muzzle flashes and sighted in, picking his prey.

Just a target. Not a person.

He squeezed the trigger. Then he pressed it again, moving the muzzle in a slow pattern around where he saw the flash.

Something heavy thumped to the floor, and he heard a groan. Success. The other guard's gun barked again, and this time the man shot at Lyle in his corner. The bullet hit the wall next to his head, only inches from his eye.

Lyle adjusted and fired at the last guard, aiming right for the barrel where he'd seen the previous flash.

A second body thumped to the floor. The firing stopped.

Lyle rolled to the side again, ducking into the darkness in case more shots came. They didn't, though. Neither guard returned fire.

"Monroe!" Andrew shouted. The phone screen dimmed again, plunging the room into blackness once more. "Monroe?"

Suddenly, the light flared to life again. Andrew lay on the ground, clutching at the phone and picking it up off the floor. He focused solely on the doctor, who lay on the ground. Andrew held up the cell, using it to see Monroe.

The doctor didn't move or respond.

Lyle pushed himself out of the corner and crept over toward the man. Andrew saw him coming at the last moment and turned to stare at him, trying to get away.

"You aren't really my type," Lyle said, bashing Andrew on the side of the head with the butt of his pistol.

The room fell quiet once again. The doctor breathed in short gasps, and one of the guards made moaning noises.

Lyle stood there, breathing in the sickly-sweet smell of blood and struggling not to cry. His hands trembled violently, and the more he tried to clear his mind, the more it seemed he would collapse into a bubbling mess on the floor.

Suddenly, the phone at his feet buzzed. It jolted him back to reality, and he almost fell trying to get away from the shrill noise. He stumbled, caught himself, and then burst out laughing.

Not regular laughter, more like maniacal panic-stricken guffaws. The uncontrollable kind that hurts more than it helps.

"I hate this, I hate this," he muttered to himself, picking up the cell. Sticky blood covered the screen.

Through the spider-webbed glass, Kate's name displayed.

Lyle clicked accept and turned on the speaker. "Hey, Kate. Can't talk right now. I'm having a meltdown, I just shot some guys, and I don't know what I'm doing and—"

"Where are you?"

"Where am I? Where am I? I don't know. The cellar. I think I'm going into shock."

"Did you get hurt?"

"No."

"Then it's not shock. You need to get ahold of yourself. I have Malcolm and the kid and am on my way."

"Cool. That's good. You need to come get me."

"No. You're fine. I hear police sirens everywhere, so you have to get out on your own."

"Are you sure the cops aren't after you?"

"Could be," she said. "But I've traded vehicles and lost any pursuit, so I feel fairly certain these ones are all yours. They're heading toward the party."

"Great."

"Just get outside. I'll pick you up on the southeast corner in the back alley."

"How much time do I have?"

"Five minutes. Tops."

"All right."

Lyle shut-down the phone and stuffed it in his pocket. Then he took a steadying breath and forced himself to relax and breathe. It was over, he told himself. All over. He was safe.

Well, safe-ish. He still needed to get out of here alive. He picked up the gun he'd taken from Monroe and wiped off his prints.

"All right," he said again, turning toward the air-gapped server inside the Faraday cage. "Let's finish this and get out of here."

A second passed.

"I guess I'm talking to myself now."

The cage had no lock, so Lyle had no trouble getting inside. At a terminal, he typed in commands. He plugged in the ethernet connection from the other computer and then turned all the connections on.

It took about thirty seconds to re-open the network and sync it back into the outside internet. Once he established a connection, he loaded his list of contacts, found the files he needed, and sent out the emails. Over one hundred news outlets would get all the paperwork and proof they could ever want in proving what Andrew and Monroe had been up to.

He couldn't wait around for the upload to finish, though. Not if he wanted to get out of here before the cops arrived. Instead, he set up the broadcast and then ran down the hallway, out of the cellar, and headed for the exit.

Without any trouble, he made it upstairs and then headed through the pantry and into the deeper manor. Out front, sirens wailed. Shouts came from the direction of the ballroom. The cops would move further into the building quickly, and no doubt,

209

some would come around the side.

Lyle found a side exit and slipped out into the night, heading for the shadows. He spotted one officer doing a sweep, but he hid behind a lawn animal until the woman had moved on. On such a dark night, staying hidden didn't pose much of a problem.

He crept through the gardens toward the outer fence and the alleyway that Kate had shown him on the map as an escape route. The sirens behind him grew nearer, but they hadn't locked down this side of the property just yet.

Kate waited for him in a beat-up old pickup truck, which sat idling in the alley. Jason sat next to her in the passenger side.

"Where's Malcolm?" Lyle asked.

She nodded over her shoulder, toward the bed of the truck. "Get in."

Lyle did as she told him, and Kate took off, heading down the alley and out of the district. A tarp covered the back, and he found Malcolm lying underneath it. He looked severely hurt—unconscious and breathing shallowly.

Lyle leaned up and opened the rear window of the truck. "We have to get him to a hospital."

"I know," Kate said. "I'm taking him to friend's place, and I have a doctor on the way. Did you get everything taken care of?"

"Yeah," he said. "I sent the emails. The information had gone out there."

"You did it, then," Kate said, smiling at him.

"Yeah," Lyle muttered, exhausted and out of sorts. "I guess so."

Wrecked, after everything that had happened—what with Malcolm wounded, and Lyle having shot two people in the cellar—he didn't feel much like celebrating.

Epilogue

1

Kate drove them north and away from the city, out of Texas, and finally, into Colorado. To stay out of sight and away from any possible road closures or police checkpoints, she used back roads.

Kate drove them to the cabin of an old friend of hers, currently out of the country. To get there through backcountry and deep woods, it took a long time.

Another car waited out front when they arrived, and a woman sat on the porch. When the car approached, she rose to her feet, frowning when she saw Malcolm's state.

"Hey, Margaret," Kate said. "Long time no see."

"You told me he was hurt, Kate, but not *this* bad. He needs a hospital."

"Not possible. Do what you can."

"Get him inside," Margaret said with a sigh. "I'll grab my equipment."

Lyle and Kate helped carry him up the stairs and into the log cabin. "Whose place is this?" Lyle asked.

"A friend's," Kate said. "Arthur Vangeest. He's a hunter."

"Like a deer hunter?"

"Something like that."

"Will he get mad at you for using his cabin?"

"He's a friend. In Europe, right now, I think. Won't come back for a long time."

They settled Malcolm in, and the doctor went to work, first removing the bullets and then treating his injuries. Kate assisted, and Lyle got tasked with boiling water and cleaning instruments. Jason helped him some, but after a while, the kid went and found a quiet place to take a nap. He looked exhausted, and Lyle didn't blame him.

Margaret had come prepared with an ample supply of blood and a trunk-load of surgical tools. It took many hours and a lot of transfusions before she declared Malcolm stable. "If he survives the night, he should be okay."

"How long will he stay out?" Kate asked.

"A couple of days. Just keep replacing the IV bags when they run empty. If he wakes, it'll take a few more weeks before he should try walking."

"Thanks," Kate said, giving Margaret a hug. She left, leaving Kate and Lyle in the living room.

"How many favors did you have to call in for this?" Lyle asked, shutting the door behind the doctor.

"A lot," Kate said. "Some of them IOUs."

"Great," he said. "We don't have any money, and now we owe favors."

"I'm sorry," Kate said, putting her hand on his shoulder. "For all of this. For everything. I'm sorry I dragged you into this."

"It isn't your fault," Lyle said. "Well, actually, yeah, some of it is. Most of it. You should have told me about Malcolm and the job. I could have helped you stop Jeff and Frank before it got started. Then you wouldn't have had to lie to him, and his team would be alive."

"It doesn't matter now," Kate said. "He knows."

"Knows what?"

"Everything, I think. I don't know if he remembered what happened or if they told him, but he'll never trust me again."

"Sure, he will."

"No, he won't," Kate said. "And he shouldn't."

With that, Kate turned and headed out of the cabin. Lyle moved to follow her and then changed his mind. Dog-tired, he needed to lie down, and she needed alone time.

Lyle explored the cabin before settling down to sleep. It disturbed him more than a little to discover a three-cell prison in the basement.

Just who the hell did this cabin belong to?

A problem for another day, he decided. Fresh out of answers and lacking the ambition to seek them, Lyle found the nearest bed and collapsed, asleep in only minutes.

2

Lyle spent the next few days working frantically to cover their tracks in everything that had gone down in Texas. He had made a lot of mistakes at Andrew's house and had left a lot of digital evidence to clean up. Luckily, Kate had triggered his safety protocols in the hotel and destroyed that lead, but he had to make sure nothing at the manor could trace back to him.

Kate hadn't returned the night before, but the truck remained out front. He didn't know where she'd gone and hoped she wouldn't stay a long time away.

Lyle didn't have the time to worry about that, though, as he had to use a satellite uplink and cheap tablet he'd found in a closet of the cabin to do his work. He'd lost his gear and would need to rebuild his custom rig and laptop from scratch. The rebuilding would take time and a lot of money—two things he didn't have.

Strangely, though, he didn't mind too much. Even having to work on the cheap hardware didn't bother him. Things you could replace, people not so much, and he felt glad to have survived.

More than that, though, they had done something good. Around the world, news reports about the flu vaccine and CDM Pharmaceuticals had gained national attention. With his uploads successful, every major news outlet ran with the story.

The fallout proved intense, and after only hours, authorities rounded up the contaminated flu vaccines for destruction. Police found Andrew in his home and arrested him. Doctor Monroe Fink remained in critical condition and soon to be arraigned, and a lot of unanswered questions lingered, as well as speculation about what had happened at the gala.

Lyle had done that. Had made Andrew's plan fail, ensuring the nefarious plot would never come to fruition. He would never receive credit for it, but that didn't matter. Just knowing they had done something good for a change gave him enough. That was why he'd gotten into this life to begin with: to stop people like Andrew.

Propitiously, his name never came up in the news reports. He did find some chatter on the dark web that included him as a possible player in the events that had taken place, but he didn't see a lot of evidence. Mostly, people viewed him as a hero and not the enemy.

The hotel shootout had a couple of mentions, but the larger story drowned it out. People had much more interest in the genetics scare.

Kate returned from her hike in the late afternoon of the second day. She stood in the doorway for a minute, watching Lyle work.

"How's he doing?" she asked, nodding toward where Malcolm lay sleeping on the couch.

Lyle shrugged. "All right, I think. He hasn't woken up yet."

"Probably won't for a couple more days, if at all."

Lyle turned back to his work, going through the security system at the manor and searching for any traces of Kate or him and deleting them.

Surprise rocked him when he discovered a hidden camera in Andrew's office. He had missed it during his first scan. Might it have caught images of him during the break-in? He hadn't noticed it in his initial scan of the systems since it didn't form a part of the original installation. Probably, Andrew had added it separately.

"What are you doing?"

"Cleaning up any evidence we left behind. All the news is talking about CDM Pharmaceuticals and what they did. The government is downplaying the danger, but they've pulled all CDM's drugs from the market already. They're giving away free doses of Tamiflu to just about anyone."

"We'll have a shortage soon."

"Yep," Lyle said. "Andrew wanted to make a pharmaceutical company rich. It just ended up being the wrong one."

"Good. I'm sorry I couldn't help you when everything went down."

Lyle lied, "It's fine. I took care of it."

"I should have been there."

"I sent you away," he said. "If anyone is to blame, it's me."

"No," she said. "It's more than that. I ..."

Lyle watched her, expectantly, wondering what she would say.

"It won't happen again," she said.

"Because?"

Kate stared at him.

"Everything worked out," Lyle said. "So, that's something."

"I mean it," she said. "I realized something important today."

"What?"

"You can take care of yourself."

"I didn't have a lot of choice."

"I know, and that's my fault for abandoning you, but you're a heck of a lot tougher than you look."

"Thanks ... I think?"

"It took me a lot to see this, but we're partners. Equal partners. I've relied on the fact that I'm more experienced than you as justification to make decisions without consulting you, and you've been gracious enough to let me. The thing is, I understand now what it means to say we're in this together."

Lyle sighed. "I still think I'd rather sit behind a computer and let you do all the heavy lifting."

"Not as easy as it looks, huh?"

"God, no," he said. "I had to fight off that doctor and then ..." His voice caught in his throat.

"I think ... I might have killed someone," he said, shaking his head.

"You didn't have a choice."

"Yes, I did," he said. "We never had to go there at all. We didn't get paid for that job, and that guy didn't have to die."

"Think of all those people you saved, though," she said. "You helped so many."

"If it's one life versus many," he said, "then I'll gladly take the one. But that doesn't make it any easier."

"No," she said. "It doesn't."

Lyle fell silent for a long moment. Then he asked, "How do you deal with it?"

"Keep moving forward. You don't actually deal with it, you move past it. I guess that's partly why I always keep to myself. Why I can't trust people. Except you."

"Thanks."

"So, tell me about this fight. You said you took on the doctor?"

"You should have seen it," Lyle said, still skimming the footage, looking for any timestamps that might cover his visit. "I think it's up ahead in the feed. We had a drag out clobber fest."

"Oh?"

"Yeah. Fists flew. Guns fired. Total mayhem. And I won. You would have been impressed."

"Is that you?" she asked, pointing at the screen. In the footage, Lyle had just walked into Andrew's office to search for the server.

"Yeah," he said, excited that the tape had caught the fight. "You'll see it in a minute."

He fast-forwarded until the moment when Monroe snuck into the room behind him. Still smiling, he hit the play button.

"Watch this," he said. "Here's where I took him down. It's one hell of a brawl."

The video played forward as the two men squared-off on-screen. Lyle grinned, remembering how their epic fight had gone. The showdown of the century.

On the video, Lyle rushed forward, and the fight unfolded.

Lyle's smile faded.

Kate burst out laughing. "Are you two slapping each other?"

"Punching," Lyle said, blushing furiously.

On-screen, though, the two of them grappled in what he could only describe as the most pathetic display of masculinity Lyle had ever witnessed. The doctor swatted at his face, he swatted back, and everything seemed to happen in slow motion.

"It seemed faster at the time."

"I'm sure," Kate said, giggling.

Suddenly, the two men on-screen fell and rolled around on the floor.

"Okay, I think we've seen enough," Lyle said, pausing the tape.

"No, no. Make copies."

"Too late," he said, hitting a couple of keys. "Already deleted."

"Ah, spoilsport."

"That didn't give an accurate representation. The footage must have become corrupted."

Kate kept laughing.

"It's not funny."

"It's too funny."

Kate rose from the seat and patted him on the shoulder. "That poor doctor didn't know what hit him."

Lyle sighed.

3

It took another five days for Malcolm to wake. Lyle had worried he wouldn't, but he was made from tough stuff. The fervor from Andrew Carmichael's escapades had died down, and things had begun to return to normal.

Kate had left the cabin, leaving Lyle to watch over the injured man until he awoke. Ostensibly, she disappeared so she could get in touch with some of her contacts and prepare for their next job, but Lyle knew the real reason.

She didn't want to be here when Malcolm came around.

In all honesty, Lyle didn't either.

Malcolm came to slowly, and Lyle helped him reorient to reality. In agony and confused, he didn't remember much of what had happened back in the hotel.

But he knew enough.

Surprisingly, though, he seemed more sad than angry.

"How could she do this?" he asked. "I thought we were friends."

Lyle shook his head. "She had restricted knowledge. They didn't tell her the full extent of the job."

"When we first worked together, she was one of the coldest and most dangerous people I'd ever had contact with. She would kill without batting an eye. That used to impress me, but after a while, it scared me instead. We grew apart. When I heard about her a few months ago, it sounded like she had changed. I prayed for her sake that she had left that person behind."

"She did," Lyle said. "She's not that cold person anymore. If you had any idea how disheartened she felt when she found out what had happened, you would understand."

"She murdered my team."

"She didn't." Lyle shook his head. "And she's tried to make amends ever since."

Malcolm sighed, disbelieving. "Too little too late."

"Maybe," Lyle said.

"What happens now?"

"I don't know. You haven't tried to kill me yet, so I'll take that as a good sign."

"You had nothing to do with it."

"I withheld information from you."

Malcolm shrugged. "I would have too. So I can't fault you for that."

"Well, then, I guess it's up to you what happens next," Lyle said. "Kate told me to give you a ride back to town if you needed one and to drop you off anywhere you chose. She also left a few thousand dollars for you to get back on your feet."

"She didn't wait here to see me off?"

Lyle shook his head.

"Probably for the best. I don't want to hurt you, but I'm not sure I could keep from going after her."

"I get it. You feel pissed at Kate for what she did, but I'm telling you, she isn't that person anymore. Underneath, she's a lovely person."

Malcolm hesitated and then said, "You love her, don't you?"

Lyle didn't answer.

"It's a mistake."

"I know." Lyle shrugged.

"You're a good person, and you've imprinted that onto her, but you have to run while you have the chance. She'll suck you dry if you aren't careful."

Lyle didn't respond. The words hit him deeply. Did they have any truth to them? If not, why did he have such a hard time dismissing them?

Malcolm said, "In the meantime, I'm starving. I haven't had anything to eat in days. What do you have?"

"Steak," Lyle said. "Frozen. Lots of it."

"Sounds perfect. You're a man after my own heart."

"Not me," Lyle said. "The guy who owns this cabin seems to like it though." Then Lyle got up and headed into the kitchen.

"What do you mean?" Malcolm asked. "Whose cabin is this?"

"I had hoped you would know."

"Not a clue."

"Damn."

Just as Lyle turned on the burners on in the kitchen to fry up the steaks, the satellite phone buzzed. Lyle said, "Hello?"

"Hey," Kate said. "Is Malcolm still there with you?"

"Yeah. I was going to cook some food and then take him back to town, why?"

"Don't," she said. "I'm on my way."

"What? Why?"

"We have another job," she said. "And it's something he'll to want to hear."

The End.
Lincoln Cole

About the Author

Lincoln Cole is a Columbus-based author who enjoys traveling and has visited many different parts of the world, including Australia and Cambodia, but always returns home to his pugamonster puppy, Luther, and family. His love for writing was kindled at an early age through the works of Isaac Asimov and Stephen King and he enjoys telling stories to anyone who will listen.

Made in the USA
San Bernardino, CA
11 August 2018